PRESENT

DARKNESS

Also by Malla Nunn

A Beautiful Place to Die
Let the Dead Lie
Blessed Are the Dead

PRESENT DARKNESS

A NOVEL

MALLA NUNN

EMILY BESTLER BOOKS

—

WASHINGTON SQUARE PRESS

NEW YORK   LONDON   TORONTO   SYDNEY   NEW DELHI

EMILY
BESTLER
BOOKS

WASHINGTON SQUARE PRESS
A Division of Simon & Schuster, Inc.
1230 Avenue of the Americas
New York, NY 10020

First Emily Bestler Books/Washington Square Press trade paperback edition June 2014

EMILY BESTLER BOOKS / WASHINGTON SQUARE PRESS and colophons are trademarks of Simon & Schuster, Inc.

For information about special discounts for bulk purchases, please contact Simon & Schuster Special Sales at 1-866-506-1949 or business@simonandschuster.com.

The Simon & Schuster Speakers Bureau can bring authors to your live event. For more information or to book an event, contact the Simon & Schuster Speakers Bureau at 1-866-248-3049 or visit our website at www.simonspeakers.com.

Cover design by Anna Dorfman

Cover art: Rhinoceros illustration © Dorling Kindersley/Getty Images

Manufactured in the United States of America

10 9 8 7 6 5 4 3 2 1

Library of Congress Cataloging-in-Publication Data is available.

ISBN 978-1-4516-1696-5
ISBN 978-1-4516-1699-6 (ebook)

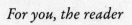

For you, the reader

ACKNOWLEDGMENTS

Love to the following: Mark, Elijah, Sisana, and my extended family. I tip my hat to Terence King for historical corrections. All mistakes and inventions are my own. Heartfelt thanks to my fabulous agents Catherine Drayton of Inkwell Management and Sophie Hamley of the Cameron Creswell Agency for their support in stormy times. To Emily Bestler and her talented team at Emily Bestler Books, my deepest gratitude for giving Emmanuel Cooper a loving home.

PROLOGUE

JOHANNESBURG, DECEMBER 1953

Friday night. A dirt lane on the outskirts of Yeoville, where cars came out of the city, then disappeared in the direction of the four-way intersection that led to the suburbs. The girl paced out the number of steps between the mouth of the alley and the vacant lot at the far end. Some men liked to lay her down in the open field. Most preferred to position her against the wall of the dark lane itself. After the urgency left them, they got into their cars and disappeared back into the flat sprawl of Johannesburg's suburbs: nice places, with names like Sandton, Bedfordview and Edenvale. She liked to feel the money in her hands for a moment before she took it to the darkest part of the alley, pulled out the loose brick she knew was there and shoved the bills behind it.

Between men, she stood halfway down the alley—in the shadows, but easy to see if one knew where to look. Squeezed

1

between high brick walls and strewn with crushed kaffir weeds, the lane's location was ideal for clients with ten minutes to spare between knocking off work and heading home.

The sweep of car headlights lit the walls of the narrow way at intermittent intervals. The moonlight was faint and partially blocked by the roof line of the adjacent building. She didn't mind the gloom. It softened the hard line of her jaw and smoothed the acne scars on her right cheek. She liked the darkness. In the dark she was perfect.

The sound of a foot crunching the dirt broke the quiet, and the girl looked up. Car lights swept past, briefly illuminating the strip. A white man stood at the end of the alley, just emerged from the vacant lot. He was tall, big across the shoulders and still. He wasn't so much standing in the alley as blocking one end of it. A chill traveled up her legs and into her belly.

"Sorry, hey. Bad timing." Fear sharpened her performance and she sounded every inch a slum-born English prostitute working for cheap. "I'm just finished for the night."

He moved toward her: big and getting bigger. Sure-footed. In no hurry. The girl backed away, worn heels scraping the dirt. Cars passed on the main road.

"Okay, wait." She glanced over her shoulder and calculated twenty steps to the safety of traffic and people, maybe twenty-two. "Wait. Let's talk. We can work something out. What is it you want?"

"Everything," he said.

On another night and with another client she might have joked, "All right. But it will cost you."

Not this time. She turned and sprinted for the alley exit. Images of a roadside trench and the cold weight of the earth covering her naked body one shovel load at a time flashed through her mind. Every drop of street cunning accumulated over the hard years told her that the big man would take her blood and her bones. But he'd pay nothing for what he took.

Seventeen, sixteen steps more to the main road. In truth, she lost count. It didn't matter. The traffic was louder, the headlights brighter. She risked a look over her shoulder. The man sauntered the dirt lane with his hands thrust deep into his pockets. He couldn't catch her at that pace. She was almost safe. Home now, quickly. Turn the handle, slip inside and lock the door.

She turned back and slammed hard into a wiry body. The impact knocked her off balance and breath rushed from her lungs. Her shoulder smacked the ground. She looked up, dazed. A second man crouched down and cupped a hand over her mouth. His palms smelled of raw sugar, such a sweet scent amid the stench of urine and kaffir weed in the laneway. Then realization came quickly. There were two men in the alley, and together, they'd netted her like a bird.

The one holding her down said, "Make sure she's white. He's strict about that kind of thing."

The man who'd blocked the exit to the vacant lot slotted a cigarette into the corner of his mouth. The flare of a match briefly lit his face, which was clean-cut and handsome with black hair combed back from his forehead.

A dream client. He squatted and held the flame inches from her face. Heat licked her pockmarked cheeks.

"White and ugly," he said, and leaned closer. "Do you want to ride home with me tonight, sweetheart?"

The wiry one still blocked her mouth with his hand. She shook her head no. Twin funnels of smoke snaked from the handsome man's nostrils and he smiled.

1

DETECTIVE SERGEANT EMMANUEL COOPER crossed the ramshackle garden, jacket unbuttoned in the nighttime heat. A fat moon tangled in the branches of a jacaranda tree and the air carried the smell of fresh-cut grass and the tree's shameless purple flowers. It was a perfect Friday night to sit with his daughter Rebekah's chunky brown arms laced around his neck while Davida sat barefoot on the stairs. Instead he was at a crime scene in Parkview, in the flashing lights of a street cruiser.

Blue police barricades encircled a brick house with weeds growing from the gutters. The barriers made a physical reminder that the inhabitants had passed through the veil of the everyday and into a darker world of blood and broken things. Emmanuel crossed the crime-scene perimeter and left ordinary behind.

"Detective. Sir." A gangly white policeman reeking of sweat and vomit moved off the house stairs. He'd been inside, Emmanuel guessed, and seen something he wouldn't forget. "Lieutenant Mason said to go straight in, Detective. Sir."

A cluster of young uniformed constables stood on the porch. Two more of them guarded the front door. Middle-class, European victims always brought the force out in force.

"Sergeant Cooper, Marshall Square," Emmanuel said to the police on door duty. They stepped aside. He stepped in.

Smashed furniture littered the entrance and ripped telephone wires snaked across the oak floorboards. Glass from a broken hall stand reflected a mosaic of light onto the ceiling. Emmanuel took a deep breath. A single phone call he'd received minutes before the end of the shift had made the difference between being with Davida and Rebekah and being here, in chaos.

"What a mess, hey?" Detective Constable Dryer, a big-boned Afrikaner with thinning brown hair combed over a bald spot, stood in a doorway to the right of the wreckage. Dryer's most useful character trait was his ability to state the completely fucking obvious.

"Uh-huh." Emmanuel made the right noises. The white and yellow telephone wires interested him. The actual telephone lay farther into the hallway, the receiver torn clean from the cord attaching it to the base. Stripping the wires from the wall might be a sign of extreme caution or violent rage. No way to tell which yet. An ambulance siren wailed in the distance.

"Animals. Who else would do this so close to Christmas?" Dryer hooked his broad thumbs into his belt, which gave his beer gut room to move. "You wait and see, Cooper. The police commissioner will work us like dogs till this case is closed. No leave. No overtime. We can kiss our holidays good-bye."

"Bad timing," Emmanuel said. Dryer liked to complain. If he'd worked for the postal service, the mailbags would be too heavy. Emmanuel let him gripe. The fleshy Afrikaner was background noise and part of what Emmanuel had agreed to endure in order to secure a short-term transfer from the coastal city of Durban to the flat sprawl of Johannesburg. He'd worked his boss, Colonel van Niekerk, hard for the transfer and knew that the favor would have to be repaid in the future—with interest. Seeing Davida and Rebekah every day, however, was worth the heavier workload, and Dryer was no worse than most of the detectives he'd worked with in other places.

Broken glass crunched underfoot and a tall man with a thin, humorless mouth stepped out of a room farther down the corridor. "Detectives," he said. Black hair, black shoes and an unwrinkled black suit gave Lieutenant Walter Mason a grim, funereal appearance.

"Cooper." Mason crooked a finger. "In here with me."

Emmanuel kept to the left of the corridor, careful to avoid disturbing the debris. A living room with a lime-green carpet, a brown corduroy sofa and a tinsel-laden Christmas tree appeared untouched. Four silver photo frames were arranged in a straight line on the mantel. Sounds of quiet sobbing came from deeper in the house.

"There's no time for delicacy, Cooper," Mason said. "The ambulance officers have to get through. Dryer, clear a path."

"But . . ." The Afrikaner started to complain. Mason's icy expression killed the words in his mouth. "Right away, sir."

Emmanuel approached the doorway where the lieutenant stood. Oak floorboards creaked underfoot. The air smelled of rusting copper after the rain. Emmanuel knew the odor well. It was the hot, wet funk of blood: a scent burned deep into his memory. He'd smelled too much of it on the battlefields of France during the war.

"Go on." Mason motioned into a bedroom bathed in bright electric light. The metal smell intensified and burned Emmanuel's throat. A shirtless white man lay on the cream-colored carpet, pale arms and legs splayed at bizarre angles. Pulped and swollen to twice its natural size, the man's face resembled a grapefruit left to rot in the field. Stained teeth showed through a split bottom lip. He had been horribly beaten. He might live to midnight.

"Ian and Martha Brewer," Mason said. "A high school principal and a secretary at the office of land management. Not the usual victims of such a violent crime. "

Emmanuel skirted the bed and found Martha Brewer. She was a tiny thing, a puppet with cut strings propped up against the mattress base. Blood clotted her dyed blond hair and stained the neckline of her pink cotton nightdress. A pulse point fluttered at the base of her neck, weak but steady. The ambulance siren howled from the front lawn and set the neighborhood dogs to barking.

"Stay here, Cooper. I'll see the medics in."

"Yes, sir." Emmanuel remained crouched and looked around. Middle-class ruin blighted every surface of the room. The wall behind the quilted bed head was sprayed with an arc of rust-colored splatter. Summer dresses and plain cotton shirts had spilled from broken dresser drawers. The wardrobe had also been rifled.

"In here." Mason directed two white men into the bedroom. Each carried a canvas-and-wood stretcher under-arm and a medical kit in hand. "See to the woman first."

Emmanuel stepped into the corridor, gave the ambulance crew room to work. They knelt on the stained carpet, stanching blood and bandaging wounds. Their hands were soon soaked, the knees of their trousers blotted red. Martha Brewer's body made a small hollow in the canvas as they carried her to the ambulance, taking a path cleared through the hallway rubble by Dryer.

"The husband is finished," Mason said when the ambulance roared onto the asphalt road with sirens screaming and Ian and Martha Brewer strapped into the back. "With God's grace the wife will survive the night."

"Yes, by the grace of God." Emmanuel made more right noises. Some days it seemed that all he did was lie by omission.

"I didn't take you for a praying man, Cooper," Mason said. The only real color in the lieutenant's face was in his eyes: they were a bright blue. Ice cubes had more warmth.

"I keep my hand in." Emmanuel examined the telephone wires to avoid discussing religion with Mason, a born-again, praise-the-Lord Christian. For twelve years the lieutenant had worked undercover operations, all the while enjoying regular access to his two great loves: sour-mash whiskey and free pussy. Then a gospel tent preacher saved him and now he served a joyless god who frowned on all forms of pleasure, even laughter.

"So it's true," Mason said. "There are no atheists in foxholes."

"I never met any," Emmanuel said. That his superior officer knew he'd been a combat soldier during the war and not part of the rear-echelon army was a detail to consider later.

"All this for a box of jewelry and a stack of bills hidden behind the underwear drawer." Mason gestured to the wrecked furniture. "The love of money is truly the root of all evil."

"The living room hasn't been touched," Emmanuel said. "There's a row of silver picture frames on the mantel. Why expend so much energy and leave those behind?"

"It wouldn't be the first time a robbery became a murder."

"True." Burglars caught in the act killed dozens of people every year and maimed a few more besides. "This level of violence seems excessive, almost personal in nature."

Sobbing came from the rear of the house.

"That's the daughter you hear." Mason stalked the length of the corridor, crunching debris. "Negus is babysitting her in the kitchen till one of the station typists arrives. She needs a female touch."

In police code, *female touch* translated to "the witness is hysterical and won't stop crying, even though we've told her to." Emmanuel followed Mason and glanced into a room with an upended single bed, a ransacked wardrobe and walls papered in a yellow canary design: a teenager's bedroom, presumably the girl's.

"The police typist is coming from out Benoni way. She won't be here for another half an hour at the earliest. " The cold-eyed lieutenant paused outside a closed door and glanced at Emmanuel over his shoulder. "I want you to get in there and try to calm things, Cooper. If I remember right, you're good with women."

"I'll try," Emmanuel said. *Good with women?* He couldn't think where Mason's comment came from.

Dryer sniggered, sure that Mason was referring to a party in Dryer's imagination at which Emmanuel and the lieutenant had shared in a repast of whores lain on by an obliging madam. Dryer was an idiot.

Emmanuel tried and failed to come up with a source for Mason's observation. They'd never worked together before or even had a beer at the local bar. The undercover operations squad was a tight unit. They believed in secrecy and money. Emmanuel had stayed far away from them his whole career—and especially since arriving back in Jo'burg.

"In here." Mason opened the door to a ruined kitchen. Silver cutlery and smashed containers littered the floor and counters. Piles of flour, rice, coffee and sugar were dumped onto the small pine table. A white girl in a cotton nightie sat in a chair with her face buried in her hands, weeping.

"Name?" Emmanuel asked before going in.

"Cassie. We got that from the neighbor who called in the disturbance. Nothing from her yet."

Negus, the detective on babysitting duty, was a solid, old-fashioned cop Emmanuel knew from the station. He would have come on duty with three things: a loaded gun, adrenaline and a hard-man face. Good cop or not, he was ill equipped to comfort a teenage girl whose parents might die tonight.

"Thank Christ," Negus mumbled when he reached the door. "I need a piss and a smoke."

The girl, Cassie, sobbed and kept her fingers tightly closed. Eyes shut, face hidden, she was trying to block out the chaos. Emmanuel walked into the room: time for Cassie to put her hands down and open her eyes.

"The local police found her in that corner." Mason pointed to a spot near a four-burner gas stove. "We've tried to get her out of here, but she won't leave."

The kitchen, at least, smelled of cinnamon and caster sugar instead of blood. There was no blood in this room that Emmanuel could see. The headmaster and his wife had been beaten in the bedroom while the house was turned over: a job for two men, minimum. He found a kettle in the debris and filled it at the sink.

"Do you want a cup of tea, Cassie?" he asked. "Or cocoa, if I can find it?"

"Nothing," she sniffed.

"You're sure?"

"Uh-huh."

She was talking. That was a start. Emmanuel left the water running and checked her for injuries. Blood running down her thighs or dripping from an elbow would have shown up in the flour sprinkled on the floor. The flour was still clean. Cassie's freckled legs and pale arms were likewise unmarked by trauma, her yellow nightgown pristine.

"Is that blood?" Emmanuel leaned closer, heart thumping. Red color smudged across the back of Cassie's hand. Christ knows what injuries hid behind those shuttered palms.

"What?" she hiccuped.

"There." He touched a gentle fingertip to the spot and noticed the red had a strange metallic shine.

"Oh." She dropped her hands to the table and rubbed at the smear with a fingertip. "I don't know where that came from."

Oh, yes you do, Emmanuel thought. It wasn't blood Cassie scrubbed away at so hard. It was lipstick.

"I'm Detective Sergeant Cooper," he said, and shut off the water tap. "Are you hurt anyplace that I can't see?"

"No." Cassie scraped the last trace of red away with a fingernail and looped a strand of frizzy ginger hair behind her right ear. She was about fifteen years old with bright hazel eyes and a wide mouth that belonged in a broader face. Freckles sprinkled her nose, neck and collarbones so her skin appeared browner than white. "I'm all right. Really."

Emmanuel gave her his handkerchief and said, "Can you tell me what happened, Cassie?"

She blew her nose and frowned, thinking.

"Take your time." He lit the gas flame under the kettle. "There's no rush."

"I . . . I was asleep in my bed and there was a . . . a big crash. Like there was someone in the house." The frown deepened, cutting a trench into her forehead. "It was dark. I couldn't see."

"Tell me what you did then." Emmanuel sat at the table. "After the noise."

"I got a fright and I got out of bed." Cassie twisted the corner of the handkerchief into a tight cylinder. "Then I hid behind the wardrobe."

"Your wardrobe?" The ripped doors and the scattered contents he'd seen from the corridor.

"*Ja.* That one."

"Did you hear voices from there?"

"What?" The question seemed to startle her and the corners of her wide mouth twitched. "I . . . I don't know what you mean."

Emmanuel said, "You were behind the wardrobe while the robbers were in your room. Did they say anything?"

Cassie took a deep breath, looked away to the kitchen window. The moon now hung lower in the branches of the jacaranda outside. Two minutes ticked by in silence.

"Zulu," she said finally. "They were speaking Zulu. I don't know what they were saying."

Footsteps shuffled in the doorway. Mason and Dryer

moved closer to catch the rest of Cassie's story. A few days shy of the Christmas holidays, the police commissioner would cancel all police leave pending an arrest. The headlines tomorrow would send a ripple of fear through the white neighborhoods: "Zulu Gang Beats European Couple to Death in Their Bed."

"It wasn't Pedi or Shangaan that you heard?" Emmanuel asked. Johannesburg was the economic powerhouse of southern Africa, and it drew black Africans of every different tribal group to the city with the promise of work. The city was an industrial Babel, with dozens of languages spoken.

"No. It was Zulu. Definitely. I . . ." Cassie buried her face in her hands and started to cry again.

Emmanuel placed a hand on her arm, hoping the warmth of human contact would calm her. It didn't. Cassie's sobs deepened. Only a little while ago, she had been alone in a corner, too terrified to move, while her parents bled out onto their carpet a few feet away.

Emmanuel stood up and put an arm around her shoulders. Her wet face pressed against his stomach. He made the right sounds yet felt no sorrow, pity or anger. He was detached, floating above the wrecked kitchen, wondering when his ability to lie had grown so deep and become so easy. Wiry hair crinkled against his shirt, curlier than his mixed-race daughter's would ever be. He'd never hold his own girl Rebekah like this in public.

"It's okay." He recited the given script. "You're safe now. You can talk to me. Tell me anything."

"I recognized their voices." Cassie's face burrowed deeper against his tear-soaked shirt. "I know who did it."

"You know their names?" Emmanuel asked.

Mason moved into the kitchen and stood at the edge of the pine table. He watched Emmanuel's ministrations with snake eyes. *If I remember right, you're good with women.* Emmanuel had been meticulous with his lies these last five weeks, especially around Mason. Talking about his personal life would send him to jail for three to six years for "immoral activity." The beauty of Davida Ellis's honey-brown skin against white cotton sheets and the sky gray of his daughter's eyes would remain his secret.

"It was boys from St. Bartholomew's College," Cassie said. "Two of them."

"Look at me, Cassie." Emmanuel waited till she did. He had to be sure there'd been no mistake. "You're talking about St. Bartholomew's College in Sophiatown?"

She broke off eye contact and licked her dry lips. "Yes."

The Anglican school and its well-known redbrick chapel were in Emmanuel's old neighborhood. The school was an oasis in the tough streets of Sophiatown for black boys who wanted to become teachers and lawyers instead of gangsters. His good friend Detective Constable Samuel Shabalala's son attended the prestigious school.

"How did you come to meet students from a native school?" Sophiatown was less than thirty miles from the neat grid of suburban streets where Cassie lived, but it might as well be on another planet in a distant galaxy.

"My father," Cassie said. "He runs an extracurricular

program for natives. He takes them to the theater and also to music concerts. Once a term they come to the house for dinner."

"To this house?"

"*Ja*. He thought it would be good for them to see how Europeans lived."

Dryer snorted from the doorway. Emmanuel stepped away from Cassie's burrowed face and squatted by her chair. She chewed her bottom lip.

"Tell me their names," Emmanuel said.

"I . . . I don't want to get anyone in trouble."

"We're just going to talk to them and clear things up. That's all." Emmanuel was surprised at having to coax the names of the culprits from Cassie. Christ Almighty. What did she care if two black boys from the townships got into trouble for beating her parents and wrecking her home?

Cassie pressed the handkerchief to her face. "Kibelo Nkhato. I think that was his surname," she said. "And Aaron Shabalala."

Emmanuel slipped back into his body, heart thumping and panic taking hold like a virus. Shabalala was a common Zulu name. Throw a net out of a bus in Sophiatown and you'd land a dozen. But two boys named Aaron Shabalala attending the same Anglican-run boarding school was unlikely.

"You're sure about those names?" Emmanuel leaned in closer to establish eye contact with Cassie. The odds against there being a personal connection between him and this crime scene were astronomical.

"Yes, of course. They were here tonight for the end-of-term dinner." The handkerchief muffled the sharp edge of her voice. "It was Aaron and Kibelo. Those two boys. I'm not making it up."

"Okay."

Her gaze flickered away to the window for a second time. With any other witness, the broken eye contact would point to a lie or an evasion. Emmanuel wasn't sure the same rules applied here. Cassie was a plain girl who, he suspected, sat in the corner at school functions with an empty dance card on her lap and a carnation wilting behind her ear. He might have overplayed the eye contact and pushed her back into her shell.

"Aaron Shabalala and Kibelo Nkhato." Emmanuel sat back down and flipped open his notebook. He proceeded as usual. Until he knew for certain that this Aaron was his friend's son, there was nothing else to do.

"Describe the boys to me," he said.

"Kibelo is skinny and light-skinned. He wears glasses and he likes to talk. Shabalala is not like that." Hot color stung Cassie's cheeks. "He's tall with wide shoulders and brown eyes. He doesn't speak so much and sometimes his face is like a mask, so you can't tell what he's thinking."

He'd never met any of Shabalala's sons in person, but a tall Zulu male with wide shoulders and the ability to keep his thoughts to himself: that might well be a description of Detective Constable Samuel Shabalala of the Native Detective Branch.

"Did your father keep money in the house?" Emmanuel's voice remained flat and cool despite his thudding heart.

"No," Cassie said. "He liked to tell the boys that the bank was the only place to keep money. You earned interest on the deposit and the money was insured if there was ever a robbery."

Solid advice, which Cassie repeated with a glazed look. Emmanuel imagined the end-of-term dinners were probably torture for the principal's daughter, having to sit politely at the table surrounded by native boys while her father divulged the cultural secrets of the white race. The neighbors wouldn't be pleased with the idea of black boys eating off china plates in the house next door, either.

"Why do you think they did it?" Emmanuel asked.

"Who?"

"The boys. If Nkhato and Shabalala knew there was no money in the house, why do you think they did all this?" He motioned to the wreckage.

"Oh . . . " Cassie's gaze flickered across the debris and her shoulders curled in. She thought a moment then said, "They took the car. That must be what they wanted."

"What car?" Mason's voice was a bucket of ice water thrown onto a fire. Cassie jumped at the sound of it.

"Tell me about the car." Emmanuel spoke over the low noise of Mason's grinding teeth. *You're good with women.* He had to figure out where the ex–vice cop got that idea.

"It's a Mercedes-Benz cabriolet," Cassie said. "Red with black leather seats."

"Nice . . . " Dryer gave a soft whistle and nodded approval. A flick from Mason's index finger sent him scuttling back into the corridor.

"Go check the garage, Cooper." Mason jerked a thumb to the back door. "See if the car's gone."

"The boys broke in, found the keys and then stole the Mercedes. I heard the engine," Cassie said.

"Make it fast, Sergeant." Cassie's certainty seemed to agitate Mason more than the assault on her parents. His jaw worked on an invisible piece of gristle between his teeth. "You'd have to be an idiot to take a car like that and expect to blend in."

Emmanuel got up, switched off the kettle and walked to the back door. Mason had it right. Two black boys in a red luxury car. The idea was ridiculous. They wouldn't get past the first roadblock.

A china fragment crunched under his shoes and he looked down. The imprint of a bare foot pressed into the floured tiles. Not a single print, but a line of them moving from the back door to the corner of the kitchen where the police had found Cassie hiding.

Emmanuel checked the door handle. The lock buckled inward but the square of glass inset into the wood remained intact. This was the point of entry into the house. A simple break and enter that started with the snap of this handle and ended in chaos. Were the car keys that hard to find?

"Make it fast, Cooper. We need to get to the school and interview those boys. That's if they're still in town."

He gave the kitchen one last glance. Cassie hunched in the chair and chewed at her fingernails. The trail of footsteps snaked around broken glass and skipped over shards of porcelain. Despite being in fear for her life, Cassie had carefully picked her way across the room to a safe corner. She glanced up and met Emmanuel's eyes.

His look said, *You are lying, girl. And I know it.*

She covered her face with her hands.

2

"CAR'S GONE, LIEUTENANT."

The ghost of a grease spot on the concrete floor was the only evidence that a vehicle had once parked in the Brewers' garage. Emmanuel crossed to the rear of the garage and stepped into the moonlight. The backyard was overgrown with fruit trees and climbing vines. Stands of wild fig and straggly banana plants made Emmanuel feel as if he might be back in a country town, like Jacob's Rest, where he'd first met Davida. An unseen animal, big enough to make a distinctive dragging sound, moved through the leaf litter.

"Something's back here," he said loud enough for Dryer and Mason to hear. "Something big. I'll take a look."

"Go with Cooper, Dryer. See what's out there," Mason said, but Emmanuel was already searching the moonlit garden. He found a narrow path behind a clothesline and followed it. Gnarled branches and knots of unpruned roses pressed in from either side and slowed his progress. The dragging sounds grew louder.

"Police." He spoke loud and clear. "Step out where I can see you."

No answer. He moved deeper into the wild garden, keeping to the thin dirt path. A noise came from a mass of plants up ahead.

"Police," Emmanuel said again, and peered into the tangled branches and stems. Darkness peered back. Revolver holster unclipped, he ducked and shuffled into the underbrush. He navigated like a blind man, using an outstretched hand to feel the way. A sharp snap came from his right. He jerked back and pressed a hand to the ground for balance. Wet leaves stuck to his palm and the familiar smell of blood rose from the soil.

Emmanuel wiped off the leaf litter and moved on as he had done during the war when every step forward might have been his last. The dragging sound came from directly in front of him now. He reached out and touched the crook of an elbow and then a bony shoulder blade. A body shuddered and collapsed under the weight of his fingers.

"Dryer!" he shouted. "Bring a light. Now."

"Where are you, Cooper?" Dryer called. "I can't see you."

"Take the path behind the clothesline. Walk into the garden. I'm to the right of the path." Every skin surface he touched came back wet and slick with blood. "Get a light in here, Dryer. Now."

A flashlight beam flicked between the tree branches. Emmanuel's eyes adjusted to the dimness. A slender black man lay on his side in the leaf litter. He bled from a deep head wound and, Emmanuel could tell, some smaller wounds in his back. His fingernails were torn and caked with dirt from crawling his way across the ground one handful at a time, looking for safety or maybe a quiet place to die.

"Call for a native ambulance," he told Dryer. "And get the local police down here with lights and a blanket. Quick smart."

The police from the porch descended on the garden, their voices high-pitched with excitement. They were young men, thrilled to be part of the unfolding drama. The black man now lay motionless on the ground, his breathing a low rasp in his throat. Emmanuel rested on his haunches and listened to the air moving in and out of the man's lungs.

"In here," he said when the local police drew near. Three flashlight beams converged on the secondary crime scene. The first policeman through the foliage made a sound of distress and stopped short. He clutched a blanket to his chest.

"Stay where you are," Emmanuel said. "The rest of you keep a foot back from the victim and form a circle."

They followed instructions, each shuffling self-consciously into place with their flashlights held high.

"Do you think it's the gardener?" one of the local police whispered.

"Maybe," another replied. "Why else would a kaffir be in a white man's backyard after sundown?"

Emmanuel was uncertain. The black man curled in the leaves wore a long-sleeved shirt and blue cotton trousers. His bare feet and hands were covered in dirt but lacked the roughness made by manual labor. And the garden grew wild. If this man was a gardener, he was terrible at his job. Emmanuel crouched low and searched the victim's pockets for identification.

"What have you got there?" Mason pushed through the tree branches and made a space between two of the local police.

"An unidentified male." Emmanuel felt around for the passbook that black men were legally required to carry on their person at all times. A pass contained the bearer's name, place of origin, a black-and-white photograph, copies of their work details, and a record of previous encounters with the police: their life story recorded in bullet points.

"No money or ID in any of the pants pockets." He lifted a bloodstained paper from the man's shirt pocket and squinted at the penciled text.

"The Brewers' address," he said.

"What the hell is an unregistered black doing in a Parkview garden?" Mason asked. "Even if he had a passbook, he should have caught the last bus to kaffir town hours ago."

Emmanuel said, "Same goes for Shabalala and Kibelo. Doubling back from Sophiatown to Parkview on public transport can't have been simple."

"They managed it somehow, maybe with the help of accomplices. You heard the girl. Those boys were in that house. She named them."

Yes, she had. And a traumatized white girl's testimony was hard to attack in court with a sympathetic European jury seated in the box.

"Any word on the native ambulance?" He rubbed his palms together, flaking off dried blood.

"It will be awhile." Mason turned to leave. "The nearest native hospital is Baragwanath and they've only got a handful of vans. Dryer might know. Assuming he asked the hospital for an estimate."

"Give me the blanket, Constable," Emmanuel said to one of the policemen, a bright-haired teenager with a face as plain as a glass of milk.

"But . . . sir . . . " the constable stammered. "I got this blanket from inside the house. It's wool. From the girl's bedroom."

"And?"

"It's not meant for one of them," the policeman said. "His blood will get all over it."

Emmanuel stood up and ripped the cover from the boy's grasp. "If the Brewers survive the night, they can burn the blanket and bury the ashes. Blood is blood. It stains the same no matter who's doing the bleeding."

"Yes, sir." The constable shuffled back a step, embarrassed. He'd offended the detective sergeant but he didn't know how.

"Stand guard till the ambulance gets here. Make sure nothing is disturbed," he said to the local police, and spread the blanket over the unidentified stranger. It drove him into a blind rage to think that Davida and Rebekah might be denied the comfort of warmth in a similar situation because they had brown skin instead of white.

He turned and walked away. Lieutenant Mason followed him onto the moonlit path with an enigmatic expression. Emmanuel stayed quiet. One word would betray the fury rising in his throat. And then Mason would know beyond a doubt that his reaction to the constable's attitude was personal.

"You speak kaffir," Mason said when they reached the house. It was a statement, not a question.

"Some," he replied. He did not advertise the fact he spoke fluent Zulu and Afrikaans and now a smattering of Shangaan, thanks to spending time with Detective Constable Samuel Shabalala, who was half Zulu, half Shangaan.

"Stay here with the local police and the injured man. If the native comes around, make a note of anything he says that might explain how two schoolboys made this mess. The police commissioner's going to need proof to back up the Brewer girl's statement," Mason said. "Negus and I will bring the boys in for questioning."

"I'll swing by the station afterward," Emmanuel said. Keeping track of the evidence against Aaron and Nkhato was paramount. What he'd do with the information once he had it, he did not know.

"Paid overtime hasn't been approved on this case yet, so if it's a few extra pounds you're angling for, then go home and get a good night's sleep."

"I work till the work is done," Emmanuel said. Mason operated undercover for months at a stretch, living and breathing the job twenty-four hours a day. In Mason's world, real policemen worked for love of the job.

Dryer stepped out of the back door and jerked a thumb in the direction of the kitchen. "Police typist is here, Lieutenant."

"Cooper's already got what we need. Let her hold the girl's hand for a while and then send her home to Benoni. The next-door neighbor, Mrs. Lauda, has agreed to take Cassie in till her aunt gets here tomorrow from north of Pretoria. Cooper, you'll walk her over when the time comes."

"Of course." There were good reasons for leaving him in charge of the primary crime scene and of Cassie, the star witness, the foremost being Dryer's idiocy. The less obvious reason was that Mason did not trust him to interview the main suspects.

The lieutenant disappeared into the Brewer house.

"Typical, hey?" Dryer spoke once the back door had closed. "Mason and Negus get the good jobs while we take care of a beaten-up kaffir and a girl."

"Any word on the native ambulance?" Emmanuel asked.

"The switchboard logged the call but it'll be a while.

The hospital vans are attending a bus crash out near Tembisa."

"It could be dawn before they get here." A bus accident took priority over a single black man bleeding out in a white suburb miles from the hospital.

"How bad off is the kaffir?" Dryer asked.

"Bad," Emmanuel said.

"Shit luck for him." The Afrikaner detective yawned and looked up at the full moon. Dead or alive, an injured native counted for little. Cassie Brewer's witness statement meant his holiday plans were all but assured—the perpetrators were practically in custody already. In a week he'd be floating in the Indian Ocean and drinking a cold can of beer while fish nibbled at his toes.

If Aaron Shabalala had instead been just some random black boy accused of robbery and assault, Emmanuel acknowledged that he might feel the same sense of relief at the easy "case closed."

"I'll check in with the police typist." He took the stairs and opened the kitchen door. A path had been swept through the debris and the rice and flour had been wiped from the tabletop. An older white woman with a helmet of blue-rinsed hair and a pursed mouth painted a violent shade of fuchsia combed a brush through Cassie's frizzy hair. Dressed in a gray wool twin set with a matching skirt and a single strand of pearls at her neck, the police typist personified the government template for a European woman.

Cassie gave Emmanuel a quick glance and turned her face away.

"Shhh . . . it's okay," the police typist soothed. "I'll take care of you, my darling. Don't fret."

Cassie eased into the woman's arms, seeking comfort. She shut her eyes and shut Emmanuel out. The police typist held Cassie close and whispered, "Let it rest, Detective. The poor thing has suffered enough tonight."

He retreated. He'd made Cassie wary with that earlier look. If he got within a foot of her without tears spilling, it would be a miracle. Cassie enjoyed being the hurt one.

"Where are you off to for Christmas, Cooper?" Dryer asked from his moonlit perch.

"I'm staying in Johannesburg," Emmanuel said. That was a lie but a necessary one. His private life was private. "And you?"

"Me, the wife and children are off to Kosi Bay. Ten days in a cabin by the sea." Dryer cast an imaginary line into the garden. "Fishing, swimming, eating prawns. It will be good. Why the hell would you stay in Jo'burg, my man?"

"I like it here," he said. This conversation, he realized, followed the pattern of every single work interaction. The other detectives gave him facts and family stories and he replied with bullshit.

"Sergeant." The milk-faced policeman appeared from the garden path, flashlight waving in panic. Whiter now, his pale eyes huge in his face, he stammered, "Come. Please. It's the man. There's a rattle in his chest, only wet. What should we do?"

"There's nothing you can do," Emmanuel said. The black man needed medical attention immediately. Not at dawn or whatever time the native ambulance arrived. "Stand guard till I come out and relieve you."

"Yes, sir." The constable retreated into the tangle of fruit trees.

Emmanuel moved to the top stair, dry-mouthed and searching for a plan. Ian Brewer was glory-bound, but Martha Brewer would likely survive the night thanks to a fully equipped "whites only" emergency ward. The black man in the garden had no such hope. He'd be dead within hours and any evidence he had would die with him. If Aaron Shabalala and his schoolmate provided an alibi for the time of the robbery, they might get clear. If they didn't, then Cassie's word would remain the gospel and every detective on the case with holiday leave pending would happily sing from her hymnbook.

There was one avenue open to him. Taking it meant stepping into the world of police who played by their own rules. He considered his situation. As a lying European detective sergeant with a mixed-race woman and daughter stashed away from public view, he broke the law every day. He was, in reality, already across the line that divided the dirty cops from the clean ones.

He said, "Head home if you like, Dryer. Things are pretty quiet. I'll stay on here."

"No way, man," the Afrikaner detective said. "Mason will have my guts if I leave before this is closed."

"Mason won't know." Emmanuel smiled reassurance.

"Go on. You have a wife and children at home. I don't have anybody."

"It wouldn't be right leaving you with all this." Dryer ducked a hand into his jacket pocket, searching for car keys, his commitment eroding.

"A beaten-up kaffir and a girl . . . Having two detectives on the scene is a waste of time. Or would you rather stay and keep me company till the native ambulance shows?"

"You sure you don't need me?"

"I'll be fine," Emmanuel said.

"All right." Dryer fished out a ring of keys and swung them around his index finger. "You should come over for dinner sometime, Cooper. Meet the brood."

"That would be nice," Emmanuel said. He'd take up the invitation right after he started performing his own dentistry for pleasure.

"I owe you, Cooper."

"Don't mention it." He clapped a hand to Dryer's shoulder and gently guided him down the stairs. It was hard to keep smiling. He wanted the Afrikaner detective gone five minutes ago.

"See you tomorrow." Dryer squeezed between the house and the garage wall and out to the driveway. Emmanuel waited till the car's red taillights faded into the dark at the end of the street and then walked quickly to the rear of the house. If he stopped to think about what he was doing, he might reconsider.

3

D<small>R. DANIEL ZWEIGMAN</small>, gray hair askew and reading glasses halfway down his nose, stitched the wound with precision and knotted the cotton thread. A circle of policemen held torches to light the outdoor surgery, including the folded sheet upon which lay the disinfectant, bandages, and morphine syrettes used for the operation. Emmanuel told the German doctor to bring everything and he had.

"The wounds are closed and the bleeding has stopped," Zweigman said. "That is all I can do with what I have." He pushed his glasses back up to the bridge of his nose. "It might be enough."

Emmanuel stood up and stretched out. The injured black man had a chance to live. That had to be worth breaking the promise he'd made just a few months previously to keep Zweigman out of danger and away from police business.

Zweigman removed his bloodied gloves and tucked the wool blanket around the unconscious patient's shoulders. The doctor's blue trousers and checked shirt were rumpled. He'd probably dressed in the dark to avoid disturbing his wife, Lilliana, and their adopted son, Dimitri, as they slept in the guest bedroom of Davida's father's house. A few months earlier, Davida had given birth to Rebekah at Zweigman's clinic in the Valley of a Thousand Hills to avoid the complications of bringing an illegitimate, half-caste child into the world.

"What now?" Zweigman asked.

"You go back to Houghton. I'll wait here for the native ambulance to arrive," Emmanuel said.

"So, that is it. 'Thank you, Doctor, and *auf wiedersehen*'?" The wiry doctor repacked the medical supplies into his leather bag and snapped the lock shut. "Once again it has been a pleasure doing business with you, Sergeant Cooper."

"I'll walk you to your car," Emmanuel said. Zweigman's involvement with the Brewer case ended here. There were still nights when Emmanuel woke in a panic at how close he'd come to losing Zweigman on a hillside in the Drakensberg Mountains a few months earlier. In Emmanuel's dreams the spear wound on the doctor's shoulder refused to heal and he died cold and alone in a cave while Emmanuel watched and could do nothing.

"Put the torches down and take a break," Emmanuel told the policemen. "I'll see the doctor out."

"Thank you for your assistance, gentlemen," Zweigman said to the constables and cut through the dense foliage. Twigs snapped under his feet. Moonlight illuminated the dirt path that led to the back door of the Brewers' house.

"I appreciate your help," Emmanuel said when they emerged from the suburban jungle and onto a patch of grass. "But I can't drag you deeper into the investigation. Not after last time."

"What will you tell Shabalala?" Zweigman ignored the reference to his own near-death experience and ducked under the clothesline. He accepted that life inflicted wounds and life healed them. Surviving the war in a concentration camp had taught him that lesson.

"If this Aaron is actually his son, then I'll tell Shabalala the truth," Emmanuel said. "I just haven't figured out the right words yet."

"There is nothing right about this situation." Zweigman pushed his gold-rimmed glasses higher onto the bridge of his nose and studied the garden. "No son of Shabalala's could inflict such a brutal attack."

"I don't know," Emmanuel said. "I ran wild at the same age and got myself into plenty of trouble."

"Drinking and riding in stolen cars with girls," the doctor guessed. "Nothing involving blood and broken bones, I'm sure."

"No," Emmanuel said. "That came later."

A pulse of bright red light blinked from the driveway. Evans, the policeman left to guard the front of the property, broke into the yard.

"The kaffir ambulance is here, Sergeant," he said. "It's in the drive."

"Show the attendants through, Evans." Emmanuel checked his watch in the glow of electric light spilling from the neighbor's window. Eleven forty-two. If he'd held steady for half an hour longer, Zweigman would still be in bed instead of attending a crime scene.

"The line between life and death is not set in stone." Zweigman read Emmanuel's mind with a glance. "The quicker a wound is cleaned and stitched, the better a patient's chance for survival and recovery. You know this from the war."

"I do," Emmanuel said. They might not have saved the man's life with their open-air operation, but they had, at least, increased his chances of surviving the night.

"Back here. Back here." Evans waved his arms in the air, excited by the coming end of the shift. With the injured black man out of the way, he and the boys could return to their homes, loosen their belts, and knock the top off a cold beer. "Come down this passage and into the yard."

Two burly black men muscled through the gap between the house and the garage carrying a canvas stretcher with a small first-aid kit resting in the folds. Zweigman motioned them to follow him into the garden. Emmanuel let them get well ahead. The handover from field doctor to hospital attendants was a courtesy Zweigman would insist on.

The ambulance men worked fast and in silence. Within minutes of their arrival, the injured man occupied a bench seat in the rear of the ambulance kitted out with donated blankets and hand-rolled bandages. The younger of the two attendants pressed Zweigman's hand in his massive paw and simply said, "Bless you, Baba."

And they were gone.

"Do they have far to travel?" Zweigman asked.

"Miles and miles," Emmanuel said, and dismissed the policemen who'd bunched together next to a beige police van. They scrambled aboard, stretching out their limbs and breaking open packets of cigarettes. The engine revved and the van jumped the lip of the curb before vanishing into the neat grid of white Johannesburg streets.

He ushered Zweigman through the front garden to a Ford sedan, glad to see the doctor depart the crime scene for his own warm bed.

Emmanuel slipped behind the wheel of his police-issue black Chevrolet and started the engine. He turned on the headlights. The houses on the street were dark now, but for a solitary window in the house next door. He glanced across the unpruned rosebushes, expecting to see the angular figure of Mrs. Lauda bordered by the wood frame.

Instead, he saw Cassie Brewer standing with her right palm pressed to the glass, her yellow nightie a splash of color under a pale face pinched tight with fear. She stepped aside and switched off the light, leaving a black void.

—

The girl took quick, shallow breaths though her open mouth. The rough cotton sack covering her face wasn't a pillowcase grabbed up from a bed and shoved into a pocket. It was designed and made for this purpose alone: to be pulled over the head and then tightened around the neck with a drawstring. The exact fit frightened her. More so than the soft purr of the car engine that sang for miles and miles of smooth, tarred road that led away from the city and all her familiar places.

The kidnappers smoked cigarettes in silence. The smell of tobacco and leather permeated the sack. The frayed end of the drawstring rubbed against her neck, irritating her skin. They'd left her hands free, but she dared not loosen the string. Any movement might attract attention and it was safer to remain quiet in the backseat, unmolested, at least for the length of the ride.

She could feel leather under her thighs. Wind rattled the passenger-side window and her dry breath caught in her throat. Seventeen years old and already an expert at running away. Charity homes, juvenile facilities, and Christian youth camps, no place held her for longer than she wanted to be there—and the interior of this immaculate car was not a place she wished to be.

Escape remained possible: a quick lift of the door handle, a hot rush of summer air and then a leap into the dark. Landing on the road would hurt. The alternative—staying with men who owned homemade hoods and prowled alleyways for lone prostitutes—would hurt multiple times more. One way or another, tonight would end in her blood.

She moved her right hand across the supple leather, slowly inching in the direction of the door. The tarmac ran smooth beneath the car wheels. The road would lead her back to the city, to the room with a single cot in the corner and a window ledge decorated by pigeon droppings: a dump made beautiful in her mind's eye.

Cool metal curled under her hand. Blood roared in her ears, drowning out the wind that rattled the window glass. Now. It had to be now. Her fingers lifted the handle. She eased sideways, ready to take the leap. A hand encircled her wrist and tugged her away from the door with a jerk.

"Do you know who I am, sweetheart?" the man who'd blocked the alleyway asked. His fingers tightened against her skin to make a handcuff.

"No." She croaked the answer. In her heart she already knew plenty about the big man. He was patient: sitting in the front seat, smoking a rollie, waiting for her to break cover like an antelope drinking at a water hole. He was not angry that she's tried to escape. He was amused. Cold enjoyment, the girl knew from experience, was worse than violent rage.

"I'll tell you who I am, sweetheart," the big man said. "I am your salvation."

4

NEGUS DOZED ON an iron cot pushed into a corner of the European detectives' room at Marshall Square Police Station. The room was a large space with cracked linoleum floors and two fans that whirred from the ceiling. Wooden desks covered with paperwork and empty coffee cups cut the space into a grid.

"No one waiting for you to get home, Cooper?" Mason stood in the enquiry room door with an unknotted tie, rolled-up shirtsleeves and damp patches under his armpits. The station interview rooms sweltered in summer.

"Just a bed," Emmanuel said, and threw his hat on his desk. The weight of one more lie added to all the others barely registered. Besides, the lieutenant asked too many questions.

"One of the boys, Nkhato, has been released," Mason said. "The senior priest at St. Bart's confirmed he was in bed at lights-out. That was at nine. He's clean. Makes you wonder what other errors that Brewer girl made."

"A bad ID on both boys is possible," he agreed. That would be a sweet result even if the police commissioner canceled holiday leave until an arrest was made.

"It's possible." Mason stifled a yawn. "I need you in with the Shabalala boy. Work your magic. Play up the born and bred in Sophiatown angle and maybe he'll tell you the truth about where he was last night."

"What makes you think he's lying?" Emmanuel asked. *The Sophiatown angle?* The lieutenant had definitely gone through the personnel files and picked up details that should have remained private.

"You'll see." Mason retreated into the corridor and proceeded to the last door on the right. Emmanuel followed. There was still a chance the schoolboy in the interview room and Detective Constable Samuel Shabalala were not related.

Mason opened the door to a windowless room painted prison green. A bright electric bulb cast a harsh light over the small wooden desk and the black youth seated with his back against the wall. Plucked from bed by the police, he wore blue cotton pajamas and polished brown leather school shoes without socks. A school blazer hung over the back of his chair, superfluous in the heat. Mason shut the door and leaned a shoulder against it.

"I'm Sergeant Cooper." Emmanuel sat down opposite the boy, who was clearly a younger version of Detective

Constable Samuel Shabalala of the Native Branch. "And
you are?"

"Aaron Shabalala. And I have already told the other
policeman everything. Many times." If Aaron knew the
name Cooper, he didn't show it.

"I wasn't here," Emmanuel said. "You'll have to tell me
where you were earlier tonight."

"I was at school, then at Principal Brewer's house, then
at home." Aaron stretched out his legs, already familiar
with this line of questioning. He was tall even when sitting
down and muscle was starting to fill out his shoulders and
chest. His broad face had no expression. Whatever his
emotions were, they were hidden behind a calm facade.
Emmanuel recognized the cool countenance and the loose
physical grace with which the Zulu youth moved.

"Do you know why the lieutenant and I are asking you
about where you were late yesterday evening, Aaron?" It
was now past midnight.

"Some men broke into the principal's home and beat
him and his wife." The young Shabalala spoke in a quiet
voice. "The principal was a good man. His wife was hospi-
table. They took us into their home and fed us with kind
hearts. I would never harm these people."

"What about their daughter?" Cassie had blushed before describing the Zulu youth. There might be something
there. "Did she also have a good heart?"

Aaron hesitated, caught out by the question. The mask
that hid his feelings slipped, and a bright flash of anger
registered in his dark brown eyes. He cleared his throat

and said with careful deliberation, "The daughter sat and ate at the table with us."

"Did you go back to the Brewers' house after you'd finished eating dinner, Aaron?" The anger Emmanuel had seen was brief but real. The Zulu youth had a temper. He controlled it well, but what might happen when that control slipped?

"I did not go back to the principal's house. I got off the bus and walked for a long time. Then I went back to my home."

Mason sucked his teeth to show what he thought of that answer. Emmanuel felt the same. The boy would have to give up a name, a location and at least one witness to back his story.

"Where did you go, exactly?" A bar crowded with drinkers, a card game, a brothel; anyplace with people would be a plus.

"Nowhere. Just walking."

Emmanuel retrieved his pen and notebook and placed them neatly on the tabletop. "Give me the name of one person, just one, who saw you wandering through Sophiatown on Friday night."

"I kept to the shadows. Nobody saw me."

"Really?"

"It is so."

Surely this boy, the son of a detective constable, understood the penalties for serious assault and theft. What part of "you're in deep shit" did he not comprehend? A knuckle rapped hard against the interview room door.

"Lieutenant," Detective Constable Negus's sleep-affected voice said. "Phone call for you."

"Take a message. I'm busy," Mason said.

"I already offered but the man says it's an emergency and you must come now, now. Something about a shepherd and his sheep."

"All right." Mason straightened up and gripped the door handle. "You're with me, Cooper. We'll give Shabalala ten minutes to think about what he really did last night and hope that he remembers the truth by the time we get back."

"I have told you where I was." Aaron flexed his right hand, testing the joints. "I was walking."

Emmanuel paused at the door and gave Aaron a look like the one he'd given Cassie earlier that night: *You are lying, boy, and I know it.*

—

The hard linoleum floors amplified the gritty sound of Lieutenant Mason's voice and the slam of the telephone receiver as it hit the cradle. Negus stood by the edge of the cot, waiting for knockoff time. Emmanuel sat at his desk, mulling over Mason's decision to pull him from the interview room. Either Mason really didn't trust him, or the ex–vice cop was so mired in a "one-man undercover" mentality that dominating all aspects of an investigation remained second nature.

Lieutenant Mason stepped into the enquiry room, jacket buttoned up and black hair slicked back. Churches of all denominations would happily invite him to join a prayer circle. Emmanuel, however, wouldn't let the lieutenant anywhere near pets or children. While Mason appeared utterly indifferent to the call that moments ago had him slamming down the phone, the tightness in his shoulders and the hard lines around his mouth reminded Emmanuel of his own father before a rage. The calm façade was a lie. Mason's icy exterior hid a violent temper fed by a decade of dirty police work.

"Back to your lonely bed, Cooper. You, too, Negus. We're done for the night. Report in tomorrow at eleven a.m."

"Right enough, Lieutenant." Negus stretched out, shoved a brown fedora onto his head and made for the door.

"Shabalala is still in the interview room," Emmanuel said. "I have a few more questions to ask him before finishing up."

A ball tightened in his stomach just as it had when his father brooded at the kitchen table, waiting for the one wrong word to justify unleashing a beating. The defenseless slum boy inside Emmanuel, who'd eaten dinner in a sweat of fear, warned him to be quiet in the face of Mason's demeanor. The combat soldier with a bullet wound in his left shoulder did not listen.

"We're not in a conversation, Cooper," Mason said with an unblinking stare. "Pack up and go home. That's an order."

"If you say so, sir." Emmanuel reached for his soft felt

trilby with a sharply angled brim and tugged it on. Soldiers and police lived and died by orders. God knows he'd followed a raft of incomprehensible commands while fighting the war, and each time he had to stop himself from asking "why?"

"Cooper." Negus stood in the corridor with bags under his eyes. "Let's make tracks, man."

"Good night, Lieutenant." Emmanuel heeded the unspoken warning in Negus's voice and left the room. Getting into a pissing competition with Mason was futile. The ex–vice cop had already taken too much of a personal interest in him.

Negus paused at the top of the stairs and said, "Here's a free piece of advice. Do not fuck with Mason. If you do, he will fuck you back in ways that would make a whore cringe."

"How is making an interview request fucking with the lieutenant? We're working the same investigation."

"It's *his* investigation, Cooper. Don't forget it. Asking a question is the same as spitting on his dead mother's grave. That's assuming Mason had a mother."

"I thought he was born-again."

"My Xhosa nursemaid had a saying, 'The rain wets the leopard's spots but doesn't wash them off.' Mason might take a shower in the blood of Jesus every morning, but he's still the same man who set fire to whorehouses and gambling rooms if they refused to pay him for protection." Negus fumbled a packet of cigarettes from his jacket pocket and slotted one into the corner of his mouth. "You just painted a target on your chest and waved your arms at a man with a flamethrower. Fade in and fit in, that's your best defense."

"I'll try."

It was too late to take evasive action or to play dead for Mason. The lieutenant had him square in his sights: from reading over his file and retaining the details, to voicing comments that implied a firsthand knowledge of an incident involving women that Emmanuel couldn't remember. There was only one course of action open to him if he had any hope of repaying his debt to Detective Constable Shabalala, a man who'd saved his life on more than one occasion: act like a diplomat but prepare to fight a covert war.

5

THE RAIN WETS the leopard's spots but does not wash them off. The proverb stayed with Emmanuel on the drive through the deserted streets of nighttime Johannesburg. How far had he traveled from the ramshackle streets of Sophiatown? he wondered. Not in miles but in time, or life, or history? Beneath the veneer of his tailored suits, polished shoes and clean hands, the white kaffir boy with a flexible attitude to the law and no allegiance to any one racial group remained.

He hid his roots well. But that invisible split between Detective Sergeant Cooper, the respectable European policeman, and Detective Sergeant Cooper, the liar with a secret family across the color line, might be the reason Lieutenant Mason had read over his personnel file. He might sense something not quite "white" about a policeman born in a slum with no apparent personal life.

Be careful, Emmanuel thought to himself. *Be careful.*

The words played in his head throughout the long drive to the wealthy bubble of Johannesburg's northern suburbs. Here, sandstone churches and elite private schools contrasted with the gospel halls and cinder-block classrooms in Sophiatown. Shade trees and trimmed hedges hid grand houses with sprawling grounds and swimming pools.

He turned right onto Fourth Avenue and then right again into a paved driveway. The night watchman, a native veteran of the El Alamein campaign in North Africa, flashed a light into the car then waved Emmanuel through the gates.

The prime half-acre spread belonged to Elliott King, Davida's father: a man cunning enough to keep a mixed-race family under one roof while simultaneously sitting at the table with members of the National Party who'd signed the racial segregation rules into law. King managed this feat by maintaining appearances. Europeans slept in the "big house." A raid by the "immorality squad," whose job it was to enforce the law forbidding interracial sex, would find the races in perfect balance. White men upstairs in the big house and brown women in the servants' hut or in the maid's room adjacent to the kitchen: a system perfected by the God-fearing Dutchmen who kept black slave wives in the Cape of Good Hope back in the eighteenth century.

Emmanuel parked at the rear of the house and sat for a moment: tired yet fully awake, hungry but for more than food. Contact with Davida and Rebekah would satisfy him. First, he had two difficult phone calls to make.

—

Emmanuel walked the path through masses of pale Madonna lilies and stands of weeping willows. Ahead, a whitewashed hut gleamed in the moonlight. He let himself in, slipped off his shoes and socks and lit a candle. From day one of his transfer to Jo'burg he'd ignored Elliott King's rules and slept in the little hut.

Tonight, he knew that a stronger man would follow the rules and retreat to the big house so Davida could get some rest. A better man would keep the mess of police work separate from his family life.

Except he felt neither good, nor strong, nor sure that he'd fall asleep before dawn. Images of the ransacked house and the bloodied bodies of the Brewers and the unidentified black man in the garden were too fresh to put away. The sadness in Shabalala's voice when he'd heard that his son was in police custody was something that Emmanuel would never forget either. He padded across cool tiles to the bedroom. Davida lay on her side with the cream sheets bunched around her hips, her hair a dark tangle in the candlelight. Rebekah slept cocooned in a yellow wicker basket with a fat baby fist curled against her smooth cheek. She was brown like her mother. My girls, he thought, my beautiful girls.

Davida eased onto her back and muttered, "Emmanuel . . . is that you?"

"Yes." He lowered the candle. "I didn't mean to wake you. Go back to sleep."

"What's wrong?" She was half in dreams.

"Nothing." He heard the lie in his voice and added, "Nothing that concerns you."

"You're tired."

"I am," he admitted. "It's late."

The thread that connected him to Davida and their little girl remained fragile. Outside of the safety of her father's private compound, interracial relationships were illegal. The new laws turned their love into something secret and precarious. If they let it, they could both feel the melancholy weight of it hanging between them . . . Detectives classified as European and mixed-race women *did* mix, but never in public. He didn't have much to offer Davida in the way of a future.

"Come on. Get in," she said in a foggy voice. "Just sleeping. It's too late for the other thing."

"You're giving me the night off?"

"Just this once," she said.

He blew out the candle and tore off his jacket and tie. Next came the leather holster holding his Webley revolver, which he laid on the side table with the butt angled for easy reach. Shirt and trousers followed. He slipped under the sheets. Davida turned onto her side again. Emmanuel placed a hand to the curve of her hip and felt the heat of her skin through the thin cotton of her nightdress. He breathed in her scent, the faint trace of rosewater in her hair. There was no place for the two of them outside of this little hut. He didn't care. Not tonight and maybe not ever.

Still, he had to be careful. If Mason or the other police

found out he'd leaked news of the investigation to a black friend and then come home to a coloured woman's bed, they'd destroy him. The boys from vice would tear down the delicate web of hope and lies that held his life together, and they'd enjoy it. Davida and Rebekah would suffer.

Be careful. The words reverberated in Emmanuel's head until he was unsure if the warning was one meant for him or for Lieutenant Walter Mason, telling him and his questions to stay away from this hut and from his girls.

—

Sunlight burned through a high window, heating a corner of the bare concrete floor. The girl crawled into the sunspot and lifted her face to the rays. Her skin warmed. The ache in her bones eased. From outside the window came the low hum of cicadas and the lonesome creak of a windmill. The air smelled of dust and of fruit rotting on the ground. She was in the country and far off the tarred main road leading back to Jo'burg. She listened for dogs and heard none. Their absence was strange. Cities had cars and farms had dogs. But the big man was no farmer. No, he was city bred with smooth, uncallused skin.

She glanced around, taking in her prison. She had an army cot with a lumpy sisal mattress covered by a scratchy gray blanket and a wooden ablution bucket. A stained and tatty pillow was the one compensation to comfort. This was no room for living, just the opposite. The hairs on her arms prickled at the thought. The long drive from a dirt alley-

way in the city to a slab floor in an isolated farmhouse might be the last journey she ever made.

A guinea fowl's incessant chirp reached her from the outside. Then, far off in the distance, she heard the throttle of a car engine traveling the rough dirt track to the house. Pain made her memories unreliable. The feel of her fingers gripping the locked door handle to the room came back to her.

The big man and his friend had had a fight. She remembered that even through the pain. After the snap of breaking furniture and a string of dirty words, they'd left the house and slammed the door shut. How long ago had that been? The stars were out and the moonlight fading. She'd tried to get out of the cell before eventually curling onto the mattress: to sleep and to heal and forget. Time blurred. Now the big man was on his way back.

She stood up and stretched for the window. It was too high to reach. Moving quickly, she pushed the cot across the floor to a space directly beneath the window. The mattress was uneven under her bare feet. Another long reach and her fingertips touched curling paint and the edge of a metal shape. The lock. It had to be. She perched on tiptoes, straining to reach the mechanism. Not quite. Another half foot and she'd get to the lock easily. An extra foot in height and she'd be able to open the window and climb out.

The engine idled at the gates to the property. Three, four minutes and the nightmare would begin again. She jumped to the concrete floor, dry-mouthed and nimble. Both the cot and mattress had to be back against the wall before the big man returned. The sound of the car grew louder.

She pushed hard and the metal legs of the cot scraped against the concrete. There'd be marks on the floor, each a telltale map of her escape plan. Car tires crunched over loose stones in the driveway and the engine cut. The girl wedged the cot against the wall, her heartbeat drumming like a tiny fist in her chest.

"You can't keep her, for Christ's sake." The smaller man's voice carried into the room, sharp with reproach. "He said to make an end to it. Finished and clear."

"I will," the big man replied, and the thud of his footsteps moved to the front of the house. "When I'm ready."

"You seriously think he won't find out that you broke your promise to get rid of her? This is his farm, Dom Kop."

"He won't know if you don't tell him," came the calm reply. "Make one more phone call and things will be finished and clear for you. Understand?"

The girl grabbed the pillow and threw it into place on the bed. Her breath caught in her throat at the icy tone in the big man's voice. He was poison, that one: the snake from the story of Adam and Eve in the Bible.

"Hey, relax. I'm just saying you have to be careful." The smaller man was cowed. The girl heard the surrender in his voice. He wouldn't help her if she escaped. One word from the big man and he'd run her down. A door creaked open and footsteps slapped the wooden stairs.

"Don't worry. I'll be finished long before he gets here for the holidays."

Hinges creaked and the door to the box room swung inward. The girl threw herself onto the rough mattress and curled into a fetal position. Sweat trickled from her forehead onto the uncovered pillow.

"Sleep well, sweetheart?" the big man asked.

"Yes, thank you." The girl forced a smile. It was important to be grateful and to speak gently. He'd taught her that last night. More lessons would soon follow this morning, each leaving a bruise.

"Sit up," he said. She did, careful to keep her chin raised, her back straight and her knees pressed together: last night's etiquette lesson had taught her the correct posture and acceptable facial expressions. Sunbeams brightened the window glass and the shadow of a tree branch made leaf patterns on the floor.

The big man clamped his hands onto her thighs and leaned in close. He was better-looking in the daylight than in the light from the lantern the night before. Nature had lavished her gifts on him. Slick black hair, fair skin, sharp cheekbones and eyes the color of the ocean. He'd win a beauty contest between them. The unfairness of it stung, but the girl pushed that thought aside.

A bird sang outside the window, calling her out of her hurting body and into the veldt.

Soon, she promised herself. You will fly.

6

THE BREWERS' HOUSE appeared shabbier in the daytime than at night. Tiny blackbirds nested in the tangle of shrubs in the garden and a rusted postbox leaned at an angle. No thieves worth a damn would target this place. The prison sentence for committing three violent assaults was too high a price to pay for a four-door Mercedes-Benz, however low the mileage.

Cassie Brewer stood by the boot of a dirty Land Rover parked in the driveway next door with her white socks scrunched around her ankles and her ponytail askew. She held a cardboard box overflowing with clothing and books.

She's still a child, Emmanuel thought. But old enough to have her word hold up in court.

A freckle-faced woman with a halo of frizzy red hair hurried down the front steps of the Brewers' house. Dressed in a brown cotton dress, black lace-up shoes with no stockings and no hat, she walked with the urgent stride of a farmer's wife who'd find her rest when she retired to an early grave. She loaded the cardboard boxes into the Land Rover's boot. A few neighbors worked their front gardens, some weeding and deadheading roses, others instructing their garden boys to do the same. They, too, watched the home.

Emmanuel moved quickly to Mrs. Lauda's driveway. Cassie saw him coming and drew in a sharp breath. She rubbed the front of her right shoe against the back of her calf, fighting the urge to run. The red-haired woman gave him a cursory glance and slammed the boot shut, raising dust.

"Detective Sergeant Cooper. Marshall Square CID." He offered his hand in greeting. "You must be Cassie's aunt from north of Pretoria."

"Delia Singleton from Rust de Winter." She shook hands quickly and checked the tires, already focused on the challenge of navigating Johannesburg's busy main roads and then the lonely dirt trails that would take her home again. "Cassie tells me you got the kaffir boys who made this mess."

"With her help we have one of the boys in for questioning," Emmanuel said. "We'll need to double-check the details of Cassie's story before laying official charges."

"The man who called last night said everything was settled. Cassie's got the case solved and I should pick her up and keep her for a while." Delia was brusque. "I've got six small ones at home and only half the fruit canning's done. I can't stay."

"One question for Cassie," he said. "Then I promise you'll be on your way."

"Make it quick, Detective." Delia crouched by the worn front tire and pressed her fingers to a patch pressed into the rubber. She ran her fingers back and forth over the surface, making sure the repair remained intact.

Emmanuel motioned Cassie in the direction of the rear of the Land Rover. She complied, reluctantly.

"Did you see Shabalala and Nkhato from where you hid behind the wardrobe or did you hear them?" he asked.

"I . . . um, I heard their voices," Cassie mumbled. The veins on her forehead pulsed blue under her freckled skin.

"And you're one hundred percent certain it was those two boys who came into your room and turned it upside down?" Emmanuel asked. Puffy-eyed and with a swollen bottom lip from where she'd bitten through the skin yesterday, the teenager clearly had passed a rough night.

"*Ja*. Sure. Completely." Cassie moved back and pressed her palms to the dusty surface of the Land Rover.

"Last chance to tell the truth," he said. The stark terror on Cassie's face as she stood framed in Mrs. Lauda's window had been real. She was lying to protect herself or someone else. "I give you my word that I'll do everything I can to find out who hurt your parents and why."

Cassie said, "I already told you. I said how it happened."

"Time to move." Delia finished the tire inspection and lifted the driver's door handle. "Get in, girl. We haven't got all day."

"Where can I reach you if I need to?" Emmanuel asked before the aunt climbed behind the wheel and sped into the hinterlands. He wondered if she'd ever had the pleasure of lying in bed until noon. Probably not.

"Clear Water Farm," Delia said, and gave instructions of major turnoffs and minor farm roads. "You can dial through to the farm on the party line. Don't use it unless it's urgent. Everyone listens in on the phone line and the whole district knows your problems. I've got enough on my plate."

"I understand." Emmanuel wrote down the phone number and instructions. Cassie stood by the Land Rover's rear bumper with her arms laced around her waist. She looked younger than her years and exhausted. He could understand why Mason and the rest of the Marshall Square detectives wanted swift justice for this fragile white girl.

"If that's all you need, we'll make tracks, Detective Cooper." Delia motioned Cassie into the decrepit vehicle. "No more tears, girl. Crying won't change anything. The doctors will fix your parents up and you'll be back to school in no time. Come, let's go."

Cassie scurried into the passenger seat and wiped dusty palms on the front of her skirt. Tears wet her cheeks, despite Delia's warning against crying.

"Safe travels," Emmanuel said when the Land Rover engine coughed to life and Delia mashed the gear stick into first. Between the farm, six children and the fruit canning, Cassie could expect to be fed and watered by her aunt, no more.

"Say good-bye to the policeman," Delia instructed. "Without the police, the black boys who put your parents in the hospital would still be walking free."

"Good-bye, Detective Cooper." Cassie cast him a nervous glance and tucked a bright strand of ginger hair behind her ear. The spot where the metallic shine of the lipstick had streaked the back of her hand had been scratched raw.

The Land Rover drove off with the main witness in the Brewer assault and robbery case huddled in the front seat. Placing a vulnerable teenager into the care of a relative made good sense, but Delia's comment that the "man who called said Cassie's got the case solved" struck a nerve. Aaron was going to get pinned for car theft and three counts of serious assault unless he came up with a credible alibi.

"How's she holding up?" One of the neighbors, a good-looking man with sandy-colored hair, green eyes and a trimmed mustache, loitered on the pavement. He wore a pressed khaki safari suit that had never been worn outside of an office, much less on a muddy bush track. Emmanuel slotted the man into the concerned-but-fascinated-with-the-crime category of civilians. Most people fell into that group.

"Cassie is fine," Emmanuel said. The scratches on the teenager's skin were self-inflicted, as if she were physically trying to erase a stain from her person. Cassie lived a hundred miles from "fine," but that was confidential information.

"My wife heard through Mrs. Lauda that you got the thieves." The man waved a brown leather satchel in the direction of a house from which a baby wailed. "My wife reckons it's two of the blacks that the Brewers had over for dinner."

"You thought the principal's native improvement program was a bad idea."

"Not just me," the tanned white man said. "Everyone on the street warned him that bringing natives into the area posed a danger. We asked him to stop. He didn't listen. And now look what's come of that experiment."

"Did Brewer get into fights over the native visits?" Emmanuel asked. The untidy garden and weed-choked gutters were another clue that the principal and his wife didn't care much about fitting into the neat streetscape. Still, they must have known that disputes over music played too loud and cars parked too long outside the wrong house could get people killed.

"Me and Mrs. Lauda had words with the principal. Mr. Allen from down the road also told Brewer, calm like, that his three daughters didn't feel safe with so many strange black boys walking the street. You know what the headmaster told him? To keep his daughters locked in the house where they'd be out of harm's way." Color rose in the man's face at the remembered conversation. "Brewer got a fist to the chin from Mr. Allen for that, but we all agreed that the principal deserved it."

"And you are?" Emmanuel asked.

"Andrew Franklin. Call me Andy." The man checked his watch, an antique piece with a battered leather strap. An heirloom, Emmanuel guessed, passed down from a distant ancestor with sweat-stained clothing and a rifle slung over the shoulder.

"I'm late for a meeting." Franklin smiled an apology. "If you speak to Cassie, tell her that we're thinking of her. She suffered a lot because of the trouble her parents caused."

"I'll let her know."

Andy Franklin walked to a station wagon parked outside a yellow house, a great white hunter dressed for the veldt but off to sell insurance in a sterile cube or maybe accept bank deposit forms. Emmanuel wrote Franklin's full name into his notebook. If Aaron Shabalala dropped off the suspects list, there'd be a number of disgruntled neighbors to interview.

The sky stretched bright blue over the orderly street. When the police barricades were struck, there'd be no reminder of last night's events, no permanent marker of the blood that had been spilled inside. The Brewer family and the black man in the garden, however, would remember that Friday night forever.

7

H E ENTERED THE European detectives' room at 10:30 a.m. with two goals: to fade in and fit in while doing what he could to solve the Shabalala case.

Negus and two undercover cops Emmanuel knew by sight but not by name smoked cigarettes at the far end of the room. Both were of average height with razor-cut brown hair and pink, fleshy faces: they might have been brothers but for the eagle nose on one and the stuck-out ears on the other.

"Christ above." Dryer shambled in, blue suit wrinkled and his tie crooked. He mopped sweat from his brow with a handkerchief. "I need a cup of coffee with four sugars to wake me up after last night."

"You're early." Emmanuel shed his jacket and hat.

Dryer consistently arrived five to ten minutes after the start of the shift and always with an excuse for the delay. "When Lieutenant Mason telephones and says, 'Be in the squad room at ten-thirty,' I make sure I turn up at ten-thirty."

"Wise move." The telephone number for the house in Houghton was on the temporary transfer sheet he'd filled out in Durban before moving to Jo'burg. The transfer sheet also listed Emmanuel's address as that of an ex-detective friend who knew to answer any impromptu visits with a simple "Cooper is out. Drop by again in a couple of hours." The real phone number and the fake address summed up his split life nicely.

"Any idea what the guys from undercover are doing here?" he asked Dryer. The fleshy-faced twins had not been picked at random: they were companions from a life that Mason had formally renounced. The lieutenant was gathering his boys.

Dryer said, "If we're short-staffed, Mason brings in extra men to help. It's normal."

"You made the early call, Sergeant Cooper. I'm impressed. I telephoned the number on your contact sheet, but the woman who answered said you were gone for the day and she had no idea when you'd be back."

Emmanuel turned to face Mason, who stood in the doorway of the room with a dead-eyed expression. He wore a freshly pressed black suit and dark blue tie.

"I never sleep late," Emmanuel said. He locked away the memory of Davida lazing in bed this morning with Rebekah at her breast. If anyone could see through the skin of a situation to the raw bone of things, it was Walter Mason.

"Fill the gaps." The lieutenant signaled the other detectives closer. "Bad news first: Ian Brewer died of his wounds an hour ago. This is a now a murder investigation. All holiday leave is canceled immediately. The police commissioner called. He wants results and he wants them quickly."

Dryer groaned. Negus sucked on a cigarette and blew smoke rings. Emmanuel felt the pit of his stomach drop to his toes. He dreaded giving the news to Shabalala, who was even now traveling on the fast mail train from Durban to Jo'burg, having been granted emergency leave by his boss, Colonel van Niekerk.

"There is good news," Mason continued. "We've received an anonymous tip-off about the red Mercedes stolen from the Brewers' house last night. In two minutes we move out to search this Sophiatown address."

Mason held up a piece of paper with the information written in blue ink. Emmanuel leaned in and read the street name and number: Annet Street backed onto the sewage works; the houses and stores were within walking distance of the front gates of St. Bart's school.

"Cooper, you're with me in the lead vehicle. You know the township, so you'll navigate. The rest of you, follow close. With the assistance of the Sophiatown police we will spread out and perform a grid search of the area. Remain in pairs at all times. Understood?"

"Yes, sir." The gathered detectives, including Emmanuel, answered in unison. He mapped the street in his mind, recalling the boundaries of the coloured school and the dense collection of shanties and rickety fruit stands that hawked single mangoes and oranges. A Mercedes-Benz in that environment would not last long. If they found a metal carcass, they'd be lucky.

—

"Wind up your window, Cooper," Mason said. "I hate the smell of this place."

Emmanuel complied. Dust whirled through the patched-together shacks and faded buildings. Populated for the most part by black Africans, Sophiatown also contained a smattering of Jews, Indians and mixed-race couples intent on breeding brown-skinned children. Sophiatown defied the racial segregation laws. The ruling National Party despised the township on principle. To Emmanuel, the place smelled alive with people, food, smoke and dreams. Fastidious whites, like Mason, found Sophiatown's lack of proper sanitation offensive.

"You've worked here?" Emmanuel asked the lieutenant, and checked the rearview mirror. Dryer and Negus followed almost bumper to bumper in the second black Chevrolet sedan, Dryer driving too close for fear of losing his way in Sophiatown's back lanes. The third vehicle carried the undercover cops.

"We mostly raided illegal shebeens. We found a few marijuana storehouses and liquor stills. The usual."

Mason had forgotten to add "and burning them down if they refused my protection." Half of Emmanuel's mind remained on the conversation while the other half scrambled to find a calm spot to work out the next best move for

Shabalala and his son. The tip-off about the Mercedes would prove to be bullshit. The investigation would find nothing: not a tire or an ashtray. That would buy time.

"This is your town." The lieutenant looked out at the rough dirt sidewalk and the gang of sweaty boys playing soccer with a ball made from cotton rags and string. It sounded like an accusation.

"Used to be." Emmanuel swung hard right into a rutted dirt lane strewn with garbage. "Not anymore."

He wasn't going to volunteer any more information. Lieutenant Mason had read his files. That was enough disclosure for Emmanuel. Colonel van Niekerk, his current boss in Durban, and Lieutenant Piet Lapping of the Security Branch kept buried the one secret Mason could not uncover: Emmanuel's voluntary resignation from the Detective Branch and subsequent racial reclassification from "European" to "mixed race" for close to a year. The missing pages were stowed away until such time as the colonel or the faceless men at the Special Branch deemed them advantageous.

Colonel van Niekerk kept his past quarantined from the likes of Mason. This protection came at a cost. Emmanuel owed the Afrikaner policeman his loyalty and remained in his debt. To Mason, his temporary boss, he owed nothing.

"You lost touch with your friends when you left the township?" Mason kept fishing for information.

"Yes. I did." That was the truth, with a few major exceptions.

"Must have been hard, being cut off from your roots."

"Not really," he lied. Moving from the grit and pulse of Sophiatown to the brooding silence of the country had been hell for a teenage boy. "I was young when I left here."

"The Jesuits say, 'Give me a boy till he's seven and I'll give you the man.'" Mason pointed his finger at the wash of life on the street. A three-legged dog hunted for scraps outside an open-air butcher with a sheep's head on the wooden table. Children played pickup sticks in the dust while men and women talked in front yards and on corners, trying to make sense of the world. "This township formed you, Cooper. Made you into the man you are today."

The implications of Mason's statement were too weighty to consider. He'd smoked his first joint on the back stoep of an illegal drinking hole not ten minutes' walk from this laneway. A twelve-year-old "white kaffir," he'd spent his time with teenage gangsters and whores, making plans, all of them bad.

8

T HAT'S IT." EMMANUEL pulled over to the curb two doors down from a brown building with the number 33 painted on the wall in yellow. A beige van with some native policemen inside was parked on the verge.

"Sophiatown foot police." Mason indicated the six black constables who jumped from the van and stood on the sidewalk.

Their bull-necked white sergeant leaned against the back door and smoked a cigarette. "We're looking for a red car hidden somewhere in this area. Stay sharp and keep your eyes open. If you find the car, blow your whistle and a European officer will find you. Get busy."

The native police spread out with bemused expressions. Did the white lieutenant not see the rusted corrugated shacks riddled with holes and patched together with cardboard? If a car was left here, it was because the owner *wanted* it stripped for the insurance money.

"Cooper, start at the end of the street and take the left-hand side. Work back in the direction of the van. Check every alley and backyard. I'll interview the people in the house."

"Will do," Emmanuel said, and moved off. Mason didn't pair him up with another detective, presumably because the inhabitants of the township would recognize him as one of their own.

Shanties sprouted everywhere. A line of black girls sat cross-legged on the scrubby verge and braided each other's hair into cornrows. Sullen boys with caps pulled low onto their heads loitered in doorways. Emmanuel searched dirt lanes too narrow for cars and neglected yards too small to lie down in. Mason was wasting time. The search proved how little he knew about township life.

A slight black boy, about eight years old and with a head doused in white louse powder, sat cross-legged on the sidewalk and angled a mirror to catch the sunlight. Reflections rippled across the walls of a dilapidated tuck shop. Emmanuel crouched beside him.

"Can I see that?" he asked. "I'll give it back."

"Promise?" Twitchy fingers tightened their grip on the object and the boy's brown eyes were large in his dirty face.

"Cross my heart." Emmanuel held out his hand. The cracked mirror was encased in metal and weighed heavily in his palm. He turned it over. Flecks of silver brushed off the surface. "Where did you get this?"

"Just there, ma' baas." The boy pointed to a space between two dilapidated shacks. "I was walking, looking on the ground for money. I found it fair and square."

"Keep it. It's yours." Emmanuel returned what was likely to be the sideview mirror of a Mercedes-Benz cabriolet to the boy and took a closer look at the opening. Chest-high scrub was piled up as a barricade. He ran a fingertip across a streak of red paint scratched into the corrugated iron wall.

He stripped away the branches. Hot color showed through the leaves. With a quarter of the barrier torn down, the curved lines of a car bonnet became visible. He pulled out more scrub and threw it onto the street. Four more big branches and he could see the whole car: a red Mercedes-Benz with black leather seats and a missing sideview mirror.

Emmanuel opened the driver's-side door and leaned inside. The interior reeked of cigarettes. He flipped the ashtray: butts smoked down to the filter spilled onto the carpeted floor. The fuel gauge needle slumped near empty.

A Sophiatown constable stopped in the alley mouth and blew his whistle to call the other European detectives to the scene. Emmanuel slid behind the wheel. The keys were still in the ignition. His knees hit the dashboard. The seat had been pushed in to allow contact with the foot pedals. The last person to drive the Mercedes had short arms and legs, a description that didn't match Aaron Shabalala.

"Make a path." The rearview mirror reflected a view of the street. Mason broke through the crowd of pedestrians who'd gathered at the mouth of the alley. Dryer and Negus and the ring-ins from undercover operations appeared next to Mason. "Police business. Move back."

Emmanuel stepped out of the car, still puzzled by its location. He'd known from the age of six which gangsters controlled the trade in stolen cigarettes, which ones did jewelry and which ones could make cars disappear. Why was this car still here? At any given time there might be three or four buyers willing to pay cash for a ride like this one.

"Good work, Cooper." Mason tapped his fingers on the car hood. "How far are we from St. Bartholomew's school?"

"About a three-minute walk," Emmanuel said. Cassie's statement and the recovered Mercedes-Benz put Aaron Shabalala on the lip of the volcano. He'd better provide a credible alibi or else get used to living out the remainder of his days in a cell with a bucket to squat over.

"The keys are still in the lock." Dryer peered through the glass. "He must have been planning to come back for it later."

Christ, Emmanuel thought, it's a miracle the car is intact. Residents of Sophiatown lived *now*, in the moment. Leaving the Mercedes for later made no sense.

"Open the boot," Mason instructed.

Dryer scrambled to obey: the silver keys dangling from his index finger allowed him a brief moment of ownership. He unlocked the boot and lifted the handle. Twigs and dried leaves covered the floor rug. Emmanuel moved closer. A seam of red dust filled the crack between the rubber seal and the metal body of the car. Sophiatown had paved roads and dirt lanes, which split into a labyrinth of paths, most of them packed hard by the traffic of carts and people. White Johannesburg largely enjoyed the benefits of loose gravel and tarred avenues. The red dust in the Mercedes's boot didn't belong to either Parkview or the township.

"Something on your mind, Cooper?" Mason asked. He stood in the lane with the stillness of an eagle watching a mouse.

"No, sir. Just relieved the anonymous call came in before the tires and the leather seats were stripped from the car."

"A religious man might see the hand of God in it, Detective Sergeant. We now have enough circumstantial evidence to charge Shabalala with the manslaughter of Principal Brewer and with robbery." Mason shut the boot and wiped dirt from his hands with a handkerchief. "The police commissioner will be pleased."

"A good result," Emmanuel agreed. Keeping a low profile was one of today's goals, but the dried mud and grass seeds embedded in the tire treads so clearly pointed to a drive across country that he couldn't stay quiet. "Looks like the car went off the tar and into the bush for a while."

Mason glanced at the evidence. "The rougher the ride, the bigger the thrill. That's how these *tsotsis* think. Consequences don't matter. They just want to feel powerful."

"True." Big Ears from undercover backed up the lieutenant's theory. "The township grows them wild, and is it any wonder? The men drink, the women whore, and there's only one shithouse for a hundred people."

Big Ears might have been describing Emmanuel's own childhood except that Colonel van Niekerk had also removed all written references to his mother's murder and his father's accusations of infidelity and miscegenation. The official record stated, "Mother deceased. Cooper leaves Sophiatown to attend 'Fountain of Light' boarding school."

"When a Zulu gets his blood up, anything can happen." Eagle Nose added. "That's the way of it."

Aaron's transformation from schoolboy to budding gangster was swift. The press and the public had a clear mental picture of these lawless boys: little more than animals, they acted out of impulse and violent instinct. Every piece of physical evidence from the clogged tire treads to the cigarette butts would be explained away with a "you know what these people are like."

"Split up." Mason addressed the group. "Cooper, Negus and Dryer collect the usual I-didn't-see-anything statements from the people in the shacks. The rest of the team and I will examine the car."

What Emmanuel heard was, "Go away and leave me and my boys alone." He exited the alley under orders. The pile of scrub cleared from around the Mercedes-Benz had thinned, scooped up by women for use as kindling and floor sweepers. On impulse, Emmanuel broke off a leafy twig and shoved it into a jacket pocket. Shabalala would identify it at a glance when he arrived in town in a few hours.

"I'll take the first five street numbers," he said to Dryer and Negus. "You two take the next ten houses between you."

They split up and moved out. A crowd of locals had gathered opposite the alley, each craning over the other to catch the police action. The native constables from the Sophiatown station formed a human chain to keep the pedestrians off the road. Three scruffy boys with distended stomachs threw stones at a yellow tomcat on the next corner.

Emmanuel talked to the ten inhabitants of the building adjoining the alley. From the buckled-over woman wearing men's boots to the smooth-skinned boy with a slick of chemically straightened hair, none of the residents had seen or heard anything unusual the night before. The pattern repeated itself: each house populated with deaf, blind and dumb residents, some of whom had trouble recalling their own names.

Emmanuel had lied to the police and to welfare officers with impunity when he'd lived in Sophiatown. The police were just another armed gang. Talking to them upset the local gangs, who, in reality, controlled the township streets. They, too, had weapons: knives, machetes and clubs.

A whistle sounded once and then again. The crowd had doubled in size by the time Emmanuel reached the lane. Ragged children squatted in front of the adults, their size allowing them the best view. An arthritic woman, balancing on two canes, sold bags of greasy fat cakes to the spectators.

Dryer leaned against the Mercedes bumper, grinning like an idiot. Mason, Negus and the undercover operations twins bunched in a semicircle, gazing at an object cupped in Mason's palm. Light refracting off the corrugated iron walls gave the alley a red hue.

"What have you got?" Emmanuel asked.

"Proof."

"Of what?"

"Come see." Mason held a lapel pin between pale fingers. "We found it under the driver's seat."

A closer look revealed the pin to be a gold-plated badge with the word *Prefect* engraved under the St. Bart's school motto, *One in Christ*. Dryer pushed off the bumper, casting a shadow.

"It belongs to Shabalala." The Afrikaner detective's fleshy face shone with sweat. "He must have lost it when he was driving the car last night."

"Are we sure it's his?"

"Shabalala is a prefect. He's also the only St. Bart's boy without an alibi for last night," Mason said. "Cassie had it right. He was after the Mercedes."

Emmanuel reached out and gripped the badge. Metal bit into his skin. An anonymous tip-off, an intact car hidden in an alley and then this treasure, dropped like manna from police heaven, together forged an unbroken chain of events leading to Aaron Shabalala's conviction. The last time he'd encountered this level of twenty-four-carat-gold bullshit was when an officer fresh from the Royal Military Academy at Sandhurst promised a quick victory on Sword Beach during the D-Day landing.

"You're disappointed." Mason palmed the school pin and slipped it into an inner pocket for safekeeping. The lieutenant's face glowed in the rusty light.

"Just stunned by our good fortune," Emmanuel said. "I can't recall a case coming together so fast."

"Lucky, hey?" Dryer accepted a cigarette and a match from Negus. The undercover guys also lit up, producing a fug of celebratory smoke. "My holiday cabin in Kosi Bay is paid up in advance. No refunds. The wife thought she'd have to drive the children there all by herself."

"I'm for Kruger Park," Elephant Ears said. "Me, my son and two cases of Castle Lager."

The comment roused laughter from the smokers. A love of holidays glued them together. In a week's time, the name Aaron Shabalala would fade away into the long list of other black boys they had arrested and imprisoned.

Emmanuel held his temper. The car search had been a setup from the outset. He schooled his expression to hide the fury that pushed into his throat and demanded a voice. Mason's disregard for the most basic tenets of the law was reprehensible. This was not the just world that he'd fought for during the war.

"Cooper has doubts," Mason said.

"What?" Dryer was incredulous: visions of the cozy cabin and the fresh-grilled fish slipping away. "The daughter's statement, the stolen car and now the school badge in the car! It's all on the table, man. Case closed!"

"Amen," the undercover cops said in unison. They turned to Emmanuel.

Emmanuel looked on their grim expressions and their tight shoulders.

"I'm not disputing the facts," he said. Mason had evidence. He had suspicions. The evidence, though corrupted, won.

"Good. You drive, Cooper." A reptilian smile tugged the corners of Mason's mouth. "We'll follow you to Marshall Square." The silver keys to the Benz arced through the air and Emmanuel caught them on the fly.

"Yes, sir." He now despised Mason with a purity that verged on the religious.

9

"*GESONDHEID.*" DRYER POURED whiskey from a bottle wrapped in a paper bag into a coffee mug. "The police commissioner called to congratulate Mason on closing the Brewer case."

Emmanuel accepted the drink, aware of the contented atmosphere in the room.

"Salute." He clinked mugs with Dryer. The whiskey burned a trail from his mouth to his empty stomach, where it bloomed warm and started to spread out. He placed the mug on the side of his desk and wrote the first five lines of the report on the discovery of the stolen Mercedes. Dryer drifted away, drawn by the group of detectives smoking near the windows. Ceiling fans whirred in the afternoon heat, moving the air without cooling it.

Emmanuel waited till Dryer had lit a smoke and then picked up the desk phone and dialed.

"Johan Britz legal services," a female voice answered. "How can I help?"

"Anna. It's Sergeant Cooper. I need to speak to Britz first thing, please."

"Anything for you, Emmanuel." Anna, the English secretary, punched the call through on the internal intercom of the tiny office located up three flights of stairs of a shabby building in the city center.

"Cooper." The Afrikaner lawyer picked up on the second ring, his subtly accented voice at odds with his reputation as a man who never shied away from a fight, especially with the police. Beaten by vindictive cops, threatened by violent husbands and shunned by the legal fraternity, Britz was the only lawyer in Johannesburg with a full-time bodyguard outside his office *and* his home. "What have you got yourself into this time?"

Emmanuel pulled the incomplete incident report closer and scribbled words into the margin. He switched to Afrikaans, Johan Britz's first language and his own. "I'm calling for some friends. Their son's being charged with three counts of assault, one of manslaughter, vandalism and theft."

"Is that all?" Britz said in a dry tone. "You think the boy might be innocent of one or all of the charges?"

"I'm not sure." Emmanuel was honest. "His alibi is full of holes and we found his prefect's badge in a car stolen from the crime scene."

"Bad start." Johan breathed down the line. "Was the search executed according to protocol?"

"I can't prove it wasn't."

"Who's in charge of the investigation?"

"I'll spell it out." Mason's name in English or Afrikaans would be easily recognizable. The Dutch alphabet made it harder to decipher. He cupped his palm around the mouthpiece and gave each letter quickly.

"Lieutenant Walter Mason," Britz confirmed after a long pause, during which the scratching of a pen on paper was audible. "That's *two* pieces of bad news, Cooper. I've never encountered this Mason myself, but he comes with a reputation."

"Anything to do with fire?"

"And brimstone. The guy is trouble. And now he's found Jesus, right? It's a hell of a case to hand me just before Christmas, my friend."

"I know."

"Are you calling from Marshall Square, right now?"

"*Ja.*" It was a risk to call Britz from the station, but Emmanuel needed to move fast to protect Aaron while his friend Shabalala was traveling to Jo'burg.

"Get off the phone right now, Cooper. I'll call at the station house later this afternoon. In the meantime, keep out of Mason's way and stay the fok out of trouble." Britz hung up.

"I'll try," Emmanuel said into the static on the end of the line. Britz's advice came too late. He was in an illegal relationship with a mixed-race girl, had a secret family and was at odds with a superior officer over a potential dirty investigation: he was already in trouble.

"You speak Afrikaans like a Dutchman." The sound of Lieutenant Mason's voice traced an icy finger down the length of Emmanuel's spine. "I bet you talk Zulu like a native, too."

"White kaffirs," Emmanuel said. "We speak a bit of everything."

"Handy for police work." Mason, jacket hitched behind the butt of his Webley service revolver, moved deeper into the room. "Marshall Square will be poorer for your loss."

"Am I'm going somewhere?"

"You're going home, Cooper. Or to wherever it is that you've booked your holidays." The bright fire in Mason's eyes held no warmth. "I bet you're heading to Mozambique. It's a good spot for a single man. You can choose from any number of activities, some of them not available here in South Africa."

Mason was fishing. He had to be; alluding to the multiracial skin diving available in the Portuguese colony was simply a crude way to force a reaction.

"Who's going to Mozambique?" Dryer appeared at the tail end of the conversation, a whiskey mug gripped in his fist. "Is that where you're heading for Christmas, Lieutenant?"

"No. The dry heat of the veldt suits me better. I was suggesting a tropical beach Christmas to Cooper."

"He'll never get a booking this late in the month. It's school holidays." Dryer rested his rump on the edge of the desk. "Besides, he's staying here in Jo'burg."

"Sergeant Cooper is free to go wherever he likes for the

Christmas break, Dryer. He's on short-term transfer to the Marshall Square Detective Branch. We locals will finish up the Brewer investigation. It's all paperwork from now on in."

"My transfer ends on Tuesday," Emmanuel said, more to cover up the fact that he'd momentarily forgotten that the sprawling mass of Johannesburg was not his town any-more. He was a Durban detective playing house in Jo'burg with Davida and Rebekah. He didn't want that game to end.

"That's your last day. I talked to your commander, Colonel van Niekerk, and we both agreed you've earned the extra three days' leave. We might not have found the Brewers' car without your help." Gratification flashed across the lieutenant's face, bright and sharp as a knife blade. "Your holidays begin immediately."

"Agh . . ." Dryer made an anguished sound. "Lucky you, Cooper."

Emmanuel smiled and accepted his apparent good for-tune. Mason's manipulations simultaneously enraged and impressed him. The lieutenant was ruthless. Mason had managed to make him seem a hero and dismiss him from the case at the same time.

"I'll finish my report and pack up."

He sat and wrote. Mason was well on the way to framing Aaron Shabalala for a murder he likely didn't commit. The lieutenant's abuse of police power flicked a switch inside Emmanuel and he felt a familiar rage begin to grow.

"A pleasure working with you, Dryer. You, too, Negus." He made the rounds of the room after finishing the incident report, shaking hands, mouthing the right words. The biggest pile of horseshit he saved for last.

"It's been an honor serving with you, Lieutenant. Have a good Christmas."

"Safe trip back to Durban." Mason's hand held his hand in a deliberate, iron grip. "Give my regards to Colonel van Niekerk."

Emmanuel left the European detectives' room with his jacket buttoned up and his temper pushed down. He imagined Mason with a broken nose and a bloodied suit, his ribs cracked by a steel-toed boot. Adrenaline pumped through him just as it had on the night his mother lay stabbed and bleeding on the floor of their Sophiatown shack. With his sister's hand clutched tight in his own, he had run barefoot and scared through the dirt maze of the township calling for help, which came too late. He'd gone to war to bury that terrified, angry boy. Mason had resurrected him, though. Well, to hell with that, he thought. I'm going back in.

"*Calm the fuck down, soldier.*" The voice of Emmanuel's old sergeant major emerged from a long hibernation inside his head. A concrete bunker of a Scotsman, quick-tempered and foulmouthed, conflict was his natural state of being. "*If you go back into that room, you will beat the skin off that bastard or worse.*"

He took a deep breath and adjusted to the presence of the phantom sergeant major. The Scotsman lived deep in a psychological trench in Emmanuel's mind, and despite it being months since his last appearance, the sergeant remained impervious to anything but a heavy dose of morphine.

"Listen to me, boyo. If Mason survives the beating, he'll have you up on charges and in the brig before you can say 'Fuck you, sir.' If he dies, you'll spend the rest of your sorry life sharing a cell with undisciplined scum, some of whom you helped put there. Either way, you lose, Cooper. You're no good to Shabalala in jail. If a police review board digs up your little secrets and charges you with immoral activity, you'll not hold Davida or your little girl again for Christ knows how long."

The Scotsman was right, but the urge to do harm remained.

"Get out of this station, soldier. Right this minute. That's an order."

Emmanuel walked the length of a corridor decorated with framed pictures of the queen and Prime Minister Malan. White noise filled his head with the roar of a distant ocean. He took the stairs, shouldered through a throng of foot police gathered in the foyer and broke out into the light of a bright, hot afternoon. City noise washed around him: car engines and horns, the clatter of trams and the shuffle of Saturday shoppers streaming along the sidewalks.

"Mason never did trust you, lad."

"He didn't shut me out, either," Emmanuel said. *"I was in the Brewers' bedroom. I interviewed Cassie and Aaron. Something changed after Mason got that phone call during the Shabalala interview."*

"Mason needed a detective with brains last night. This afternoon, he needs 'yes, sir.' He needs men who'll back up that bullshit car search without question and then piss off on holidays. You don't qualify."

"Then why take me on the search for the Mercedes?" He knew the answer but needed to hear it said out loud.

"He wanted you to find the car. Detective Sergeant Cooper, the cop from the township with a clean reputation; you were perfect for the job. Your presence made the search credible. You killed off any stink of corruption. Now Mason is done with you." The sergeant major laughed low and rough in the back of his throat. *"You've been fucked without even being kissed, Cooper."*

—

Emmanuel pushed through the uniformed police in the foyer of Marshall Square station and took the corridor that led to the holding cells. Five minutes, he reasoned. He needed five minutes to get a truthful alibi from Aaron before talking face-to-face with Detective Constable Samuel Shabalala in an hour.

"You're wasting your breath," the sergeant major said. *"The boy's sewn up tight. You'll not get anything from him."*

"I have to try."

"Then make it fast. Mason will come down on you like camel shit if he finds out you're visiting his prisoner."

"I'll take that chance."

The smell of cigarette smoke and rising damp intensified the closer Emmanuel got to the rear of the station. The grim walls and poor ventilation gave the overnight prisoners a taste of things to come should they be remanded to a proper jail: a certainty in Aaron Shabalala's case.

The duty sergeant, a bony Irishman with a thatch of graying hair, got to his feet when Emmanuel reached the tight space that housed the "nonwhites" lockup. Fitzpatrick was on permanent post at the entrance to the native holding cells, a job usually reserved for black constables who'd passed the written test but showed a poor talent for actual police work. Fitzpatrick had taken the demotion to a "kaffir" post rather than accept early retirement from the force for the arthritis in his hands. Emmanuel had worked with him years before.

"Howzit, Cooper?" The Irishman stubbed out a cigarette with his twisted fingers and automatically lit another.

"I'm in top shape, thanks." Emmanuel took off his hat and stopped in front of the small desk covered in newspapers and cigarette ash. "Is your costume unpacked?"

Next week, Fitzpatrick would play the role of Father Christmas at the annual Police and Public picnic. The highlight of his year, Emmanuel had no doubt.

"The boots need a polish but the suit is ironed and ready to go," Fitzpatrick said. "What brings you to the dragon's den, Detective Sergeant?"

"A word with a juvenile prisoner, Shabalala. He came in late last night."

"I know the one." Fitzpatrick reached for a key ring

hooked to a wooden peg on the wall. "Third berth on the right. Do you want access?"

"Yes. Better than talking through the bars." That he could, with a nod, be granted the keys and have a blind eye turned to whatever happened in the cell was standard police practice. He entered the holding area. The customary inmates of the overnight lockup filled the first two cells: drunks with their limbs sprawled across the concrete floor, thugs with skewed noses and thick necks sitting on the narrow cots and, in the the majority, ordinary black men caught without their passbooks.

Aaron Shabalala sat in the gloom and stared at his open palms. He was the sole occupant of cell three, a rare luxury that Emmanuel assumed had been granted on Mason's personal request. The prime suspect in the Brewer murder case would leave Marshall Square without a scratch. Johan Britz, the Afrikaner lawyer, would find no evidence of misconduct or police brutality that might cast doubt on the outcome of the investigation. Mason's attention to detail was chilling. Emmanuel considered himself forewarned: he was dealing with a meticulous and dangerous force.

Aaron turned at the sound of footsteps and stood up to face Emmanuel as he unlocked the door and entered the cell.

"Go in hard, Cooper. Crack him open. He has to talk."

"They found your prefect's badge in the stolen car," Emmanuel said. "They are going to charge you with murder, theft and making a false statement to the police. What do you say to that?"

Aaron stepped closer. His jaw clenched. "I say that if the Brewers were a black family and I was a white school-boy visiting their house, I would not be in this cell but sitting at home with a cup of tea. What do you say to *that*, Detective?"

"*Well . . .* " the sergeant major breathed. "*I wasn't expecting him to come out fighting.*"

"*Me neither.*" He'd seen grown men go to water at the mention of a murder charge. Aaron was made of stone—like his father.

Emmanuel regrouped. He said, "We both know that the system isn't fair or just, but you're not helping yourself by lying about your alibi."

"I have a second question for you." Aaron remained impassive. "If a black girl accused a white boy from a good school of a crime, would the police believe her and arrest that boy?"

"We can talk hypothetical situations all day long, but the justice system isn't facing a murder charge. You are."

"Then let it be so." Aaron returned to the cot and sat down. He stared into his cupped palms, seeking what, Emmanuel did not know.

"*He's angry and I think he's scared,*" the sergeant major said. "*But he's a tough little bastard . . .*"

Emmanuel let the silence fill up the room. He took a risk.

"I know your parents," he said. "Seeing you hang will break them into pieces."

Aaron looked up, surprised, and then turned his face away. A noisy breath caught in his chest. Bull's-eye, Emmanuel thought.

"You are trying to help me. I know this," Aaron said. "But I should not be here. And the men in the cells without passbooks should not be here. I hope they find those responsible for Principal Brewer's death. But it was not me."

10

JOHANNESBURG'S SLANG NAME, "E'goli," the city of gold, didn't apply in the township. Nothing sparkled or shone. Emmanuel saw only rusted iron and peeling paint from the vantage of the raised brick porch where he stood with Zweigman and Detective Constable Samuel Shabalala on either side of him. The German physician and the Zulu detective absorbed the news of Aaron's arrest on a murder charge in silence. A blood-orange sun glowed through the haze of smoke from cooking fires.

"Don't leave it like that," the sergeant major said. *"You owe the Zulu your life, soldier. Tell him that you will do whatever is necessary to get his son out of this fix. Tell him that you will break every bullshit rule to make Mason pay for framing Aaron."*

"Mason fixed that search," Emmanuel said. "I'm going to find out why."

He kept the dark turn of his own thoughts about the lieutenant to himself.

"What must we do now, now, to help my youngest born?" Built tall and broad-shouldered and with muscle where other police his age carried a layer of fat, Shabalala was not content to stand and talk in the backyard of his brother's house. He needed to move and to hunt for his son's sake.

"Let's start at Baragwanath Hospital. Mason and his team won't bother interviewing the man from the garden for his testimony now the case is solved. He could give us something." Emmanuel paused and said, "Fair warning. Lieutenant Mason is dangerous. He will come after us when he finds out we're asking questions about the Brewer case and he will not do it gently."

"When do we start?" The German doctor cemented his place in the investigation without waiting for an invitation.

"Straightaway."

"Yes, that is good." Shabalala ushered them through the quiet brick home, which had the luxury of a separate kitchen and dining area. A permanent housing shortage gripped the township, with almost every room in every house rented out to lodgers. Not so here. Emmanuel wondered what Shabalala's brother did for a living to afford such privacy.

They exited into a shallow yard with a dusty gum tree. Swallows winged through the air and dipped over the rooftops. A group of children played hopscotch on a dirt grid.

"Should the hospital visit prove unsuccessful, there is also the girl who gave the statement to you, Sergeant," Zweigman said on their way to the car. "You think she is lying, correct?"

"Yes," Emmanuel said. "I also think Aaron is lying about where he went last night. They're both hiding something."

A strained silence followed the observation while the three of them considered the reasons a black boy and a white girl would lie about an ordinary Friday night.

—

A cream-and-green hallway led to a ward packed end to end with black men on iron cots. Family groups clustered around the sick, the women fanning the air to make a breeze while children played on the linoleum floor and men smoked cigarettes to pass the time. The able-bodied sat up in bed eating boiled eggs and roast corn bought from street vendors outside the hospital gates. Others lay listless and dazed in the heat. A few slept like the dead, arms tossed above their heads, eyes half closed. Every bed was taken. Two dozen more men lay on the floor, packed together like human tiles.

"Mr. Parkview." A nurse in a red-and-white uniform and a starched cap stopped at the foot of a hospital cot and glanced at the doctor's notes. Light slanted into the ward through the open windows and gave her dark skin a copper shine.

"This one will live," she said.

Emmanuel, Shabalala and Zweigman drew closer. The man, renamed for the suburb in which he'd been found, lay under a thin cotton sheet. He'd been heavily sedated and remained deep in a dreamless sleep. Blood seeped through the bandage wrapped around his head. Zweigman leaned over the cot, batted away a feeding fly and gently lifted the edge of the gauze to check the wound.

"Please, sir. That is for the doctors to do, not the day visitors." The nurse was polite but firm, the proper combination of tones to use when reprimanding a white man in public.

"Excuse me, sister." Zweigman smiled an apology. "You understand how vain we doctors are. I stitched this cut by torchlight and wanted to check my work."

"You are the one?" the nurse asked with raised brows. Zweigman nodded. She moved off quickly to the waiting area, skirting a one-legged man in a wheelchair who wore a miner's boot on his one remaining foot.

Emmanuel crouched by Zweigman's side and looked over the third victim of the break-in at the Brewers' house. He was tall and slender with holes cut into both his earlobes for the display of ornaments; empty spools of thread and circular clay plugs were popular choices. The fashion for male ear piercing was dying out in the cities but continued in the tribal enclaves in the bush. Mr. Parkview might have traveled from the country, in which case a passbook and a travel permit were vital. A black man without the proper papers ran a significant risk of imprisonment if caught by the police.

"The head wound is healing well, but we will not get answers to our questions this afternoon," Zweigman said. "There are also the multiple wounds in his back to consider. It might be many days before he is ready to talk."

Shabalala crouched at the opposite side of the bed, shoulder muscles tense under his white cotton shirt. For the first time that Emmanuel could remember, the Zulu detective looked tired. A fifteen-hour train journey with bad news at the other end and no help from the police would exhaust anyone.

"Gentlemen, all that we have lost is time." Zweigman recognized the signs of frustration in the two detectives. "This man will live. And when he is well, the truth will be told."

A white man in his twenties moved through the ward, accepting an orange from a visiting grandmother and refusing a pinch of snuff from a bald man wrapped in a blanket. The duty nurse touched his sleeve and pointed to Zweigman.

"I'm Dr. Botha," the young physician said when he reached the foot of the cot. Dr. Botha had dark, slicked-back hair and a mouth the color of a cut pomegranate. "And you are the jungle man who sewed up a blunt-force trauma wound and four pitchfork punctures on a blanket in the backyard of a house in Parkview."

"Guilty." A faint smile touched the German's mouth. The title *jungle man* pleased him. "I had wondered what weapon made those wounds on this man's back. Now the mystery is solved."

"Look." Botha gestured to the nurse and together they rolled the patient onto his side. Four blood spots dotted the bandages wrapped around his torso. "One of my first emergency cases was a gardener who tripped over some roots and fell onto his own fork. This injury is exactly the same, only deeper."

Botha settled the patient onto his side and the nurse hitched the thin sheet around his naked shoulders. Emmanuel moved to stand next to Shabalala. Maybe the injured man *was* the gardener, inherited along with the house and the car by Cassie's mother.

"A pitchfork isn't the sort of weapon you bring to a crime scene and then carry home again. We'll search the Brewers' yard and find the fork that made those injuries."

"Take me to where you found this man and I will find the weapon," the Zulu detective said without a trace of vanity.

"We have to get there before the sun goes down," Emmanuel said. Johannesburg sprawled across miles of dry high veldt; the black hospital and the European suburbs were kept well apart by laws that split the city into white and nonwhite areas. Zweigman, however, continued a conversation with Dr. Botha.

"A surgeon. You don't say?" Botha beamed a red smile. "What are the chances of a qualified surgeon happening onto a police investigation and operating on the spot?"

"Very slim," the German replied.

Experience alone gave Zweigman the rank of senior physician. He was a graduate of the Charité Universitätsmedizin in Berlin, specialist surgeon to that city's wealthy and then general practitioner to the inmates of Buchenwald concentration camp, and his knowledge of the world and of medicine was unique.

Emmanuel edged closer, hoping to extricate the German doctor from the hospital quickly.

"You're busy, I'm sure, and I hate to take advantage but I . . . it's just that . . ." Botha fumbled for words and then spoke in a rush before courage deserted him. "I have a patient in the female ward, a Mrs. Chaza, with a stomach growth that I'd like you to examine. And there are a few other unusual conditions on both wards that might be of interest. If you have the time, that is, and if you don't mind. We could use the extra help."

"A moment please to confer with my colleagues."

"Of course." Botha moved back into the aisle with the pretty nurse. Shabalala and Emmanuel gathered with Zweigman. The golden light of late afternoon made the dust motes dance in the air.

"Stay if you like," Emmanuel said to the German. "We'll search the Brewers' backyard and swing back later."

"If you are sure . . ." The lure of diagnosing a stomach growth and of accessing multiple medical conditions was tempting. So, too, the urgent need to attend to the overflow of patients lying on the floor and the dozens more packed into the waiting room.

"You'll do more good here than crawling through the weeds with us. Two hours and we'll be back."

"You must stay, Doctor. The sick cannot cure themselves," Shabalala added.

"In that case," Zweigman said, "go well, gentlemen, and I will see you soon."

"*Sala kahle*. Stay well, Doctor." Shabalala and Emmanuel made the traditional Zulu farewell, which drew a "huh?" of surprise from the nurse, who had yet to figure out the connections between these three very different men. She watched the detectives move through the ward and disappear into the corridor with a frown.

Emmanuel stepped outside. He envied Zweigman his healing skills. Detectives made promises of restitution for rape, theft and murder while knowing in their hearts that, even with the best results, what had been broken could never be fixed.

11

THE BREWERS' BACKYARD was as Emmanuel remembered it, wild with fruit trees, climbing roses and thick grass woven through with yellow nasturtiums. Birds sang from the branches. Crickets chirped. Lizards scuttled off the dirt path and into the shade. He ducked under a branch and crouched.

"I found him here, barefoot and with no passbook." Blood-soaked leaves, now turned a dark brown, spread out like a picnic blanket. "It was dark, so the question is, where did Mr. Parkview come from?"

"I will see." Shabalala bent lower and examined the leaf litter and trampled grass. He tracked to the rear of the yard, following a trail of gouged soil. They'd come into the garden via the back gate to avoid attracting the attention of the neighbors. A black man in a suit might prompt a call to the police . . . especially after what had happened to the Brewers in their own bedroom.

"Look, Sergeant." Sprays of dried brown liquid and scuffed shoe prints were visible in the dirt path.

"Men with shoes," Emmanuel said.

"*Yebo*. Just so." The Zulu detective nodded encouragement, the way he'd likely have done when one of his own sons identified his first spoor trail. "Three men were here. Two with shoes, one barefoot."

"Mr. Parkview and two unknowns." Three unidentified males a dozen yards from the crime scene.

"The men with shoes walked in the direction of the house. The barefoot man came onto the path behind them. This is the place they met and the man you found in the bushes was stabbed."

"Parkview followed behind the two men?"

"Yes and no, Sergeant. He came from in there." Shabalala crossed the path and disappeared into a stand of mango trees heavy with fruit. A crumbling stone wall marked the boundary of a derelict orchard. The Zulu detective stepped over the barrier and peered into the shadows. Emmanuel followed and caught a glimpse of metal in the underbrush.

"Back here, Constable." Emmanuel crouched and parted the branches of a shrub with white star-shaped flowers. A garden fork lay half buried in leaves. Rust blooms and dried blood colored the prongs. "This is the weapon that was used on the man in the hospital. The spacing of the four prongs matches the stab wounds in his back."

Shabalala studied the pitchfork and said, "There is a

shed in the trees. Maybe that is where the fork came from."

"Hold on a moment." Emmanuel looked out at the overgrown fruit trees, their foliage pierced by the waning light. "Were all three men in this area?"

"No. Only Mr. Parkview, walking barefoot through the row of mangoes to the path with the blood."

"All right." He drew a crude sketch of the yard in his notebook, marking the location of the pitchfork, the path to the house and the leaf pile where the black man collapsed. "Now show me the shed."

Emmanuel and Shabalala trampled across an abandoned vegetable garden to a stone-and-iron building overgrown with climbing vines. The door was open. They peered inside. The air was musty, the walls hung with rusting garden tools. Two small windows gave dim light. An old wardrobe, a chest of drawers, broken chairs and a dozen cracked plant pots colonized the rear of the shed. A camp bed with sheets and a turned-down blanket were pushed to the left of the door in a cleared space.

"He slept in here." Emmanuel indicated a pair of brown shoes and a kerosene lantern placed neatly by the side of the metal bed frame. The floor had been freshly swept. "A space was made for the bed, but there's nothing to say he actually lived here."

"You are right." Shabalala crouched on the threshold, mapping the last movements of the mystery man. "He slept in the bed and then went out through the orchard to the path where he met the other men."

"And was stabbed. Probably with a pitchfork from this room."

"That is what I believe."

"Why was he here to begin with?" Emmanuel moved into the room, stripped the blanket from the bed and searched under the sheets and the pillow for information that might identify the man at Baragwanath Hospital. He found a pair of darned socks stuffed into the brown shoes. The shoes themselves were worn and cracked. "The Brewers must have known he was sleeping in the shed. He had their address in his shirt pocket."

Shabalala said, "Maybe the prints on the path will lead us to the other men, Sergeant."

"It's worth a try." Emmanuel left the shack, frustrated. Interviewing Martha Brewer officially was impossible now that he was "on holiday." There must be a quick way to identify Parkview and find out how he met the sharp end of a pitchfork on Friday night. Shabalala wove through the trees quickly in order to beat the setting sun. Shadows fell across the narrow path and grew longer. The Zulu detective kept a steady pace for a minute and then stopped within sight of the back fence. He peered into a stand of banana plants.

"Let's check it," Emmanuel said of a second stone-and-iron outbuilding hidden in the Brewers' urban forest. This one was smaller than the last, with a hole in the roof and no windows—possibly a disused storage shed. Shabalala pushed the door open and automatically stepped aside to allow a European first entry.

Shapes swam in the gloom. Emmanuel found a box of matches on the floor and struck a match. Light flickered over a mattress rolled on the ground and a white candle stub pressed onto a chipped saucer. Shabalala picked up the candle holder and touched the wick to the flame.

A half bottle of Jamaican rum, lipstick, a spray of pink roses in an old jam jar and an opened packet of cigarettes were set on top of an upturned fruit crate placed next to the mattress.

"What is this place for?" Shabalala asked, even though the gritty tone in his voice said he already knew.

"A girl comes here in secret. She puts on makeup and has a drink and a smoke. You roll. You slip away and come back again until the day you're caught out by her father."

The teenage Emmanuel might have found this shack and furnished it with all the essentials for sex. Shortly after giving up on being a decent Christian youth, he'd learned very fast how to be bad.

"*What's really changed?*" his sergeant major whispered. "*You still sneak through the bush to sleep with a girl you're not supposed to touch. Except that now, if Mason catches you, that little family you've made? He'll tear it apart. So you'd better decide quick smart what you're prepared to do to keep your girls safe.*"

"*Everything.*"

"*Good boy.*"

Emmanuel leaned against the wall, able to imagine for the first time the terror of having a child in danger. The thought of what he'd do if anyone, including the police, raised a hand to his daughter, Rebekah, chilled him.

"*You will go to war to protect your little girl,*" the sergeant major said with approval. "*And I'll be with you, soldier.*"

"Aaron and the school principal's daughter?" The stony look on Shabalala's face indicated he disapproved of the idea.

"Did you let your parents pick your girlfriends, Constable?" Emmanuel opened the lipstick and drew a line across his palm. The red had a bright metallic shine, the same color that had streaked the back of Cassie's hand on the night of the break-in. "You can ask Aaron yourself tomorrow when we visit the juvenile prison."

The Zulu detective lowered the candle and the semi-darkness hid the mattress, the alcohol and the cigarettes. Police uncovered secrets. The detective sergeant, in particular, had a gift for digging up big ones. A loud click in the garden caught them both by surprise. Shabalala blew the candle out and they simultaneously crouched in the dark. Emmanuel pulled the door closed, breathing deep and slow. The sound of human voices and the snap of twigs drew near.

"I don't see it," a man's voice said.

"Look again," another male answered. He was farther away, his voice faint. "Keep going in."

Footsteps crunched through the underbrush, moving in the direction of the storage room. A burnished sky stretched over the hole in the roof, glowing orange. The detectives remained tense but calm; the soldier and the hunter possessed experience enough to wait out a threat while preparing for action.

"There's nothing here but bush and more bush." The voice was close, almost breathing through the stone walls. "Are you sure this is the place?"

An indistinct answer came back, the words swallowed by the wind in the treetops. Footsteps receded. Voices trailed off into the distance. Emmanuel stood up slowly, ears straining for the sound of movement outside the storeroom.

"They have gone nearer to the house," Shabalala said in a low voice. "Two men, maybe more. Looking for something."

"Give them a minute. If Mason or his men catch us digging around here, things will get unpleasant."

"Then let us wait, Sergeant."

Tongues of dark gray colored the orange patch of sky seen though the hole in the roof. Birds roosted in the trees, calling loudly to each other about the sun going down. Minutes ticked by. The voices faded.

"Time to go," he said to Shabalala. "Keep low and head back to the path."

"*Yebo.*" The Zulu detective cracked the door and slipped into the garden. The cry of birds was deafening. They heard the chug of distant car engines. The dirt path lay empty, the twilight fading fast. Shabalala stopped by the area of blood spray and shoe prints and frowned. The soil had been brushed over, the evidence of the attack destroyed by the scrape of a heel.

Emmanuel split off the path and pushed into the fruit orchard, heart thumping. The shrub with the white star-shaped flowers shimmered in the gathering darkness. He knelt and bent back the branches.

"The pitchfork is gone," he said.

12

B USES, BICYCLES AND pedestrians streamed along the broad, flat expanse of Main Road where it entered Sophiatown. The air hummed with the sounds of thousands of people talking, singing and arguing. Tonight, the citizens of the township with money would wash off the working week in dance halls and shebeens, the illegal drinking holes squeezed into shacks and living rooms. Those without money would try to get some, by various means.

Emmanuel slowed, shifted down a gear and swung left into Bertha Street. He, Shabalala and Zweigman rode in silence. Lieutenant Mason had outplayed them. He parked in front of a wide brick house with bars on the windows. A slender youth lounged on the front stairs with his fedora pulled low onto his forehead and tilted at a sharp right angle despite the darkness.

"This is not my brother's home, Sergeant," Shabalala said from the backseat. Zweigman rode up front. "His house is nearer to the corner."

"I know." Emmanuel switched off the engine and flipped the door handle. "We need a drink and this is the safest place to park a car in Sophiatown on a Saturday night."

Zweigman and Shabalala followed him out of the Ford and onto the pavement. The man on the stairs moved to the front gate with a loping stride. He wore a baggy pin-striped suit and a grin that promised trouble.

"White man." He spoke in a high soprano voice. "You and your friends are too trusting. This is Kofifi. The streets are full of thieves who will take your ride and that fine suit also."

"It's not you that I trust. It's your boss. There's no stealing or fighting allowed on his block. This is still Fix Mapela's house, correct?"

The guard's sly fox expression faltered. He was new to the job, with more attitude than experience. "Who wants to know?"

"Tell him the white kaffir said hello and make sure nothing happens to my car." Emmanuel moved off with unhurried steps, knowing that Zweigman and Shabalala would follow. They caught up and slipped to either side of him. Lights burned at intermittent intervals along the road, brightening the houses of the lucky people with enough money for electricity.

"Who is Fix Mapela?" The German doctor wiped his

glasses with the tail of his shirt. He'd seen more patients in three hours at Baragwanath than would normally attend a full day at his medical clinic in the Valley of a Thousand Hills, an experience both humbling and exhausting.

"Fix is a friend." Emmanuel took a sharp left into a passage between buildings. "I grew up with him."

"What does this friend do that he needs a guard and bars on all his windows?"

"He fixes things. Like his name says."

Zweigman made a disparaging sound. "Does he also break things? I wonder."

"Frequently." They crossed over potholed blacktop and Emmanuel took a quick left into a narrow passage where the buildings crowded together more tightly. Rough laughter and the rattle of dice came from one direction. From another came the sound of a hymn being sung over dinner. Sophiatown brought saints and sinners together.

"Almost there." They walked the pavement of a street lined with Indian- and Jewish-owned shops selling just about anything. Two sharp lefts brought them behind a wide building with prison-style windows. A rickety flight of stairs led up to a cinder-block house with a flat tin roof. Music and the smell of beer and cigarettes came from the building.

"Sergeant," Shabalala said, "this is not a place for policemen."

"I won't tell if you don't." Emmanuel climbed to the door. The Zulu detective and the German doctor stayed put. He motioned to them. "Come on. It's a nice place. I guarantee there won't be any trouble. We can sit and plan tomorrow."

Shabalala hesitated and then took the stairs two at a time, deciding it was better to sit with the detective sergeant than to lie awake in a strange bed, worrying for Aaron's future and for his wife Lizzie's heart. He stopped halfway and gripped the handrail, waiting for a sudden dizziness to pass. Zweigman placed a hand on the Zulu man's shoulder and said, "When was the last time you ate, my friend?"

Shabalala said, "I do not remember. Maybe yesterday."

"There's a kitchen inside." Emmanuel pushed open the door. "We'll order before we sit down."

The illegal bar was a long, narrow room with scarlet walls and two cracked mirrors in place of windows. Cigarette smoke hung over the crowded tables. In the back corner, a couple clung to each other in drunken love. The clientele was a mix of louche black men and women with time to kill and enough money to buy booze. The "shebeen queen," a middle-aged battle-ax with cherry-dark skin and flat facial features, pushed through the throng. The red-and-white-checked dress and the triple strand of fake pearls looped around her neck probably came from the Indian shop, but she wore them like they were priceless. She stood in front of Emmanuel and placed her hands on her hips.

"I don't allow trouble," she said over the noise of rough laughter. "And the white men who come into my place always make trouble."

"Not us," Emmanuel said. "We're looking for a drink, food and a quiet place to talk."

"Then go to church. Or the synagogue." She winked at Zweigman and flashed a hard smile. "There is drink but no quiet place. You can stand in lovers' corner with your friends. That is the only space I have."

"We'll have a couch in the back room." Emmanuel took out his wallet and handed over a note. "One bottle of the house beer with three glasses, funeral rice, grilled chicken livers and coleslaw. Please."

"You know my place?" She stuffed the money down the front of her bra, which was more secure than a bank vault. Men had lost fingers trying to gain access.

"From when it was Mama Leslie's house," he said. "A long time ago."

"Go." The shebeen queen spoke with a grudging respect. A white man who knew the workings of her bar, the hidden room for the clients who had private business and also the most popular items on the menu. That was a rare thing. "See if there is room."

"Thank you, Mama," Emmanuel said, and moved through the crush of bodies sweating alcohol and perfume. The noise and the anticipation of immediate gratification in the patrons' faces held the familiarity of home. He pushed aside a lace curtain. Five or so mismatched sofas were squeezed into a smaller room with a painted-over window. All chairs were taken but for a dingy four-seater in the back corner. They sat down, drawing curious glances from the other drinkers, which Emmanuel ignored.

"Is it certain that the men who took the fork work for Mason?" Zweigman asked when the beer and a bowl of yellow funeral rice were set down on a small table by the kitchen help.

"It looks that way to me." Emmanuel waited for Shabalala to take some rice and then helped himself.

"The men could have been the actual criminals returning to the scene to cover their tracks," the German doctor said after a sip of beer. "They had even more to gain from the theft of the fork than the lieutenant."

"They were not the same men." Shabalala joined in. "Their footprints do not match."

Zweigman worked a mound of rice onto his spoon, thinking out loud. "The two groups must have communicated with each other," he said. "How else did the men who searched the garden know about the fork in the bush?"

"Mason." Emmanuel was certain the lieutenant was the link. "Either he's personally involved with the crime or taking money to cover up for someone else. I don't know which."

"Lieutenant Mason: two points. And us zero," Zweigman said, referring to the "successful" search for the car and the disappeared pitchfork.

"That's the score." No use denying that the day had been kind to Mason. "We'll visit Aaron tomorrow. All he needs to do is provide the name of one person who saw him walking through Sophiatown on Friday night."

"I will talk with him but . . ." The Zulu detective chewed the rice slowly, searching for the right words. "I do not know if he will speak the truth to me."

"You are his father." Zweigman leaned back while a fat-armed woman in a blue housecoat and a white head scarf delivered the rest of the food. "He is your son."

"*Yebo*. This is so, but Aaron now belongs to the oldest child of my mother. He is my brother's son through me. It was decided ten years ago."

The laughter from the front bar and the heated whispers of the couple cuddling on the adjacent sofa seemed to magnify the stillness in Shabalala's voice.

"How did he come to be your brother's son?" Emmanuel asked. This practice of "giving" children to other members of the family was a familiar concept in Sophiatown.

"The son of my mother had a wife, two children and much money. With this money he bought a car and with this car he took his family to see the ocean in Natal. On the way home to Johannesburg it grew dark and the car hit a cow on the road. The wife and children died." Shabalala took a mouthful of beer and then another. "He married again but no children, no children with the second wife. That is when my father came to me and said his eldest child was heartsore. He needed a son to make things whole again."

"Could you not refuse?" Zweigman asked. Dead children were at the heart of his own sorrow, having lost all three of his own offspring in the German death camps.

"My father lived by the old ways. For his eldest son to die without issue, that was a thing he could not stand. He said that Lizzie and I must share our good fortune and in turn Aaron would be blessed with education and with money. This man, my father, gave me life. His request could not be refused. That is the Zulu way." Shabalala cleared his throat to dislodge the hard lump that had formed around his larynx since he'd heard about Aaron's arrest. "My wife's youngest child has been well taken care of. He came home to us on the holidays, just as if he was still ours."

"Surely your brother knows where Aaron went on Friday night?" Emmanuel said. Sophiatown was not entirely the lawless free-for-all most people believed it to be. Good families still worshipped in church and drank no liquor. Their children attended school and youth clubs supervised by the clergy. Shabalala's blood son did not belong to the streets as Emmanuel had.

"The son of my father has a lung sickness." The Zulu detective opened his hands in apology. "He is at a special hospital outside Pretoria. For three weeks he has been there. On Friday morning his wife went to visit for the weekend. The priest at Aaron's school said he would keep watch over him. This was to be his first time alone in the house."

They ate amid the chatter of bar patrons and of drunken singing. Emmanuel's thoughts were equally noisy. A boy left alone for the weekend might have a girl over for a drink or hold a party for a group of friends. An empty house presented the perfect opportunity to play grown-ups. Yet Aaron, according to his own statement, chose to walk the streets aimlessly and alone. Mason had taken advantage of that lie. Could Cassie Brewer really be worth climbing the gallows for?

13

THE CURTAIN THAT divided the secret room from the public area opened and the couple on the next couch sat up, nervous as impala at a watering hole. Three men in baggy suits and two-tone shoes walked into the room with predatory grace. Emmanuel topped up the beer glasses and kept eating, hoping that his companions would follow his lead and stay absolutely calm. Zweigman scooped up more chicken livers. Shabalala divided the remaining coleslaw among the three plates. Good. They were in tune.

The men crossed the room, which emptied behind them. Emmanuel unbuttoned his jacket and took a quick look at the *tsotsis*. Their bodies slotted into three standard sizes: small, medium and large. Their looks were similarly easy to categorize: pretty, average and ugly.

"You. Trek." Medium Average ordered the lovebirds on the next sofa out of the room. They grabbed hat and

bag and rushed for the exit, glad to be let go. Laughter fil-
tered in from the front bar. It might have been noise from
a different universe. The quiet in the secret room attained
a kind of physical weight.

"What are you doing in my seat, white man?" Medium swaggered to the corner table, flanked by the others. His words were slurred, his mouth held permanently
open by a fat tongue, the tip of which protruded between
his teeth.

"I'm having a drink." Emmanuel gave Medium his full
attention. Everything about him was brown: brown eyes,
brown hair, brown skin wrapped neatly in a brown suit.
All three men smelled of beer, marijuana and sweat. "You
came at the exact right time. Ten minutes ago the place was
packed. Now you can sit anywhere you want."

"I do not want the other seats. I want this one."

"You can have it after we've finished." Emmanuel took
a swig of beer and settled back. Medium and company had
come out for their weekly Saturday-night fight. The moment they'd walked into the room, it was already too late
for diplomacy. They wanted blood. Emmanuel turned to
Shabalala and asked, "Still hungry?"

The Zulu detective patted the flat of his stomach, dis-
playing hard-packed muscle. "My wife says I have grown
old and fat. I will have more rice but that is all."

Pretty Man dug lean fingers into the funeral rice and
shoveled a scoop into his mouth. He chewed extravagantly.
Ugly laughed, but the sound had a tired feel, as if this scene
had played out too often and with the same results.

"You shouldn't eat standing up," Emmanuel said. "It's bad for your health."

"You're a doctor, now?" Butter from the yellow rice glossed Pretty's mouth. Dark-skinned with a dimpled chin, Brylcreemed hair and eyelashes a girl would kill for, he would have had to stab, rape and rob more victims than usual in order to prove his criminal worth.

"I'm not a doctor but I can tell the future," Emmanuel said. "Would you like to know yours?"

"*Ja.* What?" Ugly bit first, interested in this new twist to the routine. Truth was, some Saturday nights he'd rather stay home, brew a cup of tea and listen to *The Twilight Ranger*, the current Shadow story on Springbok Radio.

"You"—Emmanuel pointed to Medium—"will try to overturn the table, but my Zulu friend will break your arm and throw you across the room like a piece of firewood. My other friend, the little Jew, will work a knife into one of you. And I will shoot whoever is left standing. Or you can choose to change the future and just walk away."

Zweigman kept eating, not once looking up.

Medium moved fast, Shabalala moved faster. The lip of the table tilted but the Zulu detective slammed a fist onto the surface, stabilizing it, while pushing hard into Medium's chest with the open palm of his free hand. Medium flew, flipped over a couch, and his head hit the floor with a crack. Ugly grunted and swung a cabbage-size fist at Emmanuel. Emmanuel ducked and Ugly lost his balance, then sprawled across the table and knocked the plates into the air. Emmanuel smacked Ugly's head against the surface of the table and let him drop to the floor. Pretty yelped and ripped out the fork that Zweigman had speared into his right hand. He fumbled at his jacket and a flick knife emerged from his pocket. The blade flashed in the dim light and the lock on it clicked. He lunged at Zweigman. Emmanuel met the gangster's head with the butt of his revolver. Blood sprayed out of the wound on his forehead and Pretty staggered back. His knife hit the floor and slid under a couch.

"Facedown on the ground. Now." Emmanuel came out from behind the table, the Webley in his hand. He had no memory of drawing the weapon. The not-so-pretty-anymore gangster lay flat, cheek pressed to the floor. Shabalala stood over Ugly, ready for a wrong move.

"This is your idea of no trouble, Sergeant Cooper?" Zweigman pressed both hands to the tabletop, absorbing the stillness of the inanimate object while he willed the food in his stomach to stay down.

"Sorry about this." Emmanuel crossed the lounge to Medium, the trio's leader. He pushed the tip of his shoe into the gangster's ribs. Medium groaned but remained balled on the floor. "It's too early in the night for a full-blown fight, but there's no accounting for stupidity."

The lace curtain dividing the room from the front bar twitched. Emmanuel turned and aimed the Webley at the opening. His heart hammered in his chest. Maybe the three on the floor had friends outside. "Out where I can see you," he ordered the person hiding in the doorway. "Hands above your head. Now."

The curtain parted and a charcoal-black man wearing white cotton pajamas and a purple silk dressing gown limped into the room. His head seemed too large for his scrawny neck to hold it up. His smooth baby skin and a peach-fuzz beard magnified the impression of a malnourished child trapped in a man's body. Grown men had died wondering how the crippled boy could move so fast and stab a blade so deep.

"Please, don't shoot, Detective. Spare me, ma' baas." Spindly arms reached for the ceiling. The man's voice quivered. "I have a wife and ten children. My mother, she is sick with the fever, and my father, he is blind and has no hands."

Emmanuel holstered the Webley, simultaneously furious and relieved. "That's your idea of a joke, Fix? I could have shot you."

"Never." Fix Mapela limped closer and said after a long examination, "You've gotten old and unattractive, my friend."

"And you're still a cripple, I see."

"That is because God took three inches from my left leg and put it onto another part of my body. Ask your sister. She knows."

"Who else has your measurements? The pretty boy you sent to greet me, or the ugly one?"

Fix Mapela grinned and said, "Long time, my brother."

"Too long," Emmanuel responded. They gripped hands and stepped closer till their shoulders touched, a quasi-Roman greeting that Fix had invented after they'd successfully shoplifted a loaf of bread and a can of jam from Ah Ling's store. They were eight years old with bellies full of strawberry jam and heads full of plans to become the outlaw versions of Julius Caesar and Mark Antony.

"Mama Sylvia." Fix addressed the bar owner, who loitered in the doorway. "Whiskey and clean glasses. Only the best and now, now."

"As you say, Mr. Mapela." The shebeen queen threw Emmanuel a sour look. White men always brought trouble: the whole lounge was now taken over by a criminal with a heavy reputation. These men never paid. Still, giving away a bottle of whiskey beat refurnishing the entire lounge room if things had gotten worse. She retreated.

Medium groaned and tried to sit up.

"You have met my friends, Emmanuel." Fix pressed the sole of his shoe to Medium's neck and pushed hard, cutting off his air supply. The gangster gasped, eyes bulging in their sockets. Emmanuel did not interfere. Medium flailed like a hooked fish and collapsed under the pressure. Fix stepped over the prone body, the unpleasant business of punishing a subordinate for being weak now over. He continued to the corner sofa. "Now introduce me to yours."

"This is Shabalala and Zweigman," Emmanuel said. He would have preferred to keep a space between his old life and new, but the township was messy, with the good and bad, the past and the present, running together like spilled paint. "Meet Fix Mapela."

"Welcome to Sophiatown," Mapela said after shaking

hands. "Sit. Relax. My brother's friends are my friends also. That is the way it is."

"We are honored." Shabalala accepted the offer of friendship even as Medium sucked mouthfuls of air through a bruised windpipe and Pretty lay bleeding onto the concrete. Zweigman resisted the urge to help the injured men. Rules were being observed that he did not understand, and like a peasant at an aristocrat's formal dinner party, he followed the lead of the other guests.

Mapela turned to Ugly, who nursed a ballooning lump on his forehead. "Go where we cannot see you," Mapela said. "Take the others. Your weakness offends my eyes."

Ugly signaled to Pretty and together they dragged Medium to a sofa out of Mapela's sight. They propped him against an arm and then sat and stewed in their failure as instructed.

"You have come back to Kofifi with a Zulu for muscle and a Jew for money matters." Mapela lowered himself into the sofa vacated by the lovebirds and tucked his withered leg behind the good one. "What are you planning?"

"Nothing with a profit margin. We're looking into a stolen car that the police found in Annet Street this morning."

"I heard of this. Fast and red. Very popular with the Portuguese and the English."

"Any idea who might have dumped it?"

"I am finished with the old trade." Mapela pulled a tobacco pouch and three leaves of white rolling paper from a pocket and set them on the table. "That life is behind me.

Go to the front room. Ask anyone and they will tell you that I am a respectable man."

"For how long this time?" Fix left the life every few years, handing over the reins to his sister Fatty while vowing that, finally, he had made a clean break.

"Three weeks, but it is forever. No more badness." He opened the tobacco pouch and dumped a clod of marijuana onto the rolling paper. "I am married now. That is how come I was in bed when you sent greetings."

"A permanent wife or a temporary one?" Some wives were so short-lived that Emmanuel retained only an impression of their tenure in Fix's house: cigarette butts tipped with lipstick, the vague smell of perfume in the air.

"We went to the church and said the words." Mapela teased the marijuana into a line and rolled a fat joint, which he sealed closed with a lick. "I am too old to jump from one bed to the other. You, too, my brother."

"And your men? Are they just for decoration?" Changing the subject delayed the inevitable; Zweigman and Shabalala would hear, very soon, about the three wild months that he'd spent in Sophiatown after leaving his stepfather's farm.

"When Fatty runs the whole business I will let these men go and then I will live a peaceful life." Mapela placed a box of matches next to the joint. "For now I must protect myself from my enemies."

Mama Sylvia reentered the lounge with a bottle of Johnnie Walker and four cut-glass tumblers on a tray.

"Top quality from the house of a judge in Sandton," she said.

"Very good." Mapela signaled the bar owner to pour. Then he flicked a finger to the dirty plates and cutlery on the next table. "Clear the mess and bring more food, Mama. My friends and I are hungry."

"Of course. Of course." She stacked the plates and balanced them against her hip. The old ways were dying out in the city, but with certain men it was best to remain humble. She dipped her head and left the lounge with downcast eyes.

Mapela handed out whiskey shots, certain that what he had commanded would be done. They drank. Fix poured a second and third round, each glass more generous than the last. Shabalala and Zweigman drained their glasses in one mouthful and then pushed the empties across the table for more. They understood the rules of the game. Keep up with Mapela or retire to the corner with the other failures. Their innate understanding impressed Emmanuel, who watched the dropping liquor levels with a mixture of relief and trepidation.

"So you're half retired but you haven't told your wife yet." He picked up the thread of an earlier conversation, hoping to wind back to the red car before more alcohol arrived. Fix was a committed drinker.

"The truth would not suit my wife. Just like you and Ah Ling's daughter by that Sotho woman. You remember? Church one night. Grabbing cigarettes off the trucks and back to church the next night. You were tired out, man. What was her name again?"

"Pearl. And that was a long time ago."

"You can forget a backside like that? I don't think so. That was a dream." He moved his hands to re-create the swish and jig of a female rump in motion. "Such a thing it was. It must have felt good, hey? Like cupping the world in your hands."

"A near-perfect world," Emmanuel said. "Too good to last."

"That is so." Mapela sighed and lit up the joint. He drew deep and held the smoke in his lungs a long while. Fix was also a committed smoker. "If you had stayed here and worked with me like we planned, who knows? Maybe a nice house and children and that fine backside to curl around. Instead you are a policeman."

"There are worse things."

"*Ja*, like jail."

"And you'd know," Emmanuel said. "Speaking of jail. How is Fatty?"

A veteran of the South African prison system, Fix's sister had started out with short stretches in various reform schools before graduating to longer stays in facilities with better security and guards with guns.

"Fatty is fatter than you remember, but using her brains instead of her fists now that she got rid of that husband with the big nose. No problems with the police for a long time."

"Is that so . . ." Emmanuel remained sceptical. Fatty Mapela was quick to anger, slow to forgive and, in keeping with her elephantine size, never forgot a slight. "What happened?"

"One of her new husbands is a policeman from here in Sophiatown. He keeps a lookout for trouble. That is why I can leave this life . . ." Fix paused and took a second hit of the joint. He offered it to Emmanuel, who hesitated. Detective Sergeant Cooper ceased to exist in Fix's presence. That was the reason he rarely came to the township.

"Perhaps you are ashamed of me now that you have new friends," Mapela said. "Perhaps you are all police and this is a trap."

Emmanuel took the joint. He smoked. Fix relaxed and shared the remaining whiskey between Shabalala and Zweigman, inviting them back into the inner circle. A scratchy recording of Cab Calloway's "Blues in the Night" hit the player in the front room and the bar patrons sang along in drunken harmony.

"Ahh . . . Fatty, she loves this song. You must hear the records she keeps in her special house. Too good." Mapela placed a hand to Emmanuel's arm, the whiskey and the marijuana kicking in. "Anytime. Say the word and I will make a place for you here."

"Your sister might not like it."

"Ah, she is plenty busy with the three husbands. And there is the cathouse and the dance hall there by Kumalo's garage."

Emmanuel handed back the joint while Zweigman and Shabalala wisely sipped on their drinks. When the time came to stumble out of the bar, they'd remember things he might have forgotten.

"Things are no more what they used to be." Fix spoke

through the haze of *dagga* smoke. "There are too many gangs in Sophiatown: the Russians, the Gestapo, the Vultures. Each day another boy gets off the bus with a knife in his pocket and plans to be chief of the township. That is why I am getting out. These new men do not think of the future. They just grab."

"They missed that Mercedes parked under their noses."

"*Ja,* that is strange. Taking such a car from a white man's house is a heavy matter. And this Shabalala boy is not involved in such heavy things. If he had come to me, I would have paid a fair price. But to park and run, that is foolishness."

"Remember the first car we lifted? It ran out of petrol and we took off." Emmanuel smiled. "We left the doors open and the lights on."

"Man, we flew." Fix laughed at the memory. "World-record time across the field and then to your house. My leg hurt bad for a week afterward."

Emmanuel pulled the snippet of branch that he'd pocketed at the mouth of the dead-end lane where he had found the car. He placed it on the table. "The Shabalala boy parked, then covered the car with branches like this one and ran."

Shabalala Senior leaned across the table, examined the branch and then crushed the leaves between thumb and forefinger. He inhaled the odor. "*UmPhanda,* the raintree. It likes the open bushlands and rivers but grows here in the city also. I did not see this tree in the backyard of the principal's house, Sergeant."

"There weren't any raintrees near the lane where the car got ditched, either. The crack of the boot door was thick with dust and the tire treads filled with dirt."

Zweigman frowned, picking apart the elements. "If the branches were not local, then Aaron must have brought them in, knowing in advance that he was going to hide the car."

"More foolishness. To cut and stack branches when I could have found a clean space for just such a car." Fix drank the last drops of whiskey from the bottle. "What is this business to you, brother?"

"I found the car. Then I got booted off the police case quick smart. I'd like to know why."

"Of course," Mapela said. "If a man hits you, you must hit back. That is the proper way. I can help you with this."

"In order to hit back," Emmanuel said, "I need information. Not muscle."

Mama Sylvia and the fat-armed woman who'd delivered the first round of food brought dishes of roast corn, beef curry and rice to the table. Mama dished out the food and murmured, "Right away," when Fix tapped a fingernail on the empty Scotch bottle. Emmanuel, Shabalala and Zweigman ate more, not from hunger but out of apparent necessity.

"Go and see Fatty." Mapela scooped food up with his right hand, Muslim style, and licked curry from his fingers. "Once in a month she holds a dance out by the rail yards in Newtown. She will make a special place for you at her table."

That's what he was afraid of. Two Mapelas, on two nights in a row, made for a severe hangover and short-term memory loss.

"A dance in a railway yard," Emmanuel said. He pictured the scene: an old train shed with men milling around, waiting their turn with prostitutes in a warren of rooms out the back. "Sounds nice."

"No, no. I know what you're thinking. Fatty has fixed the place up proper with music and tables." Fix shoveled more curry. "Her policeman husband will be there. He has eyes and ears all over Sophiatown. He is the one you must ask about the red car."

"He'll talk to me?"

"Of course." Mapela mopped up rice. "Dress nice. Fatty's dance is for white men, so the Zulu will have to stay behind. Take the little Jew if you wish. I can pair you up with two beauties to go with. Sisters from the Transkei."

"Thanks but no." Fix's idea of beauty focused exclusively on the size and shape of a woman's behind, the bigger and wider, the better. "I'll find my own dance partner."

"As you wish."

Mama Sylvia brought over another bottle of Johnnie Walker, this time with the top already removed. Emmanuel felt certain that it was the first bottle refilled with cheaper booze. Mama leaned into Mapela with a lascivious smile to cover the switch. She poured a fresh round while Fix stroked her leg.

"Sergeant," Zweigman whispered, "I cannot drink more. I am already drunk."

"Sit on this glass. You'll have to drive us home."

"Yes. Very slowly."

An hour later, with the second bottle drained and the food gone, Mapela called for Mama Sylvia, who appeared in the doorway wearing the smile that women in her position wore when they knew what was expected of them and could see no way out of the situation other than acceptance. She slid onto Fix's lap and he kissed her full on the mouth. Or rather she let him kiss her.

"We'll leave you." Emmanuel staggered to his feet. "I'm for bed and a good night's sleep."

"Stay. Mama will find you a girl." Mapela plunged a hand between hard thighs and massaged flesh. "We'll make a party, just like old times."

"I'm too old to relive old times." He swayed against the table. The room tilted. Shabalala grabbed a handful of jacket and held him upright. "I'll drop in on Fatty tomorrow. Give my regards to your wife when you get home."

"Not so long next time." Fix's right hand was busy, so they nodded their good-byes. Shabalala guided Emmanuel out of the lounge room and through the smoke haze and noise of the front bar. The rickety stairs were perilous in the dark. Zweigman went first, clinging to the rail like a sailor walking the deck in a gale.

"Were you like that man, Sergeant Cooper? A gangster?" the German asked when they reached the bottom and staggered in the direction of the street with the Indian- and Jewish-owned shops.

"Yes, absolutely." After his escape from the physical labor and the earnest prayers on his stepfather's farm, Sophiatown was a salvation. Three months into the dissolute life, he'd woken up on a bright Saturday morning, sated but not satisfied. "The life didn't suit me, though, so I got out."

"You returned to the township?" Shabalala retraced the path to the car. He was built to absorb greater quantities of alcohol than the average South African male.

"I came back straight after high school. Seventeen years old. I had no idea where I was going. I figured I'd be like the guys I saw when I was young. You know, big cars, flash suits and girls." Emmanuel crossed the tarred road, careful to keep balance. "The price of those things was too high. I didn't realize till I was in it. Stealing I could understand. Threatening shopkeepers for protection money and collecting outstanding debts with an iron bar, that was harder. I got out, like I said."

Shabalala navigated them through the alleys and back to the Ford. Garbage blew in the wind. Rats scuttled. They emerged a few doors from Fix's house. The guard, now familiar with their presence, stayed on the stairs, too lazy to move. Emmanuel fumbled the keys from his jacket and gave them to Zweigman.

"You will go to the dance and talk to the policeman?" the Zulu detective asked. Distant music floated across the rooftops, a woman's voice backed by the blast of a trumpet and, closer still, the mewling of an alley cat.

"Of course I'll go. No question. But if Aaron talks, tells you where he was, there will be no need." Thus dodging an evening with Fatty Mapela and her select clientele of white men on the prowl. "Tomorrow. Noon. We'll head out to the prison."

"I will be waiting." The Zulu detective opened the passenger door and pressed Emmanuel into the seat like a suspect under arrest. Zweigman slid behind the wheel of the Ford and started the engine. Emmanuel directed him through the grid of Sophiatown. They passed gospel halls, empty shoeshine stands and Indian stores still open late at night. Prosperous houses and businesses thinned, replaced by corrugated-iron-and-plywood shacks along the road. The smell of wood-fire smoke, dry earth and sewage drifted into the car. Emmanuel remembered his earlier self, the young man who lurked on vacant street corners hungry for trouble, for food, for an escape from the relentless press of humanity. If his mother had survived and his links with the township had remained unbroken, he might be on those street corners still: older, leaner, infinitely more dangerous and still unable to satisfy his hunger.

14

FOUR ASPIRIN AND two cups of sweet black coffee helped soften the pound of war hammers behind his eyeballs. Slowly, the garden came into focus, bright pinks and yellows against the walls of green foliage. Bees worked the summer flowers. He breathed in the Sunday-morning stillness and tried to will the hangover away.

"You didn't come to the hut last night." Davida placed Rebekah onto his knee and sat down at the small table set up on the porch of the big house. She wore a sundress that hugged the curves of her body. A tortoiseshell clip held her dark hair in a ponytail and a simple gold bracelet encircled her right wrist. In the small, dusty town of Jacob's Rest, she'd worn baggy trousers and loose shirts and cropped her hair short to escape unwanted attention. Now her beauty was no longer a secret.

"I wanted to sleep with you." Emmanuel wondered again how long this impossible half-in and half-out arrangement would last. Not long enough. "But I was unfit for company."

"How come?"

"Police business." The words kept Davida from getting too close to the messy details of his life. Angela, his ex-wife, had stood outside the locked gate to his secrets too long and eventually walked away.

"I see." Davida glanced at the sun-flecked lawns, pecked over by an ibis hunting insects. "You come and go as you please while I sit and wait like the maid. Should I start calling you ma' baas or 'Detective sir' so things between us are clear?"

"It's not like that," he said quickly. "I don't think of you, of us, like that."

"Thinking is nice but it doesn't change the weather, Emmanuel. You come to my bed when it suits you, but now, in the daylight, you shut me out." She made deliberate eye contact. "I've been kept in a corner before and I'm not interested."

"Tell the woman where you were, for Christ's sake," the sergeant major said. *"Or you'll have to fight to get into her bed again. I'm not going to spend the rest of my days sleeping with you and the mess inside your head by myself. Cough it up, boyo."*

"I was in Sophiatown last night, drinking with Zweigman, Shabalala and an old friend named Fix Mapela." Rebekah closed a fist around his finger and squeezed tight.

"We drank a lot. Me, especially. Zweigman drove me home. I couldn't have found my way through the garden to the hut even if I'd tried."

"Sophiatown. That's mainly for them," she said, using the language of exclusion that divided the population of South Africa into legally defined "us" and "them" race groups. In this instance, "them" was shorthand for natives.

"Mainly for blacks, yes," he said. "But not completely."

"You drank with Dr. Zweigman and Shabalala at the same table?"

"Yes."

"So there are places in the township where people mix together . . ." Although Davida was the secret daughter of a white man and a mixed-race woman, her upbringing had closely approximated that of a privileged European. She had attended a good boarding school where the Queen's English was taught and the racial divisions reinforced. Her world remained sheltered and the thought of races mixing publicly thrilled her.

"When I was growing up, there was a lot more cross-over in Sophiatown," he said. "Now it's unusual."

"Lucky Emmanuel. You ignore all the signs and go wherever you like." The anger surged back, this time cloaked by a smile. "It must be nice, being a white police-man."

"We still have to obey the law," Emmanuel said. "Just not so strictly."

The child that snuggled on his lap proved Davida was right. Last night's drunken debauch in the shebeen con-

firmed it, too. He slipped between worlds, helped by a police ID and a willingness to lie. Davida's dark skin and
mixed-race beauty were extraordinary. Yet the same physical attributes also shrank her possibilities to a list of oc-
cupations the government deemed worthy of a nonwhite
woman: maid, teacher, nurse, nanny and factory worker. If
there was enough money for university, she could study to
become a doctor or lawyer, but that outcome was rare, and
she could never work in those capacities in the white
world.

*"What she said earlier was dead right, soldier. You'll
cross over the lines tonight and come home with the smell
of cigarettes on your clothes and alcohol buzzing in your
head. Meanwhile she'll be in that little hut with a baby and
no place to go. What has a whites-only area got to offer her,
besides other white men like you? That's why she's furious,"* the sergeant major said. *"If you want to keep this girl,
even for a little while, you'll have to give her more than
promises."*

"You want to come dancing with me?" he asked, the
filter between thought and speech nudged aside by a reck-
less desire to please.

"What?" She blinked, taken aback.

"Dancing. With me, tonight. Do you want to come?"

"Where's this?" Excitement mixed with apprehension
replaced the earlier flare-up of anger.

"A friend's place," Emmanuel said. Rebekah chewed a
finger with rubbery gums, a prelude to cutting teeth. "A
makeshift club, not a house."

"You sure?" Single, pregnant women kept their lost virginity and their swollen bellies secret. They disappeared from church picnics, socials and youth clubs. Davida was a mother, but still young and full of life, and hadn't danced in over a year.

"I'm sure," he lied. Leaving the walled compound brought risks. Fatty Mapela's mood and the atmosphere of the club were impossible to predict in advance. If *dance* turned out to be a euphemism for *brothel,* they'd leave — straight after he'd talked to Fatty's temporary husband about the stolen Mercedes.

"The police . . ." Davida leaned across the table and wiped the corner of Rebekah's mouth with a napkin, stalling her "yes."

"Police will be at the dance, so the chance of a raid by the immorality squad is close to zero. I'll take care of any roadblocks between here and there." Bullshitting the road patrol if they were pulled over meant flipping the ID, dropping Colonel van Niekerk's name and citing official business. They'd let him pass. The brighter officers might be suspicious, while those operating on a dimmer voltage would try and fail to hide their envy at having a sweet brown girl in their power. They'd let him go, disturbed by their own suspicions and crude fantasies.

"My mother could take care of Rebekah till we get back." Davida tentatively stroked their daughter's head, smoothing the silky strands under her palm. Her mother, Lorraine Ellis, called "Lolly" by her family, lived in the housekeeper's cottage built flush against the walls of the big house. This arrangement paid tribute to the notion of racial segregation while allowing ease of movement between the cottage and Elliott King's bedroom.

"Are you certain there won't be any trouble?" Davida said.

"I'm certain." A prudent man might calculate the cost of making a mess of this night out, but desire outweighed caution. He wanted the chance to take his beautiful girl out dancing as if they were an ordinary couple.

"Detective Cooper. Telephone for you." Mrs. Ellis, Davida's mother, stood in the doorway to the big house, gazing slightly to the right of the table. She refused eye contact, and had done so from the time he turned up at Zweigman's medical clinic after finding out that he was a father.

He arrived after midnight with nothing to offer but a desire to get close to Davida and their baby. Mrs. Ellis gave him a cold face, while Davida said nothing at all, just opened the door, lit a candle and held it close to the cradle where Rebekah slept. The child took his breath away. He'd done nothing to deserve such a perfect gift. He turned to Davida to say as much. She kissed him and stopped any discussion of the past or the future. He kissed her back, accepting her act of grace.

"Thanks." Rebekah kicked her feet in the air while Emmanuel transferred her to Davida's arms. He drank in the effortless beauty of mother and daughter, their luminescent skin and gray eyes. How long could this impossible situation last . . . ?

"Six-thirty tonight," he said.

"All right." Face buried against the soft of Rebekah's neck, Davida turned away to hide a blush.

"You can pick it up in the kitchen, Detective." Mrs. Ellis remained polite. "Or in the hallway if you want some privacy."

The words had a sting. Emmanuel knew that Mrs. Ellis believed her bright and beautiful girl was destined for something greater than a hut, an illegitimate child and a secret life with a white man that would ultimately result in heartbreak. She'd experienced firsthand the bittersweet nature of living a lie and of loving against the rules. It hurt to see her daughter repeating the mistakes she'd made.

Emmanuel picked up the kitchen phone, which lay on a table with a view through the window to the porch and bright gardens.

"Cooper," he said into the speaker. Davida blew bubbles against Rebekah's cheeks, putting off asking her mother to mind the baby while she went dancing at the illegal club.

"Are you seeing the Shabalala boy today?" The lawyer Johan Britz spoke over the barking of dogs. Besides the bodyguards, he kept two Alsatians in his yard and a mongrel bitch with an evil temper in his house for protection.

"In about an hour," Emmanuel said.

"Try to get the truth out of him, will you? I'll do my best with what he gave me, but it won't be enough to convince a white jury, not with that girl's witness statement."

"Aaron's father will be with me. That might help."

"Not good enough, my friend. Either the boy provides a solid alibi or Lieutenant Mason will see him swing. There is no in-between."

The barking continued.

"Hold on a minute . . ." Britz muffled the speaker with his hand while he settled the mongrel. "Hush, calm down. There's nobody here but me, Mouse. Take it easy now . . ."

The barking grew louder and Emmanuel's hand gripped the telephone tight. Britz's enemies were legion and now the name "Lieutenant Walter Mason" had been added to the list.

"Do you still have a guard?" Emmanuel asked.

"Always," Britz answered. The rap of knuckles hitting wood cut through the canine yaps. "Someone's at the door. Keep holding. I'll just be a tick."

"Wait . . ." Emmanuel spoke into an empty line. The phone was set down on the other end, the lawyer no longer listening. Muffled voices, barking and a loud exclamation came through. He waited. The hangover headache throbbed against his skull.

"Britz . . ." He spoke loud to compensate for the barking and growls. A door slammed. The barking faded. Mouse, the lawyer's guard dog, was no longer in the room. "Britz, pick up. Now."

No response.

"Pick up, Johan, or I'm coming over . . ."

The receiver crackled and the lawyer said, "Cooper. You still there?"

"*Ja*. Who was at the door?"

Britz's breath came hard and at short intervals.

"Oscar, my son, dropped by. Bloody Mouse . . ." he said of the mongrel bitch. "She went for him, almost took a chunk of thigh. Something's got to be done with her. It's the dog pound or the needle."

He'd do neither. Mouse was vicious and utterly devoted: the perfect combination for a man in need of protection.

"You were saying about Aaron . . ." Emmanuel relaxed, his fingers uncurling from the telephone's hard plastic cradle. The fear subsided, but a trace remained like a finger pushed into a wound. Until the connection between Mason and the Brewer case became clear, a part of him would remain alert, waiting for the inevitable attack.

"Shabalala is bright, he understands the consequences of a guilty plea. Why stick to that bullshit story?" Britz asked.

"To protect someone other than himself," Emmanuel said. Outside the window Davida and her mother stood side by side, talking in low voices. Rebekah stretched out and tore at the flowers of a lavender bush. He'd lie for his girls and do more still to protect them from harm. Who held that power over Aaron?

"Get me a name, Cooper. Get me something," Britz said, and hung up the phone, eager to make peace between Mouse and his son. Emmanuel dropped the receiver onto the cradle. Mrs. Ellis leaned close to Davida now, hands spread out in a plea. No doubt asking, "Why take a risk on this policeman?"

Color brightened Davida's cheeks. She nodded and looked away. Her mother stroked her arm, murmured soft words.

"I reckon you've lost your dance partner, soldier." The sergeant major read the body language.

"Maybe it's just as well," Emmanuel replied. Britz was safe and Mason remained ignorant of outside involvement in the Brewer case. Yet a feeling of expectation remained, as it had when the squad cleaned rifles and smoked cigarettes between battles.

"I hear it, too," the sergeant major said. *"The silence waiting to break. Mason will come after you, have no doubts. Keep your girls undercover and out of harm's way, Cooper."*

Davida held Rebekah on the curve of her hip, rocking side to side, the weight of the child both a comfort and a burden. Mrs. Ellis stepped closer, rested her forehead against her daughter's and laced her fingers through strands of her fine, dark hair. She whispered a word, maybe two, in Davida's ear then took the child from her. Davida smiled and kissed her mother's cheek.

15

EMMANUEL AND SHABALALA passed through a grim brick hall reeking of disinfectant and entered a small, equally grim room with bars on a single window. Aaron sat at a table, dressed in the uniform of the juvenile prisoners: long khaki shorts and a tucked-in khaki shirt faded by hundreds of trips through the prison laundry. He stood up when Shabalala entered, head bowed in respect.

"My father," he said.

"Son of my brother," Shabalala answered in a low, quiet voice. "Sit. Be at ease."

They took opposite sides of the table, both stiff-shouldered and uncomfortable in the wooden chairs. Emmanuel closed the door and remained standing. From outside the window came the regimented stomp of prisoners marching in the yard and forming up in rank and file. A whistle trilled. Aaron glanced across the room and frowned in recognition. He said, "My father has brought a white po-liceman to listen to our private words. How can I be at ease?"

"This man is Detective Sergeant Cooper. He is a friend. He is here to help," Shabalala said.

"A white man and a black man cannot be friends in this country," Aaron answered with resolve. "It is written in their law books. He is the boss and you are the servant."

"My child . . ." Shock hushed the Zulu detective's voice. Black men spoke these thoughts in their homes and in quiet groups, but never in front of white people. "I tell you true that this is a different matter."

"It can never be different." Aaron remained expres-sionless. "Surely you understand, my father."

"That may be so, but you are still in prison and in need of help," Shabalala pointed out. Sunshine fell through the high window and cast a brown haze into the room. The light flattened the dimensions of the furniture and people.

The boy shrugged his broad shoulders and said, "I told your friend and the other police what I was doing when the principal was beaten. They did not believe me."

"The principal is dead," Shabalala said. "The white people who sit in judgment will show you no mercy. They will send you to the hangman."

Aaron breathed in and out like a fish stuck on the beach. The muscles of his throat contracted but no sounds came from his mouth.

Shabalala leaned forward suddenly, elbows hitting the table with a thud. "Were you with the white man's daugh-ter?"

"Cassie?" Aaron paled in response. "My father cannot believe this is true."

"You are young. The young make mistakes."

"Never with that one," the Zulu youth said. "She hated us sitting at her parents' table, using the knives and forks and the toilet. I would not have touched her, or her, me."

Emmanuel caught the rapid play of emotions working across Aaron's face. He displayed plenty of anger and frustration, but not a hint of sexual attraction or the agony of lust deferred. Aaron simply disliked Cassie.

"Tell me where you were, my son. For your sake and for your mother's."

Aaron covered his face with both hands. He kept still and seemed capable of doing little more than drawing in shallow breaths. Cassie had hidden behind her palms and blocked out the world also.

A thought hit Emmanuel. "Did Cassie wear lipstick to the dinner table on Friday night?" he asked.

Aaron dropped his hands. A long moment later he said, "I saw no lipstick on her."

"For certain?"

"The principal and his wife were strict. The daughter wore no makeup. Her mother also had a clean face."

"Thanks." Emmanuel leaned back against the door, returning the room to the Shabalala men. The footprints that led from the kitchen door to the corner where Cassie had crouched with the lipstick smeared across her hand now made sense. She must have been out in the shed on the night of the assault, already in her makeup and yellow nightdress, with the mattress ready on the floor.

"One name," Shabalala pressed Aaron. "I do not care if it is a person known to the police or a loose girl in a bad house. There must be one who glimpsed you on the street."

"I kept to the shadows," Aaron said. "No one saw me."

Chair legs screeched against the concrete floor. Shabalala stood abruptly and looked down at the frightened boy; their physical resemblance was so strong it seemed the Zulu detective might be staring back in time at his younger self.

"I will come again. Maybe then my wife's child will remember where he was on that night and in whose company. Stay well." Shabalala turned away from Aaron and said, "We may leave, Sergeant."

Emmanuel opened the door, intrigued by the sight of the towering Zulu holding on to his temper by a bare thread. They had to leave immediately, that was clear, or Emmanuel feared the table would be broken to firewood and the window cracked by flying debris.

"Go well, my father." Aaron stood in the hazy brown light, the prison khaki hanging loose on his frame. He appeared smaller than when they'd first entered the room. The knowledge of the murder charge had to weigh heavily on him.

Emmanuel and Shabalala crossed the hall again, the concrete floor hard under the soles of their leather shoes. The smell of disinfectant mixed with the smell of a Sunday lunch of boiled cabbage and stewed meat. Swallows darted back and forth outside the windows. A pair of them came to rest on a mud-and-grass nest built under the eaves.

"He throws his life away . . ." Shabalala's voice hardened with suppressed anger. "For what? Lizzie and I will see him hang from the end of a rope. Still, he sits and lies."

"Aaron is lying for reasons we don't understand yet, possibly to protect the reputation of someone else."

"The principal's daughter . . ."

"I don't think so. Your son doesn't like her much, which could be the reason she named him in her statement to begin with." The new segregation laws were underpinned by the idea that the tide of physical attraction flowed inexorably from black men toward white women, not the other way around. "She wore lipstick on the night her parents were attacked. I saw it. Now the question is, if Aaron wasn't in the hut with her, who was? That person might have witnessed something we can use."

They left the hall and crossed the dirt yard to the gates. A group of young prisoners marched in rows behind them, their socks stained with dust and their foreheads slick with sweat. A senior boy gave them orders under a flat, gray sky. A white warden, dark-haired and wearing an earnest expression, approached Emmanuel and Shabalala from a demountable building. He must have been watching from a window, waiting for an opportunity to talk.

"You've been to see Shabalala." A statement addressed to the European male, as custom dictated. "The new boy."

"That's right," Emmanuel answered. "He signed in yesterday afternoon."

"At three-ten p.m., a direct transfer from the Marshall Square Police Station. I wasn't here. It's recorded in the logbook." The warden's pink face scrunched in a frown. "I wonder if there is something about the boy that we should know about."

"Such as?" Emmanuel asked.

"He came with a white lawyer, which is not common at all." The warden talked fast and low, the words rear-ending into each other like bumper cars at a fairground. "Most of our boys don't have representation beyond a welfare worker. That set the alarm bells ringing. Then there's the number of visitors. I said to myself, 'Wait a moment. This is highly unusual. What's going on with this boy? Is there some kind of trouble we should know about?'" The warden paused and took a breath. "That's why I came out of the office—to ask about the unusual circumstances."

"Tell me about the visitors," Emmanuel said.

"The inmates normally get single visitors or whole family groups coming in together. That's the usual pattern. Shabalala's had four visitors in one day, none of them family. You see what I'm saying, it's highly—"

"Unusual. Yes, I understand. Who exactly visited Shabalala?"

"Two natives came this morning, first thing, right when the gates opened. Not on foot or in a township taxi, but in a black car. That got my attention, straight off. Then there's the two of you detectives, just now. That's four visitors in four hours."

"Names and gender of the natives?" Emmanuel cut in before the warden gathered wind for more words. Shabalala stood to the side, absorbing the conversation with a passive expression. Impatience was a luxury afforded exclusively to Europeans.

"Two men in a black car with a dented fender. They parked at the gate and sat there for ten minutes, waiting for the gates to open for visitors. Both were dressed well. The younger man was a Khumalo from Alexandria Township and the older one was a Bakwena from Sophiatown. I asked them what their relationship was to Shabalala and they said they were friends of his father. So I asked, 'Where's the father?' They said, 'In the hospital.' They went to the main hall and one of our native wardens showed them to the smaller rooms. They stayed about fifteen minutes, I think. Most of our visitors—"

"First names." Emmanuel jumped in without waiting for an indrawn breath. The warden could evidently talk underwater.

"I didn't ask. They signed the visitor book with only their surnames. Should I have double-checked their passbooks, Detective? They weren't any trouble. And they came in a car, which means they were a better class of native . . . if you get my drift."

"Any physical description you can provide would help our investigation."

"All right, let's think." Another frown gathered as thoughts struggled to gain a foothold in the warden's mind.

"Brown skin and brown eyes for the younger one, white hair and broad shoulders for the older one. Both neat and polite, like I said before."

Emmanuel guessed the vague physical description meant that both men were good natives, hardly worth a second glance from the authorities. A bell clanged in the background, calling the inmates to lunch.

"I have to go and supervise the native wardens, make sure they're keeping order during mealtimes," the white warden said. "Is there something I should know about Shabalala?"

"His lawyer, Johan Britz, is big trouble," Emmanuel said. "Keep an eye on Shabalala. Make sure the other inmates steer clear of him or Britz will have you and the other prison guards in court for dereliction of duty should anything happen."

"I'll let the others know." The warden tugged his uniform straight, squared up his shoulders and set off to the dining hall. The clatter of plates and the low hum of inmates' voices drifted across the yard.

"We could go back and ask about the visitors." Emmanuel gave Shabalala the option of banging on Aaron's gates for a second time.

"No, Sergeant. That boy is truly my son. His mind and his mouth are closed. He will tell us less than the noisy white man." Shabalala glanced in the direction of the long, ugly dining hall where Aaron would sit and eat a meal of boiled cabbage and boiled potatoes served with a chunk of boiled meat. "It would be quicker to find the men who came to visit and ask them face-to-face about their business than to wait for Aaron to speak."

"If we can find them. Half the people in Sophiatown and Alexandria aren't listed on any records. There's still Fatty Mapela's dance tonight." Emmanuel opened the driver's door and spoke over the hood. "Let's head to the Brewers' house and search that storage shed."

—

She lay flat on the concrete floor, desperate to feel the cool of it in the stifling heat. It was Sunday, maybe. Time blurred in the cell. Light followed dark and then around again. She'd lost track of the turnover. Yellow light glowed through the high window, inviting her up and out into the day. Not yet. Not now. Male voices reached into the cell. Glass shattered against the outside wall at regular intervals. The big man was drinking with friends and throwing the empty bottles against the side of the house for fun, for the pleasure of the sound of a thing breaking. The little man, the coward who'd helped kidnap her, and two others whose voices she didn't recognize were in the front yard. A car had arrived on the property earlier, followed by the slam of doors, loud greetings and the slap of hands on shoulders: four good friends reunited and happy to share company. The girl hated their laughter.

She lay still and listened, caught snatches of conversation.

"Five minutes . . . quick work . . . then out . . . we'll make enough to buy a couple of animals. Maybe a lion or a couple of buffalo." That was the big man talking up a big plan. He was the boss, the one in control. Of course. Such a greedy person, the girl thought, to want more than a beautiful face, slick hair and a strong body. She would never be obedient or grateful enough to stay his hand.

". . . Be prepared for . . . not easy . . ." Another of the men added a comment and silence settled on the yard. The girl sat up, alert. Footsteps crunched gravel and a bottle clinked.

"Out of the way. Now," the big man yelled. A gunshot cracked the air, splintering glass and wood. Another shot kicked dirt against the high window, rattling the frame. The girl scuttled across the floor and slid under the iron cot. She pressed a knuckled fist to her mouth to hold back a sob. The big man had rules, so many rules. Screaming was forbidden. So, too, cursing and bad language. Signs of weakness were punished.

"Save the bullets," the little man said. *"You might need them tonight."*

"They won't fight. Wait and see . . ." The creak of the windmill covered the rest of the big man's words and gravel from the drive blew against the walls. The girl stayed under the cot, breathing deeply. Fear slowly subsided. She unclenched her fist and pressed her palms to the cool concrete floor. A metal object with a sharp point pricked her skin. Familiar ridges and shapes teased her fingertips. The girl lifted the item to the light and blew away dust. It was a

rusty hair clip with the cushioned ends missing, identical to the dozens she'd lost or mislaid over the years.

Like so many other girls, she thought. Where is the owner of the hair clip now? Gone, buried in the fruit orchard or under the windmill that sang in the wind. And others, too, she was sure, all swallowed by the ground and forgotten.

The underside of the cot, a lattice of diamond-shaped wire, loomed close to her face. She gripped the metal till it cut into her palms, causing pain and sharpening her mind. The men laughed in the yard. Bottles clinked. While they laid plans and played with guns, she was safe. After that, the big man's attention would turn back to her cell. It would be too late then to fly. She tugged at the metal, testing its strength. Pushed vertically against the wall, the underside of the cot could serve as a climbing ladder that could reach up to the window. She was light, scrawny, even. The wire was strong enough to take her weight. Worth a try tonight, while they slept off the booze and the moon sank in the sky.

A bottle smashed against the wall and a door slammed. Footsteps sounded on the gravel driveway and the wooden floors inside the house. The girl scrambled from under the cot and wiped dirt from her clothes and hands. She sat on the edge of the cot with her legs pressed together and the hem of her dress pulled over her knees. Back straight, eyes to the floor and chin tucked in, she held absolutely still, hardly daring to breathe. Every detail was perfect. He couldn't fault her. Not today. She was all and more than he'd asked for: modest, quiet and obedient. A hand turned the doorknob, testing the lock. The lock held. The footsteps receded, moving in the direction of the stairs.

The girl sat, dazed. A door closed. Car engines coughed to life and a male voice called directions. She held still. The big man might come back to judge the tilt of her head, the lank fall of her hair, the exact placement of her bare feet on the concrete floor. The cars drove off, spitting dirt and gravel from under their wheels. A lump rose in the girl's throat. Far in the distance, the car engines idled at the gates to the property and then sped away again. Tears ran down her pocked cheeks and splashed onto her hands. He was gone for sure. Everything was perfect and he'd never know. Hours of practice wasted. Hours of worry swept aside as if her hard work didn't matter, as if she herself mattered nothing to him at all.

The hair clip lay on the floor, rusted and lifeless. The owner had sat on this very cot, waiting for a chance to please the big man and receive a smile, a soft word in exchange for her efforts. The girl knew it. She got to her feet, shook her limbs out. The house was empty. The big man and his friends would be gone awhile. They had plans. The time to fly had come.

A long push and the cot slammed against the wall with the high window. She flipped the metal frame and angled it so it leaned against the wall like a ladder. Slowly, resting the weight of one foot and then the other onto the diamond-shaped wires, she climbed. Light refracted through the glass. Her fingers touched the wooden frame. Two more *footholds and she could see outside. A lonely dirt road cut through flat, bush country and ended at the gravel drive. Birds sang from the trees, the branches of which were visible at the right edge of the glass. There were no crops or live-stock. The expanse of harsh, dry country seemed to go on forever. Finding food and water might be a problem. What did it matter? The big man was stingy with food and water. He gave her just enough to keep her alive until such time as he decided otherwise. She grabbed the lock and turned the metal catch. Rust slowed the movement. She jiggled the mechanism, gaining precious inches. Finally, the two parts of the lock snapped free. Paint flaked from the windowsill and specks of blue dropped to the floor. She pushed the frame out. The wood groaned but stayed fixed. Another push. Still nothing.*

"Please . . ." A pile of earth pushed against the bottom of the frame on the outside, holding it shut. The window was stuck fast. Worse yet, two metal bars were nailed to the wood frame to secure the exit. Breaking the glass wouldn't free her.

A red-haired child with long pigtails tied with white ribbon streaked across the yard with a sack slung across her shoulder. She was fast, nimble on her feet. The girl banged a fist to the glass.

"Hey. You," she screamed. "Help me. Help me out."

Dust whirled in the empty yard. Was her vision of the child with the braids and the empty burlap sack real or a long-ago memory of her own childhood?

She climbed down and paced the cell, trying to figure a

way out. The big man might let her go. It was possible. If she was good, followed instructions, sat perfectly still and smiled at the right time, then maybe. He must know how hard she worked at being obedient now. A metal point stabbed her foot, sticking into the flesh. She leaned against the wall and checked her arch. The tip of the hairpin pushed into the skin, deeper than it should have for a quick step. Breath caught in her throat. Twice now, the pin had brought news from the dead. She pulled it free. Blood trickled from the wound and stained the concrete floor; another warning from the other side. The only way out of this cell alive was through the window.

She turned the pin over and studied the sharp point. Maybe there was a way out. It would take hours. She straightened the hairpin and climbed the bed frame. She pushed the point under the window ledge. The dirt loosened. She scraped sand into the cell and dusted it to the floor. Again and again she repeated the action. She worked on her freedom one grain at a time.

16

A DIRT LANE RAN directly behind the Brewers' house and cut through to the next street. Several homes backed onto the strip of weed-choked land with a fruiting mulberry tree growing wild at the center. Emmanuel and Shabalala entered the lane and counted garden fences along the way. Ashes from the weekly garbage burn-off were sprinkled along the green corridor.

"Four more gates and we will come to the principal's house," the Zulu detective said, and gave the rough ground a cursory glance. "Many people use this place to come and go."

"Mostly servants, I think. Whoever kept Cassie company on Friday night didn't get into the garden via the main house," Emmanuel said. "He must have come this way."

Birds flew from the branches of the mulberry tree at the sound of a wooden gate scraping against dirt. Shabalala put a finger to his mouth for quiet and pointed down the lane. The gate to the Brewers' overgrown yard opened and a black man backed into the lane. He wore the traditional patched blue overalls and dirt-splattered gum boots of a "garden boy." The man shut the gate and checked the alley in both directions, nervous. He'd spot them in a few seconds. Emmanuel stepped into the man's sight line to make sure he'd be seen.

"Police," he said. "We'd like a word."

The man wheeled around and took off, churning weeds and purple mulberries underfoot. A guard dog growled from behind the fence of a tidy brick house, its ears pinned back. Emmanuel ran through the shade of the mulberry tree and caught the man close to the street corner. He brought him down easily. The smell of marijuana and beer clung to the mat of the man's graying hair and his clothes.

"Take some advice." Emmanuel kept the man's bony shoulders pinned to the ground. "If you're afraid of the police, don't run. Don't run because we will catch you. And when we catch you we will beat you for making us run."

The black man flinched, expecting a blow. Emmanuel jerked him into a sitting position and said, "Tell me why you took off."

"I was scared, ma' baas."

"Have you got something to hide?" The question put the pressure back onto the suspect and ignored the long list of reasons that a black man might have for fearing the police. "Empty your pockets and let me see."

The man pulled out a hand-rolled marijuana cigarette and held it up with a grimace. It was tattered and gaunt, much like its owner. "I ran because of this, ma' baas. The white people do not allow such things near their homes."

"The police don't allow such things at all," Emmanuel said with the haze of last night's smoke and drink buzzing in his head. Davida's observation had been wholly accurate; being a white policeman in a country beset by rules made for a dangerous sense of freedom. "Where do you come from?"

"I am the yard boy for Baas Allen. His house is there on the corner."

"Name?" He took the joint and held it between thumb and forefinger. Possession of a banned substance and resisting arrest would put the gardener in jail for a solid stretch. This afternoon, however, he and Shabalala were hunting bigger prey.

"I am called Sipho." The gardener's gaze remained pinned to the joint and the policeman holding it as if he might, at any moment, light up and draw deep. "Sipho Zille."

"You were in Principal Brewer's garden," he stated.

"That is so, ma' baas." Sipho brushed crushed weeds and twigs from his overalls, stalling for time before answering the question "why?" The guard dog, a brown-and-black mutt, bristled, bared its fangs and barked through the chain-link fence.

"Sergeant," Shabalala called from the Brewers' garden gate. "Come. Bring the man."

"Up," Emmanuel ordered Sipho. "Let's take a walk."

The gardener sat flat to the ground with his fingers dug into the dirt. Whether trapped by fear or physically paralyzed, it hardly mattered. The dog's owner would be out to check on the disturbance soon. If the police came to investigate and took down names, Mason would find out they were running their own dark investigation.

Emmanuel crouched by Sipho and said, "Show me your passbook."

"I don't have it. It is in my hut. Baas Allen's house is just there, near the corner. I can go and fetch it."

"You could live in that mulberry tree for all I care. You must carry your passbook on your person at all times. That's the law. So, here are your choices. Walk back to the principal's garden or drive with me to the nearest police station, where you will be charged with one count of resisting arrest, one count of possessing a banned substance and one count of failing to produce a passbook. Do you think Baas Allen will hold your job for you while you're in jail?"

Sipho got to his feet and moved to the Brewers' lot. Emmanuel was glad to be free of the barking dog and the birds calling danger from the trees.

"This way," the Zulu detective said, and led the way into the wild yard. Grass, trees, climbing vines and flowers wrestled for space. Emmanuel found the chaos beautiful, nature's version of a slum township where the residents mixed in whatever way they wished. Off the path and deep in the dense foliage, Shabalala stopped at the edge of a plot of land on which chest-high marijuana plants grew in thick stands.

"Yours?" Emmanuel asked Sipho of the flourishing herb garden worked on by an army of bees and butterflies.

"No, ma' baas. Never."

"How did you find this place, Detective Constable?" He addressed the question to Shabalala, who in turn glanced at the gardener with pity.

"I followed the track of the man's boots from the lane to here, Sergeant."

"This man here?" Emmanuel placed a hand on Sipho's shoulder.

"*Yebo*. The marks of his gum boots are all around." Shabalala motioned to the prints in the garden dirt where Sipho had stopped to pull weeds. "From this place he must have seen many interesting things."

The Zulu detective pointed to the thicket that shielded the small plantation from exposure. The walls of Cassie's shed were visible through the patchwork of trees. A distance of around fifty feet separated the marijuana plot and the shed, yet it was possible to see small portions of the pathway clearly. Emmanuel turned Sipho to face the stone hut and kept his hand on the gardener's shoulder.

"You lied to us about owning the *dagga* plants." He used the slang term for marijuana so there'd be no misunderstanding. "We'll give you that one for free. We'll make you *pay* for the next lie out of your mouth. Understand?"

"I hear you." Sipho's voice thickened with fear.

Emmanuel dug his fingers deeper. "See that stone hut in the trees?" he asked.

"*Yebo*, it is clear to me," Sipho said.

"Who comes and goes there?"

The gardener swallowed hard. "The daughter of the house. She is the one who uses that place . . . and maybe there is someone else."

"Is this other person perhaps a European?" Naming Cassie's visitor right away would be rude. Servants learned to talk in wide circles to avoid dismissal or punishment for being too familiar or forward. Questions and answers needed to unfold in a cautious, roundabout way.

"Yes," Sipho said. "I have seen a white baas in this garden."

"Does this man live nearby?"

"At number thirty-seven. The yellow house with big windows. His wife and child stay there also."

Andrew "call me Andy" Franklin of the ironed safari suit and neat, trimmed mustache. The helpful neighbor who'd asked after Cassie's welfare on the morning she'd left for Clear Water Farm in Rust de Winter. Andy was more than curious. He was involved.

"Mr. Franklin lives in a yellow house," Emmanuel said.

"That is the European who comes and goes from that hut." Sipho relaxed. His tight shoulders visibly softened with relief. The name hadn't come from him. It was better, safer, to stay in the background of white people's business. "How many times the man you named came here to visit, I cannot say."

"Franklin lives two doors down." Emmanuel brought Shabalala into the conversation. "He gave me the names of neighbors who had problems with Principal Brewer's native education program but failed to mention he'd been playing with Cassie in the back garden."

"Mr. Franklin must have forgotten." The Zulu detective's tone was dry as rhino hide. "A married man has much on his mind."

"We'll have to help Andy remember." He turned Sipho around to face the lush marijuana farm. The neat rows and freshly weeded soil demonstrated a deep love of the herb. "Tell me what you know about Mr. Franklin."

"I don't work for Baas Franklin. I am the yard boy for Baas Allen."

Emmanuel's fingers relaxed. He patted Sipho's shoulder. "No problem. We'll call Mr. Allen from the police station."

"Wait," Sipho said. Stuck between white people's private business and police business made it hard for him to breathe and puzzle a way out of trouble. The tall Zulu and the lean white man could, between them, break every bone and snap every tendon in his body before throwing what remained into a jail cell.

"I am not Baas Franklin's boy, but I have heard that there is fighting in the house. There is no money. The madam is worried for the child because of the little money in the bank. Baas Franklin comes to visit the white teacher's daughter when the sun goes down. I have seen him enter the hut three times. On two Fridays and then on a Saturday."

"This last Friday night?" Emmanuel asked.

"I don't know, ma' baas. That is for sure, for real. I stayed in my hut and did not come to tend my garden till now, now."

Shabalala stood on tiptoe, dwarfing the gardener, and peered into the bush and trees. Then he crouched, taking in the low view toward the main house. "If the daughter was at the hut, she could have seen who came through the back door to her parents' home. The moon was full that night."

"We get Andy to confess and then we'll use his statement to break Cassie's story." Easier said than done. Andy had a family and a reputation to protect. Cassie was, in all likelihood, a release valve from the pressures of work, wife and baby, not his great love worth sacrificing everything for. "We'll have to push him hard to get him to admit anything."

"So it must be," Shabalala said. His son's life was like sand running through his fingers; to keep the grains safe he would have to make a fist and hold on as tight as he could.

"*Baas* Franklin is not at the yellow house. Sunday he goes to the home of the madam's parents and they come back in the night. Seraphina, the house girl, has told me this."

Emmanuel couldn't stay till dark. Fatty Mapela's dance-cum-potential-brothel in the train yard started at six-thirty. He and Davida were due to leave the compound at dusk, that time of day when the failing light turned the two of them the same color.

"You must find out about the car, Sergeant." The Zulu detective read minds and tracks in the sand with equal skill. "We will come back tomorrow."

"What time does Mr. Franklin go to work on Monday?" Emmanuel asked Sipho, whose extracurricular gardening gave him the opportunity to keep a close watch on the neighbor's movements. Cultivating a marijuana plantation in spitting distance of the homes of white children and their decent, middle-class parents took a rat's cunning.

"Eight in the morning. He works in the city in a tall, tall building. Seraphina has said so."

"Six o'clock pickup tomorrow morning," Emmanuel told Shabalala. Sophiatown was a good hour's drive away from the house in Houghton.

"I will be ready, Sergeant."

The fate of Sipho, gifted cannabis farmer and reluctant police informant, remained unresolved. Laying formal charges was out of the question. Police gossiped like fishwives; a compulsive need to exchange news and compare levels of badness became a key part of the job. If they booked Sipho, Mason would instantly learn of the *dagga* plantation found growing on his crime scene.

"The gardener knows how to keep a secret," Shabalala said of Sipho, who stared at his blooming plants in mournful silence thinking of all he'd lost: job, shelter, money and the delicious weight of Seraphina's breasts cupped in his hands. The prison wouldn't have a garden or a white madam who slipped him an extra pound of sugar on birthdays and at Christmas.

"If you tell anyone we were here, including other police, we will come for you," Emmanuel said. "We won't come right away. We'll come later, when you think you're safe and we've forgotten about you."

"I will say nothing, baas. Nothing. I swear it on the ancestors."

"Go." Emmanuel gave the gardener a shove in the direction of the back gate. "And stay away from the *dagga* till after the holidays unless you enjoy being interviewed by the police."

"I am gone, baas. No coming back." Sipho started to walk away, resigned to the fact that the policemen would steal every plant and strip each sticky resin bud to fill their own pipes. No matter. He'd start again in the New Year with seeds smuggled back from where the whites had moved his people so they could make citrus farms on tribal land.

Emmanuel's watch showed one-thirty and his breakfast aspirin had worn off. The pain in his head stirred, pulsing bright and hot behind his eyelids. Certain as summer rain, the pulse would bloom into a fist trying to break a hole through his skull. He needed a jug of water, a plate of hot, salty food and a double dose of painkillers—the good kind, laced with morphine—and soon.

"Is your sister-in-law back from visiting the hospital?" he asked.

"Not yet." Shabalala tugged a weed free from the tilled ground, his fingertips dark with soil. "My brother grows worse and I have not sent word about Aaron's troubles."

"Sorry to hear about your brother," Emmanuel said. The stiff pride with which his Zulu partner shouldered the weight of his family's problems was painful to witness. Shabalala carried his burdens as a traditional man should, alone and in silence. "I have to sit awhile. Let's drive to King's place and have lunch."

"Mr. King—"

"Won't mind. We'll eat out in the garden."

The garden, away from the big house, Emmanuel meant. The big house was where white men who supported the idea of racial segregation in public lived free of the rules in private.

"I will take some food." Shabalala stood and dusted dirt from his fingers.

"Did you eat breakfast?"

"I was not hungry, Sergeant."

"If you faint, I'm not dragging you to the car," Emmanuel said, and picked grass seeds from his trousers. He straightened the lapels of his jacket. Both he and Shabalala wore hand-tailored suits made by Lilliana Zweigman, the expensive material cut to fit them like their own skins. She'd expect to see her creations looking sharp.

"If that is so, I will walk to the car."

"After you." Emmanuel paused at the gate to the Brewers' property, the hunting grounds of Andy Franklin, left to forage for thrills in a wild, suburban garden. The exhilarating chaos of the untamed vines, the hush of the wind in the branches and Cassie's body must have been irresistible.

Emmanuel understood the addictive power of taking risks. He had felt the empty spaces in civilian life after experiencing the roar of Spitfire fighter planes cracking the sky and the boom of howitzers spitting hot shells onto the earth; your blood sang with adrenaline and every color became brighter, sweeter and more fierce in the aftermath of all that noise and chaos. Days, months and years later, you paid the price for living so far from the ordinary. Andrew Franklin was about to be presented with a bill for the moments he'd stolen from his drab suburban life.

17

EMMANUEL HANDED THE night guard twenty pence and expected no change. The guard, a fat black man with a pockmarked forehead, said, "Go down, down to the marshaling yard. Park. Then you must get out and walk straight, straight to shed number twenty-five."

Emmanuel followed instructions; found six cars, a police van and a pickup truck already parked in the gravel square adjacent to a line of dirty locomotives. A freshly painted maintenance repair shop bordered the eastern edge of the lot.

"Come." He held Davida's hand and navigated the darkening yards, keeping the grid of lay-up tracks to the right and walking "straight, straight" in the direction of the machine sheds and smaller workshops. Davida's fingers squeezed tight around his, holding on to the one familiar thing in the bleak industrial landscape. Odors of oil and diesel fuel and the crunch of dirt underfoot leached romance from the soft twilight. "Next one," he said. A long iron building riddled with rust stood up ahead, a large 25 painted on its side. Davida's steps quickened at the sound of music coming from inside. She was ready to dance and enjoy her night of freedom. A balding European man in greasy overalls sat on an upended crate and peeled an orange with a penknife. He flicked the skin onto the ground and looked up. Emmanuel pegged him right away: poorly educated, Afrikaner, rewarded with a job for life on the railroads for being born white.

"*Ja?*" The man stabbed the blade into the flesh of the orange and juice ran over oil-stained fingers. He addressed Emmanuel but studied Davida from head to toe before his stare returned to the soft, cherry-red lipstick on her mouth.

"I'm here to see Fatty Mapela," Emmanuel said in Afrikaans.

"Fatty is inside, but this is my shed. I guard the door," the man answered in Afrikaans. "How badly do you want to get inside, mister?"

"Here." Emmanuel scooped coins from his jacket pocket and held out the payment.

"*Nie.*" The doorman chewed a slice of orange with an open mouth. "A kiss from your hoer will do the trick."

Emmanuel kicked the crate hard twice and the railway man toppled to the ground. The orange rolled free, collecting dirt. He stepped around the broken crate and pushed the door open. A quick squeeze on the hand and Davida followed, leaving the leering doorman chewing gravel.

"Why did you do that?" she whispered.

"Didn't like his attitude," he said. Like most English South Africans, Davida spoke very little Afrikaans. She had no idea the doorman had called her a whore.

They walked a long corridor bordered by small cubicles, mostly empty. From behind a closed door came the sound of chatter and music. The interior door was locked. He knocked twice and waited.

"Yes?" a female asked in a gravelly voice.

"Fatty? Open up. It's the police."

A metal bolt slid back and Fatty Mapela appeared in a silver cocktail dress specially modified to fit her extra-wide hips. The tight cap of her hair was dyed platinum blond, the ends of her false eyelashes sharp enough to pierce leather. She cupped Emmanuel's face between her palms and planted him an openmouthed kiss. Davida's hand tugged free.

"How long, how long?" Fatty massaged his shoulders, digging stout fingers into the flesh.

"Too long." Emmanuel gave the expected answer and reached for Davida before she sprinted for the exit. "Fix told you I was coming?"

"Of course, yes." Fatty backed into a wide room with hurricane lamps set onto individual tables draped in white cloth. A chrome jukebox flashed yellow and blue light onto a small dance floor on which three couples swayed to a crooning love song. A half-dozen European men shared tables with women ranging in color from ebony to very nearly white. In a far corner, set hard against the rear wall, a collection of girls with glossy mouths and powdered cheeks waited for customers. Fatty had thoughtfully provided a selection of black, mixed-race, and Indian girls.

"My brother said you were coming. He did not say you were bringing a friend, Emmanuel." Fatty turned to Davida with a tight pink smile. "And such a young one, too, just out of the nest."

"This is Davida." He kept hold of her arm, felt the tension in her muscles at entering an unfamiliar world. "Meet Fatty Mapela, an old friend from Sophiatown."

"No, no." Fatty wagged a diamante-ringed finger. "More than a friend. I was your first girlfriend."

"True," Emmanuel said. "But I was not your first boyfriend."

"What can I say? The men, they have always loved a piece of Fatty." She ushered them over to a small table on the edge of the dance floor. "Whiskey and water for you and, I think, a Coca-Cola with a straw for the little girl."

She ambled over to a long wood trestle table holding a variety of drink bottles and deliberately bent over from the waist to give the room a panoramic view of her silk-encased behind.

"Don't mind her," Emmanuel said to Davida as they sat down on folding chairs. "She likes to poke fun. It's mostly harmless."

Until it wasn't, and the pokes and jabs became physical.

"Was she really your girlfriend?" The idea that a white

boy—any boy at all—would pair up with this enormous black female with a throaty, almost male voice, disturbed her. Men, she thought, gravitated to soft, feminine beauty. Fatty was a wrecking ball in high heels.

"Yes, she was my first, but it didn't last long. She was . . . uh. . . " He tried to find the most polite description of the relationship. "She was much more advanced than I was. The things she wanted us to do scared the hell out of me. We broke up after one day, which was a record even for Fatty."

"You were lucky to escape," Davida said. "She would have crushed you if she'd decided to get on top."

Emmanuel laughed and circled Davida's wrist with his fingers, enjoying the feeling of being out in the world with her. She wore a simple green dress with a scoop neck and a hem that fell well below the knee. Chosen by her mother to cool lustful thoughts, he assumed. The plainness of the dress combined with the dark fall of her hair hanging loose around her shoulders had the opposite effect of that intended by Mrs. Ellis. The sight of Davida's body moving under that layer of thin cotton was tantalizing.

"Come and dance," he said.

"Not yet." She eyed the couples on the dance floor, their hips gyrating in close contact. "Maybe later when the music is livelier."

The dancing couples groped and foraged across the racial divide with enthusiasm. Emmanuel scanned the room and the rusting iron walls. Most of the men were paired up and talking to women. A clutch of four European males leaned against the wall near the jukebox, leering at Fatty's working girls, who smiled back at them. A small door at the back of the room likely led to rows of empty cubicles similar to the ones in the front corridor. These tight spaces would later be put to use with a blanket tossed on the floor and the lamps dimmed for privacy.

Fatty brought over a short whiskey and a tall glass of cola with a straw and placed them on the table. She took a chair and sipped from the tumbler before handing it to Emmanuel.

"How is your sister?" she asked.

"Still teaching. Still single." He drank from the same glass. Both Mapela siblings practiced their own form of Holy Communion. Fix smoked. Fatty drank. If he refused to share a glass, the conversation would end abruptly.

"Still a virgin, isn't she?"

Emmanuel shrugged. "Don't know. I've never asked her."

"You are a selfish, selfish man." Fatty gave Davida a sly look. "While your sister sits with her knees pressed together, you spread the leaves of this young bush and eat the fruit."

Davida sipped at the cola, pretending indifference. She coughed when the liquid burned her throat on the way down. Emmanuel took a mouthful of Davida's drink and tasted bourbon splashed with a dash of cola.

"On the house." Fatty laughed, enjoying the joke. "I thought the little girl would like to try a grown-up drink. How long have you been out of school, child?"

"Two years now," Davida replied, gray eyes dark with anger. "But what you say is true, I am young enough to be your daughter."

"Oww . . . The child has sharp teeth. How many men have you bitten with those teeth, little one?" Fatty leaned back then and took in all of Davida. Emmanuel saw her switch to business mode, weighing up the potential worth of this beautiful, brown girl with a posh accent.

"Where's your policeman husband?" Emmanuel asked.

"There." Fatty pointed to a white man with close-cropped ginger hair. It was the sergeant from the Sophiatown search who'd leaned against the police van and smoked to pass the time. The man checked the level of a bottle then picked out some bills from the money box on the table. He rolled them up and put them in his left sock. "He is one of my work husbands. Here for business only."

"Can I speak to him?"

"After we dance, of course." The music had switched to an up-tempo swing tune with trumpets and saxophone. Two couples stayed on the floor, twirling and bopping. The bass notes rumbled through the floor.

"Next one," Emmanuel promised Fatty, and grabbed Davida by the hand, giving her no choice in the matter. She jumped up from her chair. She had come out tonight to dance and shake off a year of solitude. They began awkwardly then found a groove. Their bodies swayed, swung away from each other and then moved together again. She was good. He was good enough to keep up with her. Soon

Emmanuel's breath shortened and he broke into a sweat. He'd dance till the soles of his shoes caught fire if it kept a smile on Davida's face.

They stopped for a drink and the Sophiatown sergeant took a seat at their table. The small windows had been shut to seal in the music and the voices of the guests, and the temperature in the tin room had gone up a few degrees. Fatty stood at the door now, shouting questions to whoever waited on the other side.

"Cooper," Emmanuel said. He didn't offer an introduction for Davida, who sipped bourbon and watched the couples left on the dance floor kick a jive.

"Labrant." The sergeant drank lager straight from a tall glass bottle, leaving a crust of white foam glistening on his top lip. "What can I do for you, Cooper?"

"Anything unusual about that search for the red Mercedes?" he asked.

"Now, *there's* a question." Labrant laughed, showing his yellowing teeth. "How long have you got?"

"All night, if necessary."

"Here's what happened. We got a call at the station, a tip-off about a stolen car. Okay, I'll buy that. Then a street address and a description of the red car, which is pure bullshit if you know Sophiatown." Labrant swallowed more lager, Adam's apple chugging. "Hardly nobody has phones, for a start. If they do, they don't use them to call the police and point out the location of a luxury car. They walk down the road and talk to a cousin or a brother and the car is gone. To Mozambique, Swaziland, Rhodesia, you name it. It is not sitting alone in the township like an ugly sister at the ball. "

Emmanuel already knew all this.

"You called Lieutenant Mason about the tip-off?"

"'Course not. I mean, why the hell would I do that? Sophiatown is my town. *My* town." Labrant cast a fond glance at the money tin on the bar and the European men and dark women who danced and laughed together without any regard for the new segregation laws. "Mason called me. Said he'd got a tip-off and that we could assist in the search, but it was Marshall Square's case. We were to wait for instructions. Translation: Stay the fuck away from that car or I will have your nuts."

"And did you stay away?" Emmanuel asked. Labrant was cut from old cloth, a bull-necked cop, corrupt but fiercely protective of his rights over his own turf.

"No fucking way," the Sophiatown policeman said. "I went straight down there, found the alley with the branches in about three minutes. Then I went next door and put the hard word on a petty thief who I've had occasion to talk to over the years. The red car he knew nothing about, but he did spot two men sitting in a blue sedan parked on the corner. Two lit cigarettes, he said, and the engine still running. A couple minutes passed and two more men come from nowhere, get in the backseat and they drive off. That was just before dawn."

"Descriptions?"

Labrant shrugged. "White, maybe light-skinned coloureds. It was too dark to get a good view."

"Two men to stash and cover the Mercedes, and two for backup in a getaway car," Emmanuel said.

"That's what I figured. So I took myself off to the station and kept my trap shut. No way was that car a one-man job, but I got no proof of anything."

"And even if you did have evidence, what good would it do to interfere with whatever Mason was up to . . ." Emmanuel drank his whiskey and water, enjoying the way the alcohol mixed with the painkillers that Zweigman had given him earlier. He'd taken four white beauties before leaving King's house to put down his headache and dull the fear that came with taking Davida away from the safety of her father's compound.

"That's the truth of it. That car was Mason's business, not mine. I'm five years off the pension and I've got all this to protect." Labrant pointed to the chairs, the tables and the flashing jukebox. "New enemies I can do without. And that, my friend, is the whole story of the car."

Two men in a blue sedan and another two who might have been gambling, drinking or fucking in the township till dawn. Labrant had wisely steered clear of Mason's operation.

Emmanuel said out loud, "Looks like a setup and no way to prove it."

"Kiss the investigation good-bye, Cooper, and concentrate on more pleasant things." The sergeant winked in Davida's direction. "Life is too short to take on the likes of Mason."

Would that he could.

Fatty opened the door to a young couple, still in their teens; a nervous white youth with tanned skin and a lithe woman-child with small, high breasts. The girl's dark fingers gripped the handles of an embroidered clutch bag and the boy's hand shook when he handed over the door price. Fatty stroked his cheek, raising a blush. The couple were innocents entering a secret place to test their adult desire.

"Never too young to start," Labrant said of the youngsters, and drained the last of the lager from the bottle. "Now I've got work to do. Enjoy."

"Appreciate your help." Emmanuel shook the sergeant's hand and turned his attention back to Davida, who sipped on her spiked drink.

"You came here on business," she said, the bourbon half gone, a flush of red brightening her face.

"You are my business." He linked his fingers through hers. "Would you like to dance again, my lady?"

"This is no place for ladies, Emmanuel," Davida mocked. "But all right, let's dance."

They took to the floor a second time. Three fast-tempo numbers and then, to Emmanuel's relief, a mellow tune for slow shuffling. They moved closer, bodies in full contact. Two hearts beating together in a steady rhythm. The teenage lovers drifted by, awkward in each other's arms.

"Who are those women sitting at the back table?" Davida asked. A tall Indian girl with a thick rope of black hair to the waist disappeared into the back area with one of the men from the wall. A second white man, broad-chested with stubby legs, chose a black girl and they, too, disappeared through the rear door. "Where are they going?"

"The women are prostitutes." He saw no reason to lie. "A man chooses one he likes, they agree on a price and go back there to have sex."

Davida drew back, bright-eyed. "All together?"

Emmanuel laughed. "Generally not." He met her gaze briefly then looked away. Fatty was right. Davida was young. Sexually experienced yet strangely innocent. He, by comparison, felt jaded and stained by the things he'd seen and done in his life.

"You've been in places like that," she said. "With women like that."

"Similar. The experience doesn't have to be so . . . commercial. Dinner, cigarettes and a spare ration pack in exchange for a night. I suppose it amounts to the same thing."

There. It was out and said. He'd never shared the truth with his ex-wife, Angela. The truth was dangerous, destabilizing. Emmanuel the good husband and Emmanuel the soldier from Sophiatown lived in separate cities with no roads connecting the two.

"Do you want me to be like one of those women?" Davida moved closer, fingers linked behind his neck, her breath warm on his skin. "Just for tonight."

"I'll need more than one night."

The teenage dancers drifted by again, more relaxed now, the girl laughing. Fatty moved to answer a knock at the door. The Indian prostitute reappeared, braid undone, lipstick smudged. The jukebox arm dropped another record onto the turntable. Emmanuel barely noticed. Davida's mouth opened warm and soft beneath his, her hips and breasts pressed close. He was lost. The taste of bourbon on her tongue, the feel of her skin beneath his palms and the smell of rosewater in her hair: her body became the world. Fatty Mapela's voice cut through the music and broke the spell of Davida's kiss. Emmanuel looked over at the dance hall entrance. Fatty stood with her ear pressed to the wood.

"No. No. We are full," she said. "Come next time."

Above all else, Fatty loved money: the sound of paper notes rustling through her fingers, the solid weight of coins in her palm. She rarely turned down the opportunity to make more. Emmanuel pulled Davida closer. Hauling her to a dance in a rail yard had been a gamble and he had a feeling that he'd just lost the bet.

Boots kicked at the entry door and the wood panel smashed. The edge of the door slammed Fatty on the head. She stumbled back, platinum hair bright with blood. Two men rushed the dance hall, their faces hidden behind tight stocking masks. Two more assailants appeared, kicking the short-legged man and the black prostitute into the room via the back entrance.

"Don't move, don't scream," Emmanuel whispered to Davida. "Stay by me."

Labrant stepped from behind the bar and said, "You are making a big fucking mistake, gentlemen. Leave now and I might forgive you."

The larger of the two men at the front door unholstered a revolver and aimed it at the Sophiatown sergeant's gut. He moved the muzzle to the right and fired a warning shot into the wall. Metal groaned and men and women screamed.

Fatty hugged the floor, dazed. Labrant stood with both arms raised in surrender. The patrons of the club cowered in the shadows or hunched in their chairs.

"Everyone on the dance floor and down on your knees. Move. Now," the man at the front shouted. No doubt he was the boss, standing head and shoulders taller than the rest of the gang. His minions, dressed in cheap suits, kicked chairs and shoved patrons to the center of the room. They were empty-handed but might have hidden weapons—flick knives or holstered guns.

"Unbutton my jacket," Emmanuel said quietly. "Slow and easy. Take your time. Stay close and they won't see."

Davida freed the buttons one by one, her hand sandwiched between their bodies. The dance floor filled. Men and women sank to their knees. Labrant came over last, teeth gritted with anger. Emmanuel stepped back and to the right, taking Davida with him. The teenage lovers' table and chairs were within arm's reach, so, too, the Webley revolver holstered to his torso.

A gun was handy. The problem was the crowd, though, all kneeling, all scared. A stray bullet might find one of them in the panic. If the big man discharged his firearm again, there'd be two guns discharging in the small space. Emmanuel sank slowly to his knees and mapped the positions of the gang and their strengths and weaknesses. Four men. One, possibly more, armed. The others of medium build and average height. They ringed the dance floor. Using the Webley or a chair would have to wait for the right moment.

"Wallets out. Hold them above your heads," the gang boss said. The little guy next to him weaved through the club patrons collecting wallets from their outstretched hands. He stripped out notes and loose change and shoved the loot into a jacket pocket. Then he threw the wallets aside. Labrant reached into an inner pocket and received a fist to the head from the small man. The Sophiatown policeman shook off the blow and spat onto the ground.

"Check him," the boss man said. "See what he's got."

"He's skint." The smaller man fingered the interior of the sergeant's wallet, collected lint and an expired bus ticket. Labrant had removed all personal ID. Emmanuel wished he'd thought to do the same.

"You." Another of the gang came from behind and poked Emmanuel's shoulder. "I'll have your wallet and that watch, my friend."

Emmanuel unbuckled the watch and handed it over. He removed the money from his wallet and gave that over before letting the wallet fall safe to the ground. Davida's fingers clutched the tail of his jacket, squeezing the material tight. The three enforcers gathered around the leader with the spoils.

"Check the whores," the big one said. "They'll have cash shoved all places."

Two of the men moved eagerly to the task, pushing hands down blouses and up the prostitutes' skirts. The young black girl sobbed, her body bent almost double. Her boyfriend calmed her with "hush, hush" sounds which went unheard.

"Is that it?" The boss surveyed the booty. "This is chickenshit. There's got to be more. Check the bar and that fat bitch on the floor."

The smallest of the men rattled the box on the trestle table and spilled the change inside it. He moved to Fatty and plunged a hand down her cleavage, pulled out a few damp notes and returned to the collection point. Five years off the pension with a sock full of retirement funds, Labrant kept quiet. Not one cent would he give to these vultures.

"Fuck it . . ." The big man's mouth made a hard line beneath the stocking mask. "This won't do. We didn't come all the way out here for a couple of quid."

"There's enough," the small man soothed. "Enough to buy something small. Let's hit the road. We got what we came for."

"Not me." The boss surveyed the dance hall patrons, kneeling like supplicants before a king. "I want something special."

"No, man. Please, not this again. You've already got one."

"She's not working out." Gun hanging loose by his side, the leader weaved through the crowd surveying the women. He paused to grip the chin of an Indian prostitute and examined her teeth like a punter checking the stock before a race. "I need a new one."

Emmanuel eased back and grasped the edge of the chair leg, pulled it closer. Fatty Mapela clawed the floor and inched nearer to the bar. The gang leader crouched by the young black girl and wiped away her tears.

"Maybe," he said after a long pause to consider. "Possibly."

He continued on a sideways path and stopped in front of Davida. She turned away, kept a tight hold on Emmanuel's jacket. The boss man ran a finger down the smooth skin of her neck and across the curve of her shoulder.

"You know the rule. No crossing over." The small second in command tried again to reason. "Break the rule and he'll make you bleed for it. Forget it. Let's go."

"Fuck the rules. I want this one." He tangled fingers through Davida's hair and smiled when she winced with pain. "She smells of roses. This one is worth saving."

"Emmanuel . . ." Davida whispered when the big man pulled her up by the roots of her hair. She stumbled. Breath caught in her throat, came out in a low moan. Emmanuel let her go. He had to. He gripped the chair, got a solid hold. Fatty stopped, drew in a deep breath and crawled on. If Labrant joined in, there might be a chance they could put down these thugs.

The big man turned, dragging Davida like a toy. Emmanuel swung the chair low and hard, connected with the back of the boss man's knees. Wood splintered. The leader pitched forward and hit the ground. Fatty's working girls scattered, ran to the corners of the room. Labrant swung a fist, landed a hit into the soft part of the small man's stomach. Couples squeezed under tables and scrambled to dark places.

Emmanuel pulled Davida free and brought a heel down onto the gang leader's broad wrist. Fingers twitched, loosening their hold on the pistol, a Browning Hi-Power with a polished wood grip. He kicked it free. The black girl screamed. Fatty crawled on all fours, searching for the firearm in the low light. Labrant swung circles, punching the air, hoping to connect.

"Go." Emmanuel pushed Davida to the side of the jukebox. He flipped the big man onto his back. The stocking mask had ripped, showing a bright blue eye and the curve of a dark brow. There was something in the color, a familiarity there that Emmanuel could not place.

"Look out." Davida's voice rang sharp with fear.

A punch drove into the side of Emmanuel's face. He smelled blood, tasted it in his mouth. The room tilted. The floor slammed hard to his cheek. Pain exploded against his skull and the colors from the jukebox blurred to streaks of blinding white. The world dimmed, began to fade.

"*Get the fuck up, soldier,*" the sergeant major screamed, cutting through the pain. "*Get up and fight. You will not let them touch Davida or Fatty or any other person in this room. Fight, you slum pussy. Did I not teach you how?!*"

Emmanuel heard another voice calling from a far-off place and tried to get up. Shapes blurred and lost their form. Muscles locked and quivered. Gravity pinned him to the floor.

"*Let me in and I will make you strong,*" the Scottish sergeant said. "*Give me control, boyo. Together we will sort this mess out. Let me in, lad. Let me in . . .*"

The sergeant major's presence filled Emmanuel's head and fed fresh oxygen to his aching lungs. There was no divide. No him and me, no inside or outside. The Scottish sergeant major and the Sophiatown-born detective became one. Emmanuel spat blood and got to his feet.

"Kill the fuckers," the sergeant said.

The bandit who'd knocked him flat moved in, ducking and weaving, looking for a clear shot. Emmanuel drove two punches into the man's stomach that lifted him off the ground. He kept working, opening a cut on the cheek and then another over the right eye. A pounding right hook rocked the man back, sent the spit flying. Emmanuel kicked the bandit's legs and the man crumbled like ash. He crossed to the leader who'd dragged Davida by the hair. Blood roared through his veins. Fear vanished. Pain faded. He hit the big man with his fists, once and then again and again till he lost count. The skin on his knuckles split. He was empty of emotions and heard only the satisfying *wham* of flesh yielding.

"Jesus Christ. Stop." Labrant pulled him away. "We need the bastard alive to answer questions. Like who the fuck he thinks he is, breaking into my place."

Emmanuel's heart beat like a hammer. The world expanded and came back into focus. Fatty held the smaller man in a choke hold, her platinum hair stained red, the silver material of her cocktail dress darkened by blood. She pushed the hostage to the floor, next to the gang boss, and kicked a stiletto into his back. Emmanuel stepped aside, elated. He craved a drink, a smoke and a roll in the back room. Davida crawled out from the edge of the jukebox and slipped her hand into his.

Labrant crouched in front of the gang boss and the second in command. He ripped the stocking from the smaller man, exposing a pixie face with red cheeks and a short, sharp nose.

"Who the hell are you? One of the Christmas elves?"

The elf grit his baby-white teeth and said nothing. Labrant grasped the tattered ends of the boss man's stocking mask, ready to rip. A girl screamed, the sound high and shrill in the tin room. Emmanuel swung around, cursed under his breath. He'd lost track of the numbers. Four men. Only three accounted for. The fourth member of the gang held a knife to the teenage girl's throat, the silver blade gleaming deadly against her dark skin.

"Let them go." Flattened features and dark eyes stared out from behind the stocking mask. "Let them go or I will cut the little one. I swear it."

The voice shook; the hand holding the blade shook worse. Scared men were prone to sudden, violent moves. Emmanuel swung Davida behind him and raised opened palms.

"Wait a minute," he said. "There's no need to hurt her. We can talk. Let her go and we'll sort this business out."

"No ways. You just beat the shit out of Lenny and Crow. I ain't coming close." Beads of blood appeared on the blade. "Now let them go."

"Please . . ." the white teenager who'd paid entry for the young black girl cried out. "Please don't. I'm begging you, mister."

"It's all right," Emmanuel said. Begging would not help. The kidnapper's desperation was visible through the tight stocking mesh. "We're going to stay calm. Work things out."

"There's nothing to work out, man. Let them go or I'll cut her. So help me God, I will."

Labrant grabbed a fistful of the elf's hair and tugged till the jugular veins showed blue beneath the pale skin. Fatty brought the gang boss's revolver out from the sash of her dress, leveled the point to the crown of his head.

"You hold one card," Labrant said in a rough voice. "And we hold three. So calm down and we will sort this out just like my friend suggested."

Emmanuel couldn't imagine a worse situation than a loaded gun in Fatty Mapela's hand and a knife in a terrified man's grasp. Labrant remained calm, willing to negotiate. He threw a quick look in Emmanuel's direction, gave him the authority to break the standoff.

"We'll exchange Lenny, Crow and the one on the floor for the girl," Emmanuel said. "Three for one in your favor. That's fair."

"And we keep the cash," Labrant added.

"I . . . I don't know." A wet patch appeared on the stocking mask right were the kidnapper's mouth must be. He was licking his lips, nervously weighing up the deal.

"Surely your friends are worth one black girl and a few pounds? Do the sums. It's cheaper than burying all three of them."

"Maybe." He looked to the leader, kneeling with the barrel of a revolver pressed to his skull. "Should I, Lenny?"

"Do it." The reply came out terse and short. "And stop using names."

The boss and the petite second in command might be professionals, but the rest of the troops were amateurs, all the more reason to talk through the steps of the exchange slowly.

"We'll swap at the door," Emmanuel said. "That's fine with you?"

"*Ja*. That's all right." The captive girl sobbed and her tears splashed onto the kidnapper's fingers. The hand holding the knife gripped the handle tighter.

"Slowly. No need to rush. Walk to the door. We'll bring our hostages across. Go." The jittery robber crabwalked to the entrance, the stocking mask moist with sweat. Fatty tapped the gun barrel to the leader's head. "You. Up. To the door."

Labrant grabbed the elf by the scruff of the neck and dragged him bodily to the smashed entrance. Emmanuel crossed to the man pooled on the floor. He threw the remainder of the whiskey and water onto the man's face and brought him to.

"You're leaving," he said. "You and your friends."

The room stilled. People held their breath in anticipation of a sudden twitch of a finger against a gun trigger or the jerk of a blade against neck tendons. Emmanuel pushed the bloodied man to the exchange point and picked up his watch from the loot table on the way.

"You have two minutes to clear the yards," he said when the girl hostage staggered to her boyfriend and the four bandits retreated into the corridor. "Then we are coming after you."

Fatty released the safety on the boss man's gun and said, "*One* minute."

The men turned and ran. Emmanuel gave them a thirty-second start. Fatty and Labrant followed him down the corridor and out into the yards. A lone security light cut through the darkness. A vast tangle of tracks and sheds spread out in the moonlight.

"Agh ..." Labrant made a disgusted sound and pointed to the body of the Afrikaner railway worker sprawled in the dirt. The flecks of fine coal dust suspended in the air of the yard had speckled the red hole that leaked blood on the bib of his overalls. "We should have shot them in the corridor, made an end to it."

"Gunning down four white men in front of two dozen witnesses would be the end for us as well." Emmanuel checked for a pulse and got nothing. The wound was fatal, the Afrikaner killed with a neat thrust of a knife. "There's no way to clean up that kind of mess and hope to keep it quiet."

Labrant grunted agreement and said, "Let's get this one out of the way before the guests see. They'll connect us with this for sure and put us in the frame for it."

Emmanuel agreed. Better to be cautious than sitting in a police station writing up a false statement. Fatty tucked the revolver into the sash of her dress again and grabbed a limb. Labrant took the other arm and Emmanuel the legs. They lifted the dead man's weight and shuffled to the corner of the shed. The space between the shed and the next building made a snug, black, temporary casket. Perfect. They laid the body down and walked around to the front.

Emmanuel stopped, crouched and wiped blood from his shoes with a handkerchief. Shadows flickered in the entrance. He looked up. Davida stood in the dimness, fingers pressed hard to her mouth to stifle a cry. She'd seen them dump the body. He was certain.

"Come, little girl." Fatty's voice carried a sharp edge. "This is no place for a child. Let us leave the men to their business."

Davida retreated in silence, her upper arm held in Fatty's grip. Emmanuel paused and worked again at the shoe leather. Only warm water and soap would remove the stain, he realized. No amount of scrubbing would clean Davida's mind of the things she'd witnessed. The Afrikaner's slack body, the strange dance they'd performed while carrying the bleeding corpse to the passage and the peeled orange in the dirt; all were burned deep into her memory. Time would chip away at the images, soften their edges, but she'd never forget. He knew. He'd tried.

18

I T WAS THE big one who did the stabbing. The pissant who grabbed the girl didn't have the guts," Labrant said. "I reckon Vickers knew them, let them in to rob the place."

"That was his name?" Emmanuel pocketed the bloody handkerchief, which would now have to be thrown away or burned.

"*Ja.* Vickers Steyn." Labrant blew out a loud breath. "Should never have trusted him. I saw him beat his dog once."

"It's finished," Emmanuel said. The time for analysis had already passed. "We have to move. The thieves won't come back after the beating they've taken, but they might call the police or get the vice squad down here."

"Right." The sergeant glanced to the black spot where the body lay. "I'll take care of Vickers, find him a resting place in the Orange Free State."

"We could leave him and call the body in to the police tomorrow morning." That presented the least illegal option. "He might have family."

"Lucky for us, Vickers had no family and no friends: just a job and a boss who'll report him missing when he fails to show up for three shifts in a row. A miserable death for a miserable man," Labrant said. "I'd shed a tear but I'll be too busy digging up a bush grave on my brother-in-law's—"

"Don't say any more," Emmanuel interrupted. "I don't want to know. Let's clear the place, first. Get everyone out."

They reentered the corridor of shed twenty-five. Patrons streamed out as if they were running from a burning building; their valuables clutched in their hands, faces drawn with fear, elbows shoving to clear a path.

"Calm down, people," Labrant shouted. "The thieves are gone. Move to your cars and leave in an orderly fashion."

The crowd gave no sign of having heard. In less than five minutes, the room and the corridor were empty. The teenage hostage and her white sweetheart were the last out, their arms wrapped around each other.

Dust motes swirled in the light of the hurricane lamps, stirred up by the rush of departing couples. Fatty's working girls bunched together, smoking and chattering in high-pitched voices. Sergeant Labrant would eventually escort them back to the southern edge of town, where they lived together in an isolated house screened from the road by tall slash pines. Davida stood by herself, deep in thought or in shock.

Labrant stripped three tablecloths and rolled them into a ball. He said, "Ready, Cooper?"

Emmanuel walked out to help remove the body.

—

Half an hour later the jukebox had been wrestled onto the back of Fatty's pickup truck and the prostitutes packed into the rear of the police van. Vickers Steyn, rolled in tablecloths, occupied the space farthest from the door. A road patrol would see the girls, not the body. Emmanuel said his good-byes and returned to the shed to collect Davida. At the very least, he'd spared her the sight of Fatty's girls joking with each other in the presence of a corpse.

"*God above,*" the sergeant major said when Emmanuel entered the emptied tin building. "*This is, without a doubt, the worst first date in the history of mankind.*"

"*Agreed,*" Emmanuel replied. What was he thinking? Taking Davida to an illegal dance in a railway yard? His intentions had been good: get her out of the house so she could dance with him while their baby slept safely at home. His decision to expose her to the underbelly of South African life spoke of desperation, of having no more to offer her than snatched moments of normality in abnormal situations. She deserved more than that.

A single hurricane lamp lit the darkened room. Davida stared into the yellow flame, breathing in and out with deliberation.

"Come," Emmanuel said. "Let's go."

Davida continued to stare; the fire cast a spell that blocked the smell of blood mixed with perfume and the echoes of the black girl's sobs. Emmanuel had witnessed this internal retreat several times during the war. He had lost good men, fine soldiers to shell shock. A mind under pressure sometimes built walls too thick to breach.

"We have to go." He laid his fingers on Davida's arm. "It's not safe to stay here." She punched him in the chest, hard. Emmanuel staggered back, absorbed the pain. A high blow caught him square in the mouth, drawing blood from an earlier cut. He grabbed her wrist, instinctively blocking another blow. She fought on. Emmanuel reined her in, let half the hits connect. They slammed into the corrugated iron wall. He turned and pinned her against the metal sheeting, exerting control. She kicked and twisted until her breath came in short, exhausted gasps.

"Why did you bring me here?" She slumped against the iron wall and gave up the fight.

"To dance with you," he said.

They stood in the softly lit darkness, their bodies pressed close together, their hearts beating in rough time. Emmanuel thought to step back, to break them free of the rush of adrenaline mixed with desire. They'd entered dangerous territory, where only breath and flesh mattered. Davida's hips flexed, inviting closer contact. He tried to physically break the spell, give them room for rational actions. Her hands and his lips had other ideas. He kissed the pulsing heartbeat at the base of her neck, the line of her jaw, her open mouth. Fingers found buttons, ripped cotton, touched heated skin. The wall bucked against their pressure.

Emmanuel pushed the fabric of her skirt above her waist, exposed smooth brown thighs and white silk underwear.

"Here?" he asked.

"Now," she said.

—

Nighttime and the sky was crowded with a million stars. Grain by grain, the gap under the windowsill grew bigger and the outside world closer. Hour upon hour she'd labored, stopping to rest aching fingers and quivering muscles. An embedded rock had taken most of the afternoon to excavate and even now it lay loose on top of the soil. She pushed the window out to its full extension. The gap was small, four hand widths at most. She'd have to breathe in and tunnel under like a worm.

Perched on the top rung of the iron cot, the girl pressed her head and shoulders under the rail. She gave one last push against the top on the iron cot, which crashed to the floor. Chin pressed to the dirt, she inched forward. Fresh air touched her face, a luxury after the heat and stillness of the cell. The wooden rail scraped the top of her head and snagged the material of her dress. Outside, a yellow moon lit the yard and deepened the shadows under a scraggy line of fruit trees. One inch more and then another and another: the slowest escape in history. She scraped more dirt to clear a path and spat sand from her mouth. The scent of sage-brush and the sour tang of rotting citrus grew stronger. Soon the land would be hers, the open sky, the wide hori-zon and the finger of dirt road leading to a bigger road and then to the city. A night owl hooted and the soft whistle of wind called her out. Then came the sound of a car engine, still far off but getting louder. Twin headlights glowed in the darkness: the big man and his gang were on their way home.

She wiggled, pushed and clawed. The window rail scratched her skin and bruised the muscles on her back. The curve of her bottom snagged on the low wooden bar, hold-ing her half in and half out of the small window. The head-lights danced as the car tires bounced over the road's surface. If there was a God, He was a cruel one, to let her feel the wind on her face and smell the open bushlands just to take it all away now. The girl stopped, drew a shudder-ing breath and arched her body like a cat, bringing the full force of her spine and hips to the rail. Nerve endings screamed with pain. She repeated the move, obeying a pure animal instinct to escape.

How fast cars were, even in the dark, she thought. Speed gave the big man an unfair advantage and he al-ready had the upper hand. Not tonight, the girl decided. Tonight I will prevail. She bucked and flexed, moved for-ward. The car stopped at the gates. There was time, maybe.

The gates closed, the headlights were so bright. Fear tore through her. Animals chewed through their own limbs to get free. She snapped her body up against the bar, willing to exchange broken bones for an inch more space.

The car reached the gravel drive, a black shape menacing, like a predator. She twisted her hips and the wooden bar gave just enough room for her to slip under. Light swept the forlorn yard and the drought-stricken orchard. She lay still, waiting for the engine to die and for darkness. The car parked. Raised voices came from the interior, a fight between the big man and the little one. No sign of the other vehicle carrying their friends. The lights went out. The girl cleared the low bar. Her ankle snagged against the wood. No, please. There'd be no second chances. She had to succeed or die in the attempt. She kicked at the window and smashed the glass. The car lights switched on, illuminating the house. The girl kicked again and broke free. Glass cut her skin, the pain only a faint whisper, barely registering.

Then she ran.

Male voices shouted filthy words, all of them familiar to her. The engine coughed to life and the tires gripped the gravel. They were coming after her. She jogged right and sprinted into the fruit trees.

"Get back here," the big man shouted. "Now."

She glanced over her shoulder, saw the car stalled between two gnarled trunks, the headlights shining into a part of the orchard where she was not. The big man hung an elbow out of the window.

"You know where you are, girl?" he called out. "A hunting reserve. The animals will tear you apart if I don't get to you first."

She'd take her chances with the wild animals. The night closed around her body like a shawl and she tore into the darkness.

19

EMMANUEL WOKE BRUISED and aching. The split skin on his knuckles and the pain in his feet from kicking ribs reminded him of the hard fight the night before. The fight itself he barely remembered. Muffled sounds, flashing colors and the sensation of hot blood burning through his veins were all that remained in his mind.

His palm rested on the sleek curve of Davida's naked hip. Details of what they'd done against the wall in the rail yard, and again when they'd arrived home, were burned into his memory, and would, Emmanuel suspected, remain undimmed until the pyramids turned to sand. With the exception of Rebekah, who was probably still sleeping beside Mrs. Ellis in the cottage adjoining the big house, this small hut contained all he needed to live and die happy.

Footsteps crunched the garden path outside, breaking the bubble. He slipped out of bed, reluctant to face the world. The footsteps grew louder. He pulled on trousers, shoved the Webley into the waistband and shrugged on a shirt. He left the bedroom with a quiet tread and peered out of the front window. Dr. Zweigman, wearing a plaid dressing gown, blue pajamas and slippers hurried through the garden. Emmanuel opened the door before he knocked and stepped onto the porch. He closed the door with a soft click.

"The night duty guard rang the alarm." Zweigman's German accent intensified under stress, trampling vowels and elongating consonants. "There are men at the gate. They've asked for you, Detective Cooper."

Emmanuel hit the path barefoot and in wrinkled clothes. Ribbons of soft pink colored the sky as the sun rose through the trees. From the rear of the big house he saw them: three white men in dark suits. Their purposeful stride and tugged-down fedoras indicated law enforcement. He moved out to meet them. Zweigman came along, bulking up the odds to two men against three.

"Fuck . . ." Emmanuel recognized Mason, flanked by the undercover detectives who'd helped search the Mercedes. Mason had crossed the threshold into Emmanuel's private life and had brought the fight over the Shabalala investigation right to his doorstep. He quickened his pace, hoping to keep the lieutenant far from the big house.

"You know them?" Zweigman asked while trying to tamp down strands of explosive white hair.

"Unfortunately, yes." And they now knew where he lived, had found out somehow. Emmanuel confronted the trio halfway up the drive, realized only then that his shirt was unbuttoned, the Webley revolver tucked, township gangster fashion, into the waistband of his trousers.

"Cooper," the lieutenant said. "You appear to have spent the night fighting and fucking."

Mason, by comparison, must have used the dark hours to wrestle the top off a whiskey bottle or three. His pallor matched the gray dawn and red veins webbed the whites of his eyes. The lieutenant had fallen off the wagon hard and lost his born-again certification.

"What can I do for you, sir?" Emmanuel hooked up buttons to cover bruised and scratched skin. He could do nothing to conceal the blue mark left by a blow to the head during last night's fight. Mason's companions smoked in quiet, waking up with the help of nicotine; one wore mismatched socks and the other a gravy-stained tie. They'd been dragged from sleep and tumbled into clothes on short notice.

"Is there a place to talk, Cooper?" Mason asked.

"It isn't my house, so right here will do fine."

"Pity." The lieutenant held up two splayed fingers, signaled for a cigarette. "I'd like to have seen how a sugar baron lives."

So, Mason knew the Houghton estate belonged to Elliott King, sugar-mill proprietor and owner of vast tracts of South Africa. Davida and Rebekah's names might also be penned into Mason's notebook. The thought brought a cold rush of fear, which Emmanuel pushed aside. Fresh from bed as he was, barefoot and physically hurting from the fight at the club, projecting a confident demeanor was imperative.

"Find out why he's here," the sergeant major's voice said. *"Doesn't smell right, does it? Him walking through the front gate, hungover, pale as a cut onion. And the other two have no bloody idea what's going on."*

"Is this a social or a police call, Lieutenant?" Emmanuel asked.

Mason accepted a cigarette from the flap-eared detective and touched the tip to the lit end of the detective's stub. He drew deep and held in the smoke before letting it drift through barely opened lips. "Where were you between eight and midnight last night, Cooper?"

"Here," he said. "In the house."

"You have a witness, I suppose?"

"I was with this man. Dr. Daniel Zweigman. We discussed the war." Using Elliott or Winston King's name to plump up a lie was out of the question. They held the keys to the little hut, to Davida and Rebekah. He threw Zweigman a look, sent a subtle request for cooperation.

"You talked for four hours?" Mason said.

"It was a long war," Zweigman replied.

Mason fixed the Jewish doctor with a sharp gaze. Zweigman returned the scrutiny with brown, unblinking eyes. He hadn't talked about the war with the detective sergeant last night, but he'd lived it and witnessed the rise and fall of tyrants. It took more than a cold stare to intimidate a Buchenwald survivor.

The lieutenant abruptly switched focus and said, "Do you know a man by the name of Vickers Steyn, Sergeant Cooper?"

"No." Emmanuel spoke too quickly, a fraction too loud. Fear bit deep. Mason had, by some means, made a connection between him and the shifty Afrikaner sitting outside shed twenty-five, and all before breakfast. How?

"Calm down, breathe deep and deny, deny, deny," the sergeant major instructed. *"Hold your ground and don't say another word. Let Mason cough up the information."*

Emmanuel stretched out and yawned. Three people alone could tie him to the doorman. No way had they talked. Fatty Mapela and Labrant were in the business of making money; the financial rewards for turning police informants were considerably less than one night's takings from their illegal operation. They'd stick with the cash flow. Davida he could personally vouch for.

Zweigman scratched an unshaved cheek and flicked a twig from the hem of his dressing gown. Cars drove by on the street, loud in the silence.

Mason said, "I will ask again and this time take a minute to think before you answer, Sergeant Cooper. Do you or did you know a man by the name of Vickers Steyn?"

"I've not heard that name before nor have I met any man by that name." There. That should be clear enough. "Why do you ask, Lieutenant?"

"A white male matching your description was seen talking with Vickers last night."

"*Bullshit. Johannesburg is the biggest city in Sub-Saharan Africa. How many males matching your description do you reckon there are? Hundreds, probably thousands, yet Mason zeroes in on you,*" the Scottish sergeant said. "*What the fuck is he really doing here?*"

"It must have been a detailed description to bring you out at dawn and with backup," Emmanuel said. In reality, the backups had backed away and now stood with hands thrust deep into their pockets, waiting to leave.

"Perhaps your witness made an error," Zweigman said. Dawn's low rays caught the frame of the doctor's gold-plated glasses, refracting a sparkle of light. "Detective Cooper and I were in the house until late last night. He could not have been in two places at once."

In less strained circumstances, Emmanuel would have smiled. Given the chance, the German doctor could easily have been a private investigator or perhaps a vaudeville actor.

"There's been no mistake." Mason aimed two fingers directly at the German's heart, the smoke from his cigarette clouding the air. "You are lying to cover up for Cooper. I don't know how things work in kraut land, but here in South Africa, providing a false statement is a punishable offense."

"Are you familiar with Yiddish, Lieutenant?" Zweigman found more snagged twigs on his garment and picked them off one by one. "It's a colorful language with many interesting expressions. Here is one that I particularly like: 'A mewling cat catches no mice.' If your claim has teeth, then stop making sounds and do something."

"Lay charges or leave," Emmanuel translated for the haggard police detective. Mason studied the doctor's wild white hair and parchmentlike skin with a bleak expression. The scrutiny served to condemn and to warn Zweigman that he had committed every physical detail to memory.

"Sir?" Big Ears nudged when the silence stretched to an uncomfortable length. The sun rose higher in the sky, the world waking up and getting to work. If they left now there'd be time for a decent breakfast before the start of their shift.

"Are we finished here?" Emmanuel asked.

The damage done by a solid night's drinking showed clearly on Mason's face. He looked old, worn out. But not quite: beneath Mason's hungover pallor and squinting eyes lurked a dark core of something that Emmanuel could not quite define.

"We're done for now. See us out, Cooper."

They walked to the guardhouse and left Zweigman alone on the curve of the driveway. The guard cradled a phone to his ear, talking to the big house, confirming the presence of law enforcement on the grounds. Emmanuel quickened the pace, decreasing the distance to the street. Davida might be awake now and wondering at the empty tangle of sheets and the rumpled pillow where he'd been. If she left the hut and came out of the garden and into plain sight in nothing but a thin cotton dressing gown, Mason would know, even through the blur of stale whiskey, that she was important. He'd connect her to Emmanuel in a second.

Emmanuel greeted the watchman with a nod, ducked under the boom gate and turned right onto the sidewalk. He stopped in the shadow of the walls and waited. Now, at least, the house and grounds were out of sight. A group of white schoolgirls in blue smocks and knee-high white socks streamed in the direction of a bus stop on the street corner. The scent of shampoo and soap perfumed their wake. The backups stayed to the grass verge and waited for the girls to pass.

Mason threaded through them, some with arms full of books, others pushing strands of silky hair under the brims of their wide hats. The girls broke apart, the hum of violent energy emanating from Mason pushing them aside as if repelled by a magnetic force.

"Something's chewing a hole through that bastard's guts," the sergeant major said. *"I still don't know what the hell he's doing here. Have you figured that out?"*

"Not yet."

"Then stop skulking around corners, boyo. Stick the boot in and shake some teeth loose. Get the fucker to react."

"Poke a stick into the hornet's nest, you mean?"

"Affirmative."

Mason veered off the footpath and into the shade of the boundary wall. He stood with both hands resting on his hips and the butt of his Webley revolver visible in its holster.

"Cut him down, soldier."

"Stay off the bottle, Lieutenant," Emmanuel said. "You look like shit."

Mason's lips thinned. He hitched a thumb in the direction of the King family compound. "Hide behind these walls and that rich man's money, but remember that when you leave I'll be waiting. I will find you and that coloured bitch you were dry-humping on the dance floor last night. That is a promise."

"It sounded more like a threat, but I catch your drift. Here's some advice for you, Lieutenant. Don't come to this house again or that rich man will have your police card, your firearm and your pension with a single phone call. That's a promise, not a threat. You understand the difference?"

Mason swam in a small slime pond. Neither a member of the feared security police nor highly ranked enough to manipulate government ministers, he drew power from a tight gang of undercover police. He could inflict damage, though.

"That advice goes for you guys also." Emmanuel widened the threat of legal action to include the two detectives working backup. They shuffled their feet, scratched at their necks and glanced away to the traffic of native servants streaming to work in European-owned houses. They'd heard enough to be uncomfortable, which suited Emmanuel fine.

"Warm up the car, boys," Mason said. "I'll be along in a moment."

The detectives crossed the tarred road to a police sedan parked under the branches of a red-blossomed flame tree. Mason twirled a finger in the air. Big Ears cranked the engine, turned on the radio and left the motor running. Orchestral music drifted from the vehicle and across the road; the choice surprised Emmanuel.

Mason leaned close, blue eyes gleaming. "Get the fuck out of my town, Cooper. You have twenty-four hours. After that, I will come after you. That is not an idle threat. It's a guaranteed certainty."

He walked to the car, got in and slammed the door. The black sedan pulled away from the curb, carrying off its deadly cargo to the strains of a classical symphony.

—

Barefoot and with a firearm tucked under wrinkled clothes, Emmanuel stood awhile to contemplate Mason's warning. Aaron Shabalala and the Brewers hadn't been mentioned or even alluded to. The fight at Fatty's illegal dance hall and Vickers Steyn's murder were the reasons behind the dawn visit.

"*Mason knows the men who took a beating at the club last night,*" the sergeant major said. "*How else could he connect you with an Afrikaner doorman working the arse end of a rail yard? That bullshit 'man matching your description' story is true. The lieutenant had eyes and ears at the dance. And Davida called your name out once that I recall.*"

Emmanuel scrambled to remember if he'd made the same mistake and identified Davida to the masked thugs.

No. He'd been careful. Only Fatty Mapela knew her name and she'd sooner chew through her own tongue than talk to the police.

"Davida's safe for now, but not for much longer. Mason wants you out. He'll be back and he will tear this house apart."

—

"The infamous Lieutenant Mason." Zweigman and Emmanuel walked the wide curve of the drive with the sun falling warm on their shoulders and the sky turning a deep blue overhead. "I did not expect him to be so tall or so sad."

"Sad?" That description felt a hundred miles in the opposite direction from the truth.

"Yes," Zweigman insisted. "And scared. More scared even than you were, Detective."

"Mason came armed with a gun and death threats." The doctor's smudged glasses must have distorted reality. "Do you really expect me to have sympathy for the devil?"

"No, but think on it. Half drunk, stumbling through the dawn to make unsubstantiated allegations . . ." Zweigman laid a gentle hand to Emmanuel's arm. "Those are the acts of a desperate man, not a strong one."

"Zweigman has something," the sergeant major said. *"If those were Mason's men at the dance club, he'd be furious but also shit scared right now. So frightened he practically confessed to a personal involvement in last night's balls-up."*

"All right." The Scotsman and the German made good sense. "Scared, I understand. It's sad that I'm still having trouble with."

"I saw it behind the bluster and the aggression. Many of the SS officers at the camp carried this unhappiness also, as if all the power in the universe could not fill the hole in their chests where other men had hearts," Zwiegman said. "Why *did* Mason come here?"

"To warn me off."

"The Brewer case?"

"No. Mason's confident that the Brewer investigation is closed. He came to frighten me into leaving town."

"Why?" Zwiegman asked the obvious question. "You pose no threat to him."

Emmanuel thought through the elements and said, "Some masked men tried to rob an illicit dance club last night. I was there. They killed the doorman on the way out, probably to stop him identifying the ringleader. The men left with broken ribs and no money, but I did see one of them clearly enough to pick him out in a lineup."

"Why would Mason come out at dawn to protect these robbers?"

"They were his men," Emmanuel said. "Had to have been."

"Interesting . . ." The doctor stopped and tapped his fingers together while the cogs of his brain turned. After a long while, during which the sun lit up the windows of the big house like mirrors, he said, "Could the robbers who broke into the Brewers' house and the robbers who broke into the

dance hall be the same men? That would explain Lieutenant
Mason's erratic actions. He feared you'd dig into the dance
hall incident and connect him to both crimes."

"*It's possible,*" the sergeant major said. "*Good help is
hard to find, even for a dirty cop. How many men would
Mason have on his books? Six at the most, I reckon.*"

"Your theory makes sense," Emmanuel said to Zweigman. "We'll stick with the Brewer investigation and hope-
fully find the link to Mason."

"*Heads up, soldier,*" the sergeant major warned. "*In-
coming. Twelve o'clock.*"

Winston King, Davida's brother, stood on the driveway, his tanned skin lit golden by the dawn. A beautifully
formed mixed-race man living and passing as white, a thug
with enough charm to talk the birds out of the trees, Winston could give lessons in living a lie.

"Friends of yours?" Winston asked of the three departed detectives. He, too, wore pajamas and a dressing
gown: fine Egyptian cotton thread handwoven by nuns in
a high-altitude cloister, Emmanuel imagined, and then
dyed a color that might be called Amalfi blue or perhaps
Caribbean wave.

"I know them," Emmanuel said. "They're cops, which
is how they got on the grounds. The guard couldn't have
stopped them."

"There is one way to make sure they never come back
here and that's for you to pack up and get out of my father's house," Winston said. "This experiment in happy-
ever-after is over, Detective Cooper. Time to leave."

"Davida will decide whether I stay or I go," Emmanuel said. However impossible his dreams were of a stable relationship, they could not be dismissed by the flick of a rich youth's hand. "Ask her. See what she says."

"I don't think I will." Winston prowled in a semicircle, taking in the rumpled shirt, cut knuckles and bruise-darkened skin on Emmanuel's cheek. "Women confuse sex with love and I'll bet you're good in bed, aren't you, Detective? Plus my sister has a weakness for rough white men with guns, which makes her opinions completely invalid."

"This from a glorified drinks waiter! You will not take orders from a spoilt child, Cooper."

"I'll go when Davida tells me to." Emmanuel turned and walked in the direction of the hut. Between Mason's ultimatum and Winston's threat of eviction, the morning had unraveled in spectacular fashion. He had miscalculated. The case had crossed into his personal life and now he had twenty-four hours at most to break the case against Aaron Shabalala or he ran the risk that Davida and Rebekah's identities would be revealed.

"What would Mason do in similar circumstances?" the sergeant major wondered. *"How would he ride out this shit storm?"*

Emmanuel knew.

20

ANDREW FRANKLIN'S BODY contorted into a U-shape. He dug his heels into the concrete driveway and threw his weight from right to left like a horse bucking a rider. "You can't do this. I have work. I have obligations."

"I'll write you a note." Emmanuel pushed Andy into the Brewers' empty garage and threw him into a chair. Shabalala stepped out of the shadows and pressed the full weight of his palms to Andy's shoulders, locking him down.

"This is kidnapping. It's against the law."

"Asking questions is completely legal." Emmanuel crouched and made eye contact with Cassie Brewer's next-door neighbor. "Carnal knowledge of a minor, on the other hand, is definitely illegal."

"What are you implying? I have a wife and a child, for heaven's sake. I don't have time to listen to this rubbish."

Andy tried to shake off Shabalala's grip, but the Zulu detective's fingers flexed, giving Franklin a taste of the power that lay behind his palms.

Emmanuel said, "You're not going anywhere until you tell us about your relationship with Cassie Brewer."

"There was no relationship."

"Are you sure about that?"

"*Ja*. Completely."

"All right, then." Emmanuel gave Shabalala a quick nod. The Zulu policeman grabbed Andrew Franklin's wrists and pinned them behind the chair in a viselike grip. Andy strained and jerked against the tight hold but could not break free. Emmanuel laid his hands on Andrew Franklin's knees.

"Stop struggling and listen to me closely," he said. "I don't have time to scratch around for the truth. I need the truth and I need it now."

"I'm a married man, I—"

Emmanuel's right hand flashed up and he gripped Andy's throat, cutting off the air supply. He slowly tightened his hold. "Have I got your full attention, Mr. Franklin?"

Andy gasped, his eyes bloodshot and terrified. He gargled a wet sound, his body flexed against the wooden slats of the chair.

"I've killed better men than you, Andrew: husbands and brothers fighting to keep their loved ones safe in a war. Those men are buried and gone. And now you are standing in the way of something I need. That makes you expendable. Do you understand?"

Andy nodded, or tried to, before the steely grip of Emmanuel's fingers forced his head back again. Shabalala steadied the chair and kept his eyes fixed on the oil stain on the concrete floor. His son had not stolen the red car from this garage. Nor had he beaten Principal Brewer to death. This terrified white man might be the key to Aaron's freedom. If his friend Emmanuel Cooper could open the door to the truth, Shabalala would let the interrogation run as long as it needed to.

"Friday night, you and Cassie Brewer played house in the back shed." Emmanuel eased his hold on Andy's throat in order to give him enough oxygen to talk. "Then what happened?"

"Sounds," Franklin croaked. "Voices in the garden."

"You saw who it was?"

"No . . ." Andy hesitated, on the verge of revealing an uncomfortable detail. "Cassie thought it might be the kaffir who was visiting her parents from up north. She figured he was opening the back gate so his friends could come in and rob the place. She went to check."

"While you stayed in the hut?"

Andy squirmed under Emmanuel's disapproving gaze. "I . . . I had the most to lose if we got caught out. Cassie volunteered."

"And you let her."

"She knew the lay of the land . . . it was safer that way."

"Safer for you, certainly." A mix of youth and inexperience rendered Cassie incapable of seeing beneath Andrew

Franklin's bland good looks to the cowardly heart beating at his core. "What then?"

"She came back to the shed and said it wasn't the kaffir. It was two white men, a big one and a little one, walking very quietly to the house. She didn't like the look of them, the way they moved in the dark." Andy swallowed and winced in pain. "I suggested we end things for the night and meet again in a few days. So we split and I went home."

Andy's one saving grace was providing a detail that tied the assault on the Brewers to the murder of the Afrikaner doorman. A big white man and a little one had led the break-in at Fatty's club. Zweigman's theory could be right.

"You left the girl alone and in danger," Shabalala said to Andy. "You who are the elder. The man."

Red crept into Andy's cheeks: that a kaffir should talk to him with such contempt felt worse than an openhanded slap or a bruised windpipe. He threw his head back and tried to pin Shabalala with a cold stare.

"Watch your mouth," he croaked. "A kaffir in a suit is still a kaffir."

"I am half Zulu and half Shangaan," Shabalala answered with good humor. "And you are not even worthy to be called a man."

"Are you going to let him speak to me like that?" Andy played the white-men-against-the-natives card and got a shrug in reply.

"I'd let him break your arm if he wanted to," Emmanuel said, weary of Andrew Franklin's smallness and vanity. "Now tell me about the black man who came to visit Cassie's parents."

Andy remained sullen in the face of his own impotence. He said, "The kaffir came from the country. Cassie's mother was helping out with a land problem. I don't know the details."

"Any idea where the man came from exactly?"

"Up north."

Delia Singleton, Cassie's aunt, lived on a farm north of Pretoria. That might explain how Mr. Parkview came to have the Brewers' address in his pocket.

"So," Emmanuel clarified, "you saw nothing and you know nothing because you hid in the shed and then ran off home while two men broke into the Brewers' house and beat one of them to death. Is that the sum of it?"

"I told Cassie to wait till the men had left. I said to be careful."

"A true gentleman." Emmanuel signaled Shabalala to release Andy. They moved to the garage door and stepped out into the garden, leaving Franklin sweat-stained and cowering in the chair.

"Where to, Sergeant?" the Zulu detective asked.

"Sophiatown." He crossed the lawn with car keys rattling. "Let's find out why Aaron is lying."

They were going to burn through every lead to break the Brewer case and put Mason and his men first in line for the gallows.

—

Emmanuel, Shabalala and Zweigman gathered around a pine table covered with breakfast plates and dirty crockery. Fix wore his standard uniform—striped pajamas and a dressing gown with a silk collar.

Emmanuel had explained the gangster's unusual apparel on the path leading to the plain brick house. "He thinks that wearing pajamas in public will make him unfit to stand trial if he's ever caught and charged. Knowing Fix, he read that in a law book while actually in jail."

Penny, Fix's church-sanctioned wife, poured coffee. Half a dozen years, at most, separated her from the school playground. The pretty woman-child with a shy smile and doe eyes was too sweet for a township gangster. It was probably what Fix loved most about her.

"Go now," the gangster said to her. "Leave the men to business."

Penny slipped out of the room and shut the kitchen door. Apart from a soft "hello" when introduced, she'd said not one word or made eye contact with anyone at the table, not even Fix. It might as well have been 1835, when traditional men expected modest and obedient wives.

Emmanuel sipped the bittersweet coffee and said, "I've got two names. One of them lives here in Sophiatown."

"I will help you if I can." Fix spread a thick layer of butter and plum jam onto a slab of burned bread, a taste he'd acquired from living on the streets and cooking over an open flame. "Tell me the names. Everything you know."

"What I know isn't much." Emmanuel flicked to the page where he'd penned the key points of the prison warden's rambling monologue. "First we have an older man with white hair and broad shoulders who goes by the name of Bakwena. He drives a black sedan with a dented front fender. The second man is a Khumalo with brown hair and brown eyes and younger than Bakwena. Both of them neat and well spoken."

"Bakwena is from Sophiatown?"

"Yes."

Fix crunched down on the blackened toast and chewed slowly. Shabalala and Zweigman drank coffee and waited, hoping the flimsy descriptions would transform themselves into names and addresses for the men who'd visited Aaron in jail.

"There is one man . . ." Fix licked jam from his sticky fingers, savoring the taste. "A Bakwena who owns the Eternal Rest funeral parlor on Morris Street. He has a dented black car and white hair. He is a big noise here in the township and likes to speak against the government whenever there is a meeting or a strike."

"We'll call in and say hello." They'd knock on every door and check every name like prospectors searching for gold in a river. "Which end of Morris Street?"

"Eternal Rest is near the open land at the far end. Come, I will take you." Fix stood up and grabbed the edge of the table with a startled expression. Twenty-seven years with a stunted right leg and its shortened length still surprised him every time he got to his feet. Use the word *cripple* within earshot, though, and he'd introduce you to the sharp end of a knife, free of charge. "Bakwena will answer questions quick, quick with Fix Mapela by your side."

Bad idea. A truly terrible idea. Fix didn't ask questions, he interrogated and he intimidated until answers spilled out . . . along with blood and other fluids. Emmanuel pretended to weigh the offer before answering.

"Stay. Spend time with that pretty wife of yours. This business with Bakwena will take ten minutes, tops. You'll be bored." Fix and boredom were mutual enemies.

"Remember, I am your blood brother. Brothers stick together through thick and thin."

"Of course." Had he known at the age of six that the slice of a penknife blade across his palm would have real and actual consequences in the future, he'd have declined. Or perhaps not. Fix had made a nightmarish childhood bearable and had even stolen shoes and pens for Emmanuel's sister, Olivia, so she could concentrate on school instead of the empty money jar on the kitchen counter. Fix *had* been a brother: a wild, tearaway sibling who lived on the streets but a brother nonetheless.

"All right." Emmanuel relented. "But no knives or guns."

"You take your gun," Fix said. "I will bring a knife. A small one. Just for show. That is fair, no?"

Zweigman gave a groan and Shabalala stared at a crack in the linoleum floor with a blank expression. Emmanuel saw beneath the mask. The Zulu detective disagreed with the decision to include Fix Mapela in the investigation, feeling, perhaps, that they'd already used up a week's worth of violence and intimidation when questioning Andy Franklin earlier.

With Mason poking fingers into his private life, Emmanuel did not have the time or the inclination to explain the complex web of childhood dreams and poverty that tied him to a township gangster. Besides, Fix was right. Bakwena would answer their questions with Fix in the room.

"Let's go," he said.

"We will take my car." Fix clapped hands like a child invited to a party. "In matters of business, it is best to arrive armed and in style!"

21

PAINTED HEAVENLY BLUE, the Eternal Rest funeral parlor contained a stout brick hall and a long, woodworking shed for the construction of the simple pine boxes in which most of the township dead were buried. The smell of sawdust and the clank of hammers reached the street.

Fix led the way into the main building. His trade made him well acquainted with township funeral homes. Some gangsters got public farewells with a casket and flowers, others a shallow grave on vacant land with only the sky to say good-bye.

"In here." Fix pushed open a door to a stifling-hot office with a polished cross hanging on the back wall. A broad-shouldered black man with a scrim of white hair clinging to the back of his skull sat behind a desk, reading a newspaper. All the major newspapers in fact: English language, Afrikaans, Zulu and Xhosa.

"Mr. Mapela." The man stood up and tugged his waist-coat straight. "One of your colleagues has passed and I'm sorry for your loss."

"No, no." Fix grinned. "I bring you three live friends with questions in their mouths."

Bakwena's attention shifted from Emmanuel to Zweigman and then to Shabalala, as if mentally fitting their bodies into the right-size caskets. He appeared to give up trying to connect these three, disparate men and said, "I will be happy to answer whatever questions you have regarding the passing of a loved one. Put your minds at ease, gentlemen. Eternal Rest provides only the best service."

Fix snorted. "Who do you think they've come to bury—their sister?"

Bakwena forced a smile and indicated a row of seats in front of the desk. "Be seated, gentlemen. I will help if I can."

"Very wise," Fix Mapela said. "To refuse my friends is to refuse me."

Bakwena sat and linked his fingers together. He nod-ded, giving permission for the questioning to begin.

"What's your connection to Aaron Shabalala?" Emmanuel asked, having seen a dented black car parked outside Eternal Rest and witnessed firsthand Bakwena's overly polite manner. White men in authority generally lapped up this "good native" drivel and the prison guard was no exception. The funeral director pursed his lips to consider the question.

"The name is unfamiliar to me," he said in his deeply timbred voice. "I do not know this Aaron Shabalala."

A hard, metal click broke the silence that followed Bakwena's denial. Emmanuel glanced sideways. Fix wiped the blade of a flick knife against the leg of his pants and then proceeded to dig dirt from under his fingernails with the tip. He remained relaxed, an apex predator passing time before a kill. Zweigman blew out a small breath, stunned by the sudden, subtle escalation of tension. Shabalala studied Bakwena's face, probing for the truth.

"I'll ask you again, just to be sure," Emmanuel said. "What's your connection to Aaron Shabalala?"

Bakwena breathed deeply and looked down at his linked fingers. He said, "I am sorry, gentlemen. I don't know the Shabalala of whom you speak."

Emmanuel pulled out his notebook at roughly the same time that Fix lunged across the desk and slammed Bakwena's right hand flat to the wood surface. The motion sent newspapers scattering across the floor. Sweat broke out on the funeral director's brow. The Fix effect was instant.

"You lie to my brother, you lie to me. It is the same thing, and liars, they make me nervous." Fix held the knife at eye level and the blade danced from side to side in his agile fingers. "When I am nervous, I make mistakes."

The point of the blade sliced down between Bakwena's splayed thumb and index finger. Fix stabbed the point into the surface of the desk between the next two fingers and then the next. Metal found flesh on the last stab and blood leaked from the cut. Bakwena yelped in pain: a strange, high sound coming from a man of such solid build.

"You see?" Fix gestured to the blood. "That is the kind of mistake that happens when I am nervous."

Zweigman shuffled forward but Emmanuel raised a hand, signaling him to stop. There would be time to doctor the wound after Bakwena told the truth about knowing Aaron, and not before. Besides, Fix never left a job half done. Calling him off was nearly impossible. Emmanuel leaned across the desktop and noticed that Shabalala had not moved an inch or flinched away as a result of Mapela's attack.

"Last chance to tell me everything before my brother trims your fingers for you," he said. Fix laid the flat of the knife blade against the first and then the second knuckle of Bakwena's index finger, then flipped it so the sharp edge touched bare skin.

"I hardly know the boy." The funeral director blinked away the trickle of sweat running into his eyes. "We met only a few times."

"Go on."

"He was a new member of the Call to Action Group. I thought him too young to join, but the others said we needed new blood and fresh minds. He came to three of our planning meetings."

"What does this action group plan on doing?" The name suggested something rash.

"Fighting fire with fire," Bakwena said. "The National Party and the Dutch only respect what they fear. We have been too peace loving and it has gained us nothing. If we resist, the government will take notice of our grievances. To win this fight with the government, we must be an army. We must go to war."

"Spoken like a man who's never been in the army or gone to war," Emmanuel said. A battle plan on paper and an actual battlefield strewn with disassembled bodies were only distantly related: one remained a neat idea while the other reflected a flesh-and-blood cost. Still, he could hardly argue the point. Fix had loosened Bakwena's tongue in minutes. Violence worked.

"What exactly were your plans?" Emmanuel asked. Action took effort while talk cost nothing. The Call to Action Group might have been merely a forum for complaints.

The funeral director squirmed and clamped his lips together to seal in a confession. Fix flipped the knife into the air, caught it on the fly and stabbed the blade at Bakwena's right eye. The tip stopped inches from the dark pupil. Bakwena's eyeball reflected in the silver surface.

Emmanuel tensed but sat still. He breathed. He let the knife do its work. Neither Shabalala nor Zweigman moved.

"A train line supplying the gold pits . . . not a passenger train, you understand?" The funeral director remained glassy-eyed and unblinking. "We wanted to strike fear into the government and the rich barons who own the mines. We weren't going to harm the mothers or their children, just destroy the equipment that keeps the white man in power."

"Clean fights don't exist," Emmanuel said. "Somebody always gets hurt."

"Aaron was there when you talked of destroying trains?" Shabalala asked. The penalty for treason was life imprisonment with only annual visits from loved ones.

"He came to the planning meeting on Friday night. We studied a map and made a list of places to destroy the track."

Fix withdrew the knife and tucked away the blade. "Heavy business," he said. "Kicking the white man in the wallet. I like it."

Bakwena wiped his forehead with a handkerchief and instantly soaked the thin cotton.

"Better to kick the white man there than to kill his women and children," he said.

Shabalala leaned across the desk edge so the funeral director had no choice but to meet him eye to eye. "Why would the boy join a group such as yours? He is from a good family with a good mother and father."

"It was because of the father that he joined," Bakwena explained. "The white hospital refused to treat his father's lung sickness even though they have many machines and empty beds. The father offered money but the doctors sent him away. Now the father is dying far from home."

"A great hurt make worse . . ." Fix mused philosophical. "That is the white man's way."

"This explains Aaron's weak alibi," Emmanuel said. "Telling the truth meant putting everyone else at the planning meeting in the dock for treason. Aaron limited the danger to himself."

Would Bakwena have done the same? Emmanuel wondered.

"I understand," the Zulu detective replied. "He stayed quiet to save the others from prison."

"How committed are you to the revolution?" Emmanuel asked Bakwena.

"The revolution is my life's work." The funeral director's rich voice was perfectly suited to giving church sermons and delivering fiery speeches from the political stage. "I will not rest till every black African is given equal rights in all things. I am not alone in this. There are many, many more who feel as I do."

"Good," Emmanuel said. "You have a chance, right now, to turn your words into actions. Go to the Sophiatown Police Station and make a formal statement. Tell them that Aaron Shabalala came to your house on Friday night at around nine-thirty and stayed for an hour. That's all it needs to be. Sixty minutes. Give him an alibi."

Bakwena said, "My politics are well known to the police. I myself am very well known here in Sophiatown. The police will use this opportunity to question my friends, my family . . . everyone that I know. The Call to Action Group will be in danger."

"Tell them that Aaron came to discuss the cost of a funeral. His father is sick. It makes sense."

What would it take to move this armchair revolutionary from behind a desk? A miracle, Emmanuel suspected.

"The risk is too great, my friend," Bakwena said. "One wrong word and the Sophiatown police will call in the

Security Branch to investigate. Every chain has a weak link. The Security Branch will find that link and break it. All of us who were at the planning meeting will be condemned to life in prison. Better to sacrifice one life than five."

"So long as that life isn't yours." Andrew Franklin's cowardice and Bakwena's ruthless self-preservation were symptoms of their broken country. "Aaron didn't break during questioning, but you, the great leader, can't promise the same."

"Shabalala is strong. He will keep his silence while we work to overthrow the government. We will achieve our goal and South Africa will be free. Shabalala's sacrifice will be remembered in the history books. I gave him my word."

"For what it's worth," Emmanuel said. The funeral director had the voice of a revolutionary but lacked the necessary courage to save one of his own men from the gallows.

Fix twirled the knife, ready to end this endless talk, talk, talk. "Five minutes," he said. "I will make this man do as you please, brother."

"I don't doubt it, but we can't control him once he walks into the police station." They needed a definitive solution to Aaron's dilemma—one that didn't call Lieutenant Mason's attention back onto the Brewer case. A statement quietly lodged over the Christmas break would likely go unnoticed until well after Johan Britz, the Afrikaner lawyer, had had the time to unpick the police investigation.

"*Two* minutes," Fix begged. "Our dove will sing the right tune."

"Mr. Bakwena has no power but in words," Shabalala observed. "First he will sing for us then he will sing for whoever has him trapped in a cage. He will exchange the lives of the others to save his own. Of this I am sure."

Emmanuel rubbed the back of his neck, easing the tension there. If Lieutenant Mason or the Security Branch offered Bakwena a deal, he'd likely take it. The funeral director didn't have the strength to pull Aaron from the fire. They had to find another way.

"The girl." Zweigman spoke up for the first time. "She is the true weak link. We know that she lied. We have proof. Now we must get her to tell the truth."

Mason would, sure as summer rain, present the red Mercedes-Benz and Aaron's school badge into evidence. If Cassie withdrew the statement naming Aaron, the lieutenant had little more than a receiving-stolen-goods charge. Six months in a juvenile facility was preferable to waiting out a death sentence in the company of hard criminals. Johan Britz could whittle six months down to three if Cassie reneged on her statement.

"She's our best chance," Emmanuel agreed. Especially now that Andy had confessed to their relationship.

"Shit, man." Fix slid off Bakwena's desk with a click of his tongue. "You are too soft. You must be tougher than your enemies and more cruel, or you will never win."

"*Remember that piece of advice when next you meet Lieutenant Mason,*" the sergeant major said. "*The prize for second runner-up will be a free trip to the hospital or six feet under.*"

"I'm going to be the last man standing," Emmanuel responded to the voice in his head. Aaron's freedom and Davida and Rebekah's safety depended on it. He gave Bakwena a last fleeting glance on the way to the door. That Shabalala's son had lied to protect other people, no matter how unworthy they were of the sacrifice, was a small compensation and provided only little comfort in the circumstances.

Bakwena slumped in his chair and patted a handkerchief to his sopping brow. He straightened the material of his waistcoat and breathed deeply, slowly rebuilding the façade of a successful businessman with the courage to talk openly against the government and the police.

"We're done here," Emmanuel said, and left the office. What they'd do next was none of Bakwena's business.

"The daughter will speak?" the Zulu detective said when they'd regrouped on the cracked pavement outside the Eternal Rest funeral parlor.

"We won't give her a choice," Emmanuel said. "Clear Water Farm is three, maybe four hours north of here, depending on how the road is. We'll leave in an hour. Pack for an overnight stay, just in case."

Fix held up pale palms like a man being robbed in daylight. "Me and the bush do not mix. There is too much quiet. A man needs noise to think and make plans. I will not set foot where the corn grows."

"Then stay and keep Sophiatown in line while we're away," Emmanuel said.

Fix had once spent five days digging rocks from the fields and subsisting on a diet of thin porridge and a daily piece of bread after being illegally transferred from police custody to a dust-bucket farm named Shiloh. It took Britz, the Dutch lawyer, three days to track him from the police lockup to the slave labor farm.

Britz brought charges. The police officers involved were reprimanded and the farmer given a suspended sentence for "mistreatment." Fix returned to the township with an abiding hatred for the countryside and a true appreciation of just how little the law cared for his interests.

"Go well, my brother." Fix slapped Emmanuel's shoulder and gave the traditional farewell. "Enjoy the countryside, but remember to take your gun."

—

An ugly yellow sun blazed above the stunted trees and red anthills. Parched land stretched out to the far horizon. The girl huddled in the shade of a boulder and licked her cracked lips. Her leg ached. She'd picked out all the glass she could find in the cut, but there might be more buried where she couldn't see: she imagined tiny shards encrusted with dirt, poisoning her blood.

No: she shook off the thought. The real problem was water, or rather the lack of it. After kicking in the window, she'd run into the night and kept running. She'd moved through brush and dried grass, spiked thornbushes and stone outcrops until dawn. The grunts and growls of unseen animals prowling the dark had spurred her across the moonlit veldt.

She struggled to her feet and searched the surrounding area. She could sleep off the exhaustion of the long night, but her dry mouth and raw throat needed water to heal. Three gentle hills broke the flat horizon. The distance to the hills was impossible to gauge, but they called to her with the possibility of rock pools to swim in and groves of shade trees to sleep under. She'd be safe from the big man there. A day or two to rest and she'd move on to search for the road that led back to the city.

22

EMMANUEL ANGLED THE sun visor to block the harsh light that hit the windscreen. Thirsty land, flat and brown, flashed past the car windows. Spiked thorn trees, gnarled wild pears and yellow grass cried out for a ground-soaking thunderstorm.

"The rains are late," Shabalala said of the dusty fields and the gaunt cattle huddling in the gray shade of the acacia trees. "If they do not come soon, there will be hard times."

Emmanuel imagined the hard times had already begun for those without a permanent source of water on their property. A dry summer meant a lean and hungry winter.

"Five more miles to the turnoff." Zweigman checked the odometer and peered through the heat waves that shimmered on the horizon. The blank sky and harsh terrain were alien to his European eye, yet he found a strange and powerful beauty in the blooming prickly-pear trees and the blue, distant hills. One wrong turn, though, and you'd die of dehydration or loneliness.

"There . . ." The doctor pointed to a weathered signpost with an arrow that indicated a bumpy dirt road. Three properties shared the sign: WELKOM, LION'S KILL, and last on the list, CLEAR WATER FARM.

"I hope that name isn't wishful thinking." Emmanuel turned onto the rough track. "We have no water on us. Or food."

They had stopped to eat at a roadside cafe with a solitary "nonwhites" table covered in a fine red dust. One mouthful of the "special beef stew" and they'd agreed, the three of them, that eating dirt might be a tastier option. They'd arrive at Delia Singleton's house thirsty, hungry and with a long list of questions for her niece. The harried farmwife would be well within her rights to turn them off the property before sundown; what were three grown men but just more mouths to feed in what looked like a time of deprivation?

The road bisected the veldt, brightened at intervals by flashes of green foliage and red aloe flowers. Five miles in from the main turnoff came a faded sign for Welkom, the first of the three properties to share the access road. At seventeen miles, another sign, painted in bright red, pointed to the second property.

"Lion's Kill," Zweigman mused aloud. "That is a strange name for a farm."

"I think it is a hunting reserve," Shabalala said. "Rich men pay much money to hunt lions and buck."

"The returns are better than planting corn, that's for certain." Emmanuel shifted to low gear to better navigate the washboard gullies and potholes. The road had not been graded or patched up in a long while. A wire fence marked the beginning of a new property boundary line. An elegant wrought-iron sign pointed the way to Clear Water. A sprawling white farmhouse appeared two miles off the turn, the high silver roof peaked against the sky. The distance from the homestead, and the scope of the landscape around it, created the impression of a prosperous European estate growing out of the African bush.

Reality hit at the mouth of the gravel driveway. Tall weeds grew in the dusty garden at the front of the house and strips of rust ate away at the iron roof. Rows of withered corn rustled in a field to the east and the baked lawn spread out like a brown rug.

Whoop . . . whoop . . . whoop . . . The sound came from a stand of mature mango trees planted on the right side of the drive. Emmanuel checked the branches. Four dirty white children hung from tree limbs and howled as the car drove by. A scraggy, red-haired teenager sat barefoot and shirtless on the front stairs and whittled away at the end of a stick with a penknife. Emmanuel parked the car.

"Huh . . ." Shabalala made a sound that encapsulated their joint surprise. This vision of white ruin populated by feral white children was the last thing any of them had expected when they'd turned off the tarred road at the signpost to Rust de Winter.

The boy on the stairs stood up with the sharpened stick and the penknife held in opposing hands. He pushed thick-rimmed glasses up the bridge of his nose and squinted at the multicolored passengers in the car through smudged lenses. "Who are you?" he asked in a polished English accent, which sounded odd coming from the mouth of an unwashed urchin.

"I'm Detective Sergeant Cooper, this is Detective Constable Shabalala and that man is Dr. Zweigman." Emmanuel made the introductions when they'd alighted from the car and stood facing the boy. "You are?"

"I'm Jason Singleton." He closed the penknife and slipped it into his pants pocket before offering a handshake to each adult, including Shabalala. "Pleased to meet you."

The children in the orchard dropped from the branches like ripe fruit and tumbled onto the driveway. All four youngsters had wild hair and crusted red eyes, which they rubbed with grubby fists.

"Conjunctivitis." Zweigman made the diagnosis in a low voice. "Highly contagious but easily treated."

Jason Singleton pointed to each child in turn. "The little one is Jodea but we call her Jodie, then there's the twins, Aries and Hector. The last one is Bramwell. Our other sister, Julie, is out someplace I don't know."

The Singleton clan shared Cassie's hair color and freckled skin, but their small, tight mouths fit just right into their pinched faces. Jason remained on the bottom stair while his younger siblings circled the visitors and examined their clean fingernails, pressed suits and lace-up shoes.

"You're from the city," Jodie, the youngest child, said with an equally posh accent. "People from the city are cry-babies like Cassie."

"These men are police." Jason corrected the girl. "They're like soldiers. They don't cry. Ever."

"Where are Cassie and your mother?" Emmanuel asked. The children were content to mill around, dirty and barefoot and without adult supervision.

"My mother is baking in the kitchen," Jason said. "Would you like to speak to her?"

"If we could."

A small hand belonging to either Aries or Hector, Emmanuel couldn't tell which, reached out to touch the butt of the Webley revolver holstered to his waist. He brushed aside the crusty fingers and took the stairs. Jason opened the door to a wide corridor furnished with antique chairs and discarded shoes. A pile of unopened mail covered the surface of a side table with ornately carved legs.

"Where's your father?" Emmanuel thought to ask. Delia hadn't mentioned a husband during her brief rescue trip to Johannesburg, and the farm, like the Brewers' garden, had gone back to its natural state.

"My father is dead," Jason said on the way through to the rear of the house. "He passed away during the first term of school."

"What happened?" Emmanuel thought about how a man might die out here: some sort of farming accident, probably—crushed by a tractor, kicked in the head by livestock or cut by the blades of a thresher.

"A hunting accident. He went on a shooting weekend at Lion's Kill next door and his gun misfired while he was cleaning it. Ma runs the farm now."

Or tries to. The dead lawn and emaciated crops suggested that Delia had lost control of Clear Water. Emmanuel knew well the day-to-day demands of tending to the land. He didn't wish a life of crop failure, flood and drought on anyone who didn't wish it on himself—or herself, in Delia's case.

"I'm sorry to hear about your father," Emmanuel said, and followed Jason into the kitchen at the back of the homestead. Large windows gave uninterrupted views of a shady porch and an in-ground swimming pool filled with green-slimed water. Delia and an elderly maid wearing a brown housecoat and a tatty wig punched down mounds of dough at an oak table. Another maid, also in domestic uniform, poured white sugar into a pot of boiling water to make syrup for the jars of pink guavas lined up on the bench top.

Delia looked up from kneading the pastry. "What is it, boy?"

"Police," Jason said. "And a doctor."

"Mrs. Singleton." Emmanuel stepped into the room and into Delia's direct line of sight. She looked as if she had a million things on her mind and the energy to deal with only one of them at a time. Shabalala and Zweigman remained inside the doorway.

"Oh, it's you, Detective Cooper," Delia said, and pressed the dough across the floured surface. "The hospital told me that the police commissioner wants an autopsy report on Ian and that his body will be ready for pickup in a couple of days. I'm just making sure there's enough food for when Cassie and I go down to arrange the funeral."

"It will take more than a few days for the autopsy report," Emmanuel said. Add Christmas holidays to the usual list of holdups and Ian Brewer's body might be held over until well into the New Year. "Don't rush on account of the medical examiner's office. They'll give you plenty of notice about when it's time to pick up the body."

"Oh." Delia's shoulders softened, but her hands never ceased working. "Is that what you've come for? To tell me about the autopsy?"

"No, we were hoping to talk to Cassie if she's around."

"Where's your cousin?" Delia asked Jason, who shrugged his freckled shoulders and broke off a pinch of dough to eat.

"Probably down at the river," he said. "That's where she goes to have a blubber most days."

"There's a running river?" Emmanuel asked. Clear Water Farm actually had clear water and still looked like it was in the middle of a drought.

"The irrigation pump broke three weeks ago." Delia tucked a strand of red hair behind her ear and shaped the dough into small buns. "I've been meaning to get it fixed, but with the children on school holidays, the trip to Jo'burg and the funeral . . ."

The maids tutted and shook their heads at the madam's endless worries. Bad luck had flown into the farmhouse roof, built a nest and refused to leave.

"The river is down there." Jason pointed to a dip in the land visible through the kitchen windows. "I can show you if you like, Detective."

"If that's where you think Cassie might be," Emmanuel said. He'd spent years soldiering through a myriad of human tragedies and then moving on to the ultimate goal: Allied victory. Swooping into Delia Singleton's clearly unraveling life and then leaving almost immediately brought back uncomfortable memories.

"*Jesus Christ . . .*" the sergeant major seethed. "*Stop wasting time with feelings, Cooper. Get a fresh statement from Cassie and then get the fuck out! You copy?*"

"*I do.*"

Delia said, "I need to give the little ones a bath and then start making the soup. Find Julie to get her to help you bring up water from the river."

Jason took a bucket from the younger maid and said, "Julie's out in the bush with her kaffir pals. It will take me the whole afternoon to carry enough water for a bath. The others won't help. They run off whenever there's work to be done."

"You're the man of the house now." Delia opened the oven and peered inside with a distracted air. "The others are still children. You have to lead them. Teach them the right way to do things."

Small chance of that, Emmanuel thought. The younger Singleton children were happy hanging from tree branches and playing in the fields. They'd never give up their freedom for farm work. Shabalala stepped closer to the table and caught the older maid's attention. She narrowed her dark eyes and regarded the tall Zulu and his white companions with suspicion. Shabalala smiled and gestured to the bucket in Jason's hand, then held up three fingers to make a silent request for three more. To make a verbal request of a white woman's servant would be inappropriate.

The maid ducked under the table and produced two more wooden pails with rope handles. She handed them to Shabalala with an expression that said, *I'm not impressed with your suit or your white friends, but thanks for helping with the water.*

"Come," Jason said, and skirted the table on the way to the back door. Once outside, they followed a trampled grass path that ran along the edge of the slimy swimming pool. Farther along, they passed three elderly black men crouched in the shade of a yellowwood tree. A young woman in traditional dress breast-fed an infant a few yards to their right. The small gathering looked to the back door of the farmhouse with stoic expressions.

"My father used to meet people under this tree to discuss their problems," Jason said. "People from the farm and the native location still come here, even though my mother stays in the house and won't talk to them. They still wait for her. "

The men called out greetings and the young mother dipped her head to acknowledge the passing of three European males and a tall native who must also be shown deference. Emmanuel suspected that the patience shown by the group would be wasted. Delia was barely hanging on. She had no time for them or their complaints.

They meandered through a cornfield and down to the banks of a clear river embedded with white, marbled boulders. Flowering bulrushes grew thick and wild by the water's edge. Downstream, a muscular black woman scrubbed laundry on a rock while three naked children splashed in the shallows. No sign of Cassie, though.

"She's normally right there." Jason pointed to a smooth rock ledge jutting out into the water: the perfect spot to dangle your toes in the flow. "That's her favorite place to sit. She cries a lot."

"She has just lost her father. Perhaps she has good reason for tears," Zweigman suggested.

"No, that's not the reason." Jason dipped his bucket into the river and filled it to the brim. "She cried from the first day she got here."

"Any idea where she could have gone?" Emmanuel asked. Flat country spread out under blue sky. The Singleton farm likely stretched for miles with the horizon shifting ever farther away with each step into the inhospitable veldt.

"She'll be back before long," Jason said, and wrestled the heavy bucket onto his shoulder like a native porter carting goods from a supply train. "She hates the country, so she can't have gone too far."

In what direction? A sensible city-bred teenager would stay close to shelter and a source of water. Emmanuel shaded his eyes and searched through the heat haze on the plains. He did not feel especially confident about Cassie's levelheadedness.

Shabalala set the buckets down and walked across the sand to the flat rock. He crouched, scanned the riverbank and said, "A girl wearing sandals left from this place many hours ago."

"When did you see Cassie last?" Emmanuel asked her cousin, who swayed with the effort of keeping the overflowing water bucket balanced on his shoulder.

"Breakfast," Jason said. "She ate half her porridge and left in a hurry."

"Go and find her," Zweigman urged. A city girl wandering the bush alone for hours rang a warning for all three of them. "I will use the time to rinse the infection from the children's eyes. Milk and honey will clear it up."

The doctor picked up the empty buckets and stooped by the water's edge, his energies shifting to the inhabitants of Clear Water homestead in need of his care.

"One hour," Emmanuel agreed; he and Shabalala would track Cassie across the veldt and Zweigman would tend the children. "If she stayed close to water, we might be away longer than that."

He nodded the go-ahead to Shabalala, who tilted his hat in farewell and walked along the riverbank with quick strides. He crouched again by the rock and examined the sand and twigs nearby. Zweigman and Jason retraced the grass path to the homestead, their steps slowed to compensate for the weight of their buckets.

"The boy is right. His cousin came here many times to sit at this place. This morning she stayed and then moved in that direction." The Zulu detective pointed along the crooked spine of the river to a point beyond where the washerwoman lathered soap onto a scrubbing brush.

"At least she's got sense enough to stick close to water," Emmanuel said, and fell into step with Shabalala. Silver light reflected off the farmhouse roof. If Cassie were lost, that wink of civilization could act as a beacon, drawing her homeward.

"Have you seen the young white missus?" Emmanuel stopped to ask the washerwoman who scrubbed away at worn cotton sheets. A hint as to Cassie's state of mind would be helpful. The woman looked up, glad for the break.

"The sad one was here when I came with my first load, ma' baas. I greeted her but she turned her face away from me. When the children came to play in the water, she got up and ran away—quick, quick, past the bulrushes and then on till I could not see her anymore."

"My thanks." Emmanuel caught up with Shabalala on a bend in the river. Cassie had taken off long before they'd arrived at Clear Water with their questions. What reason did she have for running?

"The girl moved fast and then rested here against the tree trunk." The Zulu detective indicated a hollow in the sand and tracked the soft scoops left in the riverbank by Cassie's sandals. A few minutes later they came to another dip in the sand where the teenager had again sat down to rest.

"She runs and stops. Runs and stops, yet there is nothing chasing her," Shabalala said when they'd tracked her long enough to establish a pattern. On the opposite bank a tall boy drove a herd of cattle down to the river. The sun blazed hot. Shabalala and Emmanuel removed their ties and jackets, rolled up their sleeves and wet their heads and faces with handfuls of cool water. They moved on.

Ten minutes later they came to a trampled patch of grass stained with drops of dried brown liquid. Shabalala rubbed the substance between thumb and forefinger to confirm what they both already knew.

"Blood. Only a small amount and just dry . . ."

Emmanuel stepped back to get a clearer view of the area. A hard object crunched underfoot. He knelt down and lifted a black-handled steak knife from the grass. Rust-brown liquid stained the serrated blade. White noise roared in his ears. Cassie held the key to open Aaron's jail cell. Unless she retracted her statement, Lieutenant Mason's tainted evidence would make it to trial. Her life was precious, yet she'd decided to throw it away. He turned a quick circle, searching for a body, and realized that the roaring sound in his head had an external source.

"A waterfall," Shabalala said, and loped off. Emmanuel matched his pace. They rounded a sharp bend. Five feet ahead the land dropped away and the river plunged over the edge of a steep cliff. Cassie stood on the lip of the precipice with her arms pressed close to her sides.

"No . . ." The word came out short and strangled from Shabalala's throat.

"Wait!" Emmanuel shouted over the crash of falling water. He sprinted to close the gap with the lonely figure balanced on the edge of the cliff.

Cassie jumped.

23

EMMANUEL HIT THE WATER. His left shoulder bounced against a submerged boulder and pain tore through his body, sharp and dull at the same time. The force of the cascading river pushed him down to the bottom of the deep pool at the base of the falls. Bubbles escaped from his mouth as the impact pushed all the air out of his body. His left arm hung useless by his side. The world spun in a dark swirl of leaves, sand and silt. He kicked hard toward the surface. The sheer weight of the falling water held him down. He tried again, right arm extended to its maximum length to search for a fingerhold above the surface. A hand gripped his wrist and pulled him up to the light. Shabalala, soaked to the skin and hatless, treaded water just outside the impact zone.

"Cassie?" Emmanuel shouted over the roar of the water, and tasted mud and algae in his mouth. He and Shabalala had jumped over the edge together, falling like leaf litter into the pool.

"I will find her." The Zulu detective dived down through the white spray and disappeared into the churning falls. Emmanuel clung to a craggy rock ledge, his teeth gritted against the pain of bruised muscles and a dislocated shoulder. The last he'd seen of Cassie Brewer was a bright flash of her red hair and a white hand sinking out of view.

"Don't black out just yet, soldier. If anyone can get the girl out, it's the Zulu," the Scottish sergeant major said. *"He'll find her."*

"Dead or alive?"

"That's out of our hands. All we can do is pray . . . even though you and I know there's no one listening."

A long minute later Shabalala broke the surface of the water and scissor-kicked out of the foaming spray. Pale limbs thrashed in his wake as he dragged Cassie Brewer to the side of the pool and propped her body against the rocky edge. She spat up brown sludge and moaned low in the back of her throat.

Emmanuel moved around the edge of the pool, clinging to the bank with his right hand. Shabalala sucked in great mouthfuls of air and held Cassie afloat despite the effort he'd expended dragging her up from the bottom.

"Climb out," Emmanuel said. "I'll keep her above the surface."

Shabalala brought himself out of the water in one

graceful push, then crouched in the sand. He took two deep breaths and exhaled slowly, focusing on dragging the white girl's deadweight over the edge of the pool and onto the riverbank.

"I'll push. You lift." Emmanuel braced against the rocky bottom and wedged his good shoulder under Cassie's body. She coughed up a twig and her eyes flew open, wide and panicked. "Now."

"*Woza* . . ." Shabalala breathed the Zulu exhortation, which meant "go, get up, move." Workmen all over the country used the word to give them extra power when their energy had drained. The Zulu reached down and fit his hands under Cassie's armpits and then applied the full measure of his strength to pull her from the pool. Emmanuel pressed upward, ignoring the pain that stabbed across his shoulders and into his neck. Cassie's body lifted and then sloshed over the rock edge like a fish on a hook. Emmanuel heard retching and hiccups. Shabalala appeared again at the pool's perimeter.

"Give me your hands, Sergeant. I will pull you out."

"Can't," he said. "Hit a rock on the way in. Dislocated my shoulder."

"I see . . ." Shabalala peered into the water and pointed to a boulder wedged hard into the rock wall. "Come over here. Climb on. I will lift you onto the bank."

He stepped onto the curved rock and grabbed a tuft of straggly grass to keep his balance. Shabalala took hold of his good arm and pulled back slowly. The muscles of both Emmanuel's right and left shoulders ached and flexed. He pushed up hard through the water and Shabalala dragged him over the lip of the rock and onto the coarse sand. Cassie Brewer lay a few feet away, curled into a tight ball and shaking in shock.

Emmanuel flipped onto his back, jaw clenched tight. "You'll have to push my shoulder back into its socket," he told Shabalala. "I'll tell you how, but it might take a couple of tries."

He had limited experience in readjusting dislocated shoulders, having done it only once before and under the instruction of an injured field medic who'd tripped over an empty ammo box and refused to wait for trained help to arrive.

"One of you'll have to fix my shoulder," the medic had said to the squad. "I'll guide you through."

Emmanuel volunteered. Medics saved lives. They brought morphine to the injured and carried the shot, the burned and the shell-shocked to safety. One medic down translated to multiple losses on the battlefield. He'd snapped the shoulder back into place under a barrage of enemy fire. Now, lying on a peaceful African riverbank, he hoped he remembered the right steps in the right order.

"Bend my shoulder at a ninety-degree angle and rotate my arm to my chest. Good. That's it . . ." He stopped and thought through the next stage, drops of sweat and river water forming on his brow. "All right. Now move the arm outward and try to coax the bone back into the socket."

Shabalala followed the final instructions and deftly eased the dislocated bone back into its socket. Relief came instantly, though the bruised muscle would take days to heal.

"Thanks. You got it first time." Emmanuel slowly rotated his shoulder, testing the movement of the joint. The bone stayed in place. He got up and walked over to where Cassie lay curled up on the sand. She had red scratches on her wrists and forearms from where she had tried to cut herself with the steak knife.

"Cassie . . ." Emmanuel crouched in the sand with Shabalala at his back. He pushed away the knowledge that pursuing this child over the precipice could have cost Shabalala and him their lives. But for a few lucky inches, the submerged boulder could have easily broken a skull or snapped a spine. "Come. Sit up."

Cassie burrowed deeper into the sandy bank with her eyes squeezed shut. Goose bumps appeared on her skin and wet strands of hair lay plastered against the side of her face. He placed a hand on her shoulder and felt the soft, shivering flesh.

"You need to get warm," he said. "Let's get you into the sun."

Cassie remained limp and unmoving. Shabalala stepped closer and said, "Over there on that patch of grass, Sergeant?"

"Yeah." Emmanuel moved aside. The Zulu detective scooped Cassie up and carried her into a warm spot just outside the spray of the waterfall. The river flowed on—a slender, yet powerful, vein of silver that cut through the dry land. The two detectives crouched either side of Cassie and raised their faces to the heat like sunworshippers in an outdoor temple. They'd be close to dry in a few minutes and ready to walk back to the farmhouse. Emmanuel waited for Cassie's ragged breathing to ease. Her eyes flickered open, but she remained flat on the ground and expressionless.

"Our friend Dr. Zweigman is waiting at the house," he said. "He'll take care of any cuts and bruises from the jump and he'll make sure that you're all right. Can you walk?"

"I don't want to," Cassie said.

"You don't want to walk or you don't want to go back to the farm?"

"Both."

Shabalala sank down onto his haunches, preparing for a long wait. He didn't mind the time it took to get the unhappy white girl up and moving. She was alive, and through her, Aaron stayed alive also.

"Fuck this . . ." the sergeant major seethed. *"Get your Zulu to carry the crazy bitch back to the house or drag her by the hair if necessary. It's well past the time to play nice, Cooper."*

"Flogging a sick horse never makes it go faster," Emmanuel replied. *"Same goes for teenage girls."*

"This is what Mason meant when he said, 'You're good with women.' You don't mind the time it takes to get them warmed up and talking. I'd sooner have a wound sewn up with a blunt needle."

The source of Mason's observation about women still remained unclear. Emmanuel's hat had blown off during the jump and the sun beat down so that the hard light seemed to shine directly onto the back of his retinas.

"We have to go back to the homestead if we want food and shelter for the night," Emmanuel said. "You don't have to walk. Detective Constable Shabalala is strong enough to carry you most of the way . . . if you'd like."

Cassie lifted her head off the sand and looked outside her anguished self for the first time since jumping over the edge. Shabalala nodded encouragement and held out his hands to help her to her feet. She sat up slowly, all the while studying the tall black man intently.

"He looks just like you," she said.

"I am Aaron's father," Shabalala replied. "I am sorry to hear the news of your own father's passing. He was loved, I am sure."

Cassie dug her fingers into the riverbank and gathered the sand into fists. "It's my fault that he died," she said. "I lied about the St. Bart's boys and God punished me. He took my father away . . ."

Emmanuel said, "The European men who broke into your parents' house are to blame for what happened. You weren't even there. You were in the little hut with Andrew Franklin when they came to the house."

"How do you know that?" She tilted her head back and blinked hard.

"We spoke with Mr. Franklin this morning." Emmanuel left it at that. He had yet to gauge the high-water mark of Cassie's feelings for her neighbor. Love with a capital *L* would make getting a true statement difficult. Conflicting emotions flashed across the teenager's face: joy, apprehension and then a desperate flicker of hope.

"Will Andrew come for me?" she asked.

"No," Emmanuel said. "I don't believe he will."

"He promised that we'd be together." Cassie sucked in a breath, accepting the truth of the detective's statement. "I lied about being in the house to help him. He said we'd be together soon. Now my father is dead."

"Here." Emmanuel squeezed water from his handkerchief and gave it to Cassie, who wiped away tears. She pushed back strands of damp hair and blotted drops of river spray from her arms.

"I don't care about politics or native education," she said. "That's all my father used to talk about: bus passes and passbooks and fighting segregation. He's up in heaven now and he's telling my grandfather that I'm a liar. His spirit will hate me for eternity. I know it."

Such were the dark thoughts that had pursued her along the riverbank and then pushed her over the edge of the waterfall. Shabalala leaned closer and rested his elbows on his kneecaps, graceful and easy in his six-foot-plus frame.

"The dead have no cause for hate," he said to the grief-stricken girl. "Your father's spirit wishes for your suffering to end. He cares only for your happiness."

Cassie rested her cheek on her forearm and focused on the Zulu detective, who crouched at arm's length. Andrew Franklin had never regarded her with loving-kindness and neither had Aaron. One person alone called her freckles "sun kisses" and insisted that her too-wide mouth was beautiful. Now it felt that this strange but familiar black man was looking at her through her father's eyes.

"My dad was good, like you," Cassie said to the Zulu detective. "He'd want me to tell the truth, wouldn't he?"

"Your heart already knows the answer to that question," Shabalala said.

—

The girl sank to the ground and clutched her knees to her body. Disappointment sapped the last of her energy. The blue-green mountains, so cool and inviting on the horizon, offered no refuge from the heat now that she was here. There was no sign of water. Reality dawned on her. She would die in this barren land, watched over by a cloudless sky.

If thirst didn't take her, then the cut in her leg certainly would, only more slowly. This morning's ache had progressed to a sharp, stabbing pain in the flesh. It hurt to move. It hurt to swallow. It hurt to look across the land. She'd exchanged a dungeon for an open-air prison with no water or food. Just my luck, she thought.

She lay down on the ground. Small brown birds sang from the thorn trees, and high above, an eagle soared on outstretched wings. A tiny flower sprouted from the earth at her eye level, its bright petals short and spiked. A thought nudged into her head. There was beauty in this harsh place: small and hidden, but it was there. Better to die in the fresh air than in a dark alley crushed between brick walls.

"Hey . . ." *A finger jabbed her ribs. "Hey, you."*

She stirred and blinked into the light. A freckled white girl with ginger hair plaited into two messy braids crouched in the dirt with her head tilted sideways like a curious bird. Two black children, a boy and a girl dressed in a mishmash of traditional skins and castoff European clothing, watched from a safe distance. All three carried slingshots made of rubber bands and Y-shaped sticks. The boy asked a question in a native tongue and the white girl shrugged.

"She's alive, but I don't know her name."

Another question, this time from the black girl, who scanned the hills and the arid plains with a nervous glance. The freckled girl answered in the native language and then said in English, "I'm Julie. You're from the Lion's Kill farmhouse. I saw you in the little room."

Of course, of course, the girl's sluggish brain made the connection. She remembered now. This red-haired child had run across the dirt yard in front of the basement cell with a hessian sack slung across her back.

"Water . . . please . . ." The words come out in croaks. "Help me."

The boy spoke in a harsh voice and rubbed his palms together in a gesture that said, Wash your hands of this problem quickly. *The black girl nodded agreement and they spun on their heels and took off at a run across the hard land.*

"Don't." The girl reached out, tried to grab Julie's hand. "Stay. Please."

"Can't." Julie dipped into the pocket of her grubby cot-

*ton dress and pulled out three speckled bird's eggs, the size
of walnuts. She cracked the eggs together to break the
shells.*

"Quick," she said. "Open wide."

*The girl worked her jaw apart and felt silky egg whites
and the taste of yolk coating her tongue and then running
wet into her throat. She swallowed and opened her mouth
for more.*

*"All gone. I'll try to bring some more later." Julie stood
up and looked in the direction that her playmates had run.
She threw aside the crushed shells, wiped her sticky fingers
on the front of her dress and took off at a sprint, her braids
swinging from side to side in rhythm with her steps. The
girl struggled to a sitting position in time to see Julie's di-
minishing figure winding through the anthills.*

"Alice," the girl said. "My name is Alice."

*A warthog trotted through the thorn trees and stopped
to dig up a tuber with its curved tusks. It continued snuf-
fling for food then raised its ugly head at the sound of a car
engine shifting gears. Alice rose to her feet and shaded her
eyes. A red line cut through the veldt—a road.*

*No sign of the car yet, but its destination had to be the
farm at the end of the road. She squinted into the light and
recognized the stunted orchard and the gravel yard of the
house where she'd been held captive. A rusted windmill
turned lazy circles in the air, the lonesome creak of its blades
terrifyingly familiar. A whole night and a day of running
for the three hills had gained her a scant few miles from the
concrete cell.*

The warthog grunted and took off with its tufted tail raised like a flag. A blue car appeared on the road and traveled at top speed in the direction of the farmhouse. The driver knew the way, it seemed to Alice, or had experience navigating rutted dirt tracks in third gear. Under different circumstances, she might have run across the ground to beg for help from the driver, but her injured leg and her intuition kept her still.

The last visitors to the house had smashed beer bottles against the walls and fired guns. She doubted the big man knew good people, the sort who'd pick up a battered girl and race to the nearest hospital without questions. Having escaped the cell once, she dared not risk being delivered back into the big man's hands like a piece of lost luggage.

Alice crouched down and gripped her knees tight. Pain throbbed deep in the cut on her leg. She barely noticed. There'd be no more eggs or water or help, no matter what the girl Julie said. Her earlier premonition would come true. This ground would be her grave.

24

EMMANUEL AND SHABALALA stood on the rear porch of the Clear Water homestead and drank rooibos, red bush tea, from mismatched cups. The elderly maid had made a big show of offering the fine china cup to Emmanuel and then a chipped tin mug to the citified Zulu with no business wearing a suit. The detectives drank in silence and paid the offended servant no mind.

"You did well," Emmanuel said of the written statement from Cassie Brewer exonerating Aaron and identifying two European males, one big and the other small, as the prime suspects in the robbery and deadly assault on her parents. "We'll give the new statement to the lawyer, Britz, first thing. He'll make short work of the police case. The pressure will be on Mason to explain the school badge found in the stolen car."

They were ahead of the game for once, the end of the line now in sight.

"My thanks, Sergeant." Shabalala touched the folded paper in his jacket pocket again. Each word written by the school principal's daughter carried a magic charge. "I am in your debt."

"Let's call it even," Emmanuel said, remembering the time fifteen months ago when Shabalala had spirited his broken body away from a beating at the hands of Piet Lapping of the Security Branch.

"Gentlemen." Zweigman carried a tray of freshly baked buns out of the farmhouse and joined them on the porch. They ate quickly, inhaling the warm bread slathered in butter and honey.

"How is she?" Emmanuel asked when the last bun had been eaten and the crumbs thrown under a bush for the birds. The doctor had taken Cassie into his care the moment they'd arrived back, sun-kissed and badly scraped, from the waterfall.

"Exhausted," Zweigman said. "I expect she will sleep through till dawn."

Emmanuel hoped to be gone from Clear Water long before that. He said, "We have enough time to make the drive to Jo'burg before nightfall. Have the children been treated?"

"The boy Hector has so far eluded capture. His siblings are hunting him down as we speak. Give me one more hour, Detective, and I will be ready to leave."

"We'll wait," he said. If they left immediately, Zweigman would spend the long drive back to the city worrying about Hector's red rabbit eyes while calculating the likelihood that the treated children would become reinfected. He took his duty of care seriously.

Jodea, the smallest of the Singleton children, flew around the corner of the house with a freshly scrubbed face. She waved to Zweigman.

"Come quick, Doctor. We have Hector under the mulberry tree. Jason says to bring the medicine."

The German hurried after the girl, determined to rid the farm of conjunctivitis. Emmanuel could not imagine Zweigman lying in the sun and sipping a fruit cocktail in Mozambique. He'd find patients no matter where he was; even on Elliott King's island resort, he'd discover a waitress with an infected toenail or a gardener fighting the flu.

Shabalala threw the dregs of his rooibos into the garden and took the empty tray back to the kitchen. Afternoon light lent the arid plains and the outline of the three distant mountain peaks a stark beauty. The number of natives gathered under the yellowwood tree to seek an audience with Delia had swelled to six since setting off to look for. Cassie. Emmanuel recognized the old men and the young mother, who now held her sleeping baby wrapped in a cotton shawl.

"So much to be done," Shabalala said when he returned. The neglected crops and deserted cattle yards cried out for attention.

"I'm not touching that pool," Emmanuel replied. The dirt-poor farm boy inside Emmanuel who'd dug up tree roots and hunted rabbits with a slingshot thought the pool a useless indulgence built so close to a river.

"The generator," Shabalala suggested.

Emmanuel picked up his hat, which he'd found covered in dirt a few yards from the waterfall, and pinched a fresh crease into the crown. He couldn't imagine Shabalala lying around doing nothing either. Sometimes it seemed that the Zulu detective and the German doctor's practical goodness kept him grounded in the world.

"Lead on, baas," he said, and took off his jacket.

Shabalala smiled.

—

Fixing the generator's clogged fuel line took ten minutes and left the pungent taste of diesel in Emmanuel's mouth. Shabalala plucked grass from the edge of the path and handed Emmanuel a few stalks.

"Chew on the white end," he said. "It will cut the taste."

They walked and chewed, having both taken turns unclogging the fuel line. The woman they'd seen earlier stood on the edge of the path jiggling her baby from side to side on her hip.

"How long has she been there?" Emmanuel asked. The woman must have followed them from her spot under the yellowwood tree and awaited their return in the afternoon heat. Her mute patience was yet another reminder of the years he'd lived on his stepfather's farm and waited for rain, for sun, for seeds to sprout, and waited, especially, to get the hell out of there and back to Sophiatown.

"*Umjani, mama.*" Shabalala slowed down and acknowledged mother and child with a nod. The woman smiled and ducked her head but remained quiet. Emmanuel took the lead.

"The madam cannot talk with you today," he said. Better to hear it now than realize that fact after dark.

"I see that the madam's door is closed. It is you that I wish to talk to, ma' baas," she said in a quiet voice.

"How can I help?"

"The matter concerns my husband. He is missing now for two days." She rocked side to side to calm the infant. The baby arched its back, kicked out its legs and let out an extended howl. Birds flew from a nearby tree and escaped across the fields at the sound.

"Shhh . . . Shhh . . ." The woman rocked faster, desperate to shush the noise. The white man and the black man who dressed like a white man would not stay and listen to the story of her vanished husband if the child continued wailing. Shabalala held out both hands, asking for permission to take the baby.

"Give the child to me," he said when the woman hesitated, unsure that she'd read the gesture correctly. "I promise I will not drop the little one."

She relented and Shabalala cradled the infant in his arms with an ease that spoke of long experience. He swung back and forth in a steady rhythm. The child's sobs quieted to intermittent hiccups.

Emmanuel said, "Tell me about your husband."

He feared that now, as always, a missing person report would prove nothing more than an effective time waster.

"He went to Johannesburg on the express bus and has not come back. He is gone now for three nights."

"He left to find work?" If that were the case, then the husband might already be lost to this pretty woman and her child. The flow of the city absorbed country migrants into the urban stream and cast them adrift from their home places.

"No, ma' baas. He did not go to seek work. He is a teacher at the farm school." This she said with a shy pride before adding, "And he is a deacon at the church."

"Why did he go to Johannesburg?" Religion and education were unreliable defenses against the temptations of Jo'burg and Sophiatown.

"He went to speak with the madam's sister and her husband, who is also a schoolteacher."

Shabalala stopped swaying and sent Emmanuel a look that said, *Could it be?*

"Describe your husband to me."

"He is a good man, ma' baas. Softly spoken and—"

"What does he look like," Emmanuel interrupted, impatient to have his suspicions confirmed.

"Tall," the woman said. "Taller than you but not so high as that man with you."

"His ears?"

The woman frowned, not fully understanding the question. Ears were ears unless they were missing altogether.

"Are they cut like this?" Emmanuel traced a slit onto his lobes with a fingernail to illustrate the point.

"*Yebo*. They are cut just as you show. The sister of the madam said he must remove the clay plugs so he did not stand out in the city, where few men keep the custom."

"Mr. Parkview," Shabalala said with certainty, and continued to rock the fretting child from side to side. "What is your husband's name, mama?"

"Abraham Zolta," the woman said. "That is what he is called."

"What business took Abraham to Johannesburg?" Emmanuel asked. Four hours of driving on gravel and dirt roads in a private car translated to six hours or more of rough travel in a dilapidated bus with the misleading name "Fast Boy" or perhaps "Quick Time."

"He went about the river and the land and to see where the government has drawn its lines."

"What lines, mama?" Shabalala inquired.

The woman blushed and pushed bare toes into the sand. Abraham usually answered questions about white people's business.

"The lines that are drawn on paper," she said. "The sister of the madam knows where these papers are kept."

"Martha Brewer worked for the Office of Land Management," Emmanuel told Shabalala. The new segregation laws created a great deal of work in redrawing town and city boundaries that would formally split the entire country into physically separate "white" and "nonwhite" living areas. Whole suburbs were being reassigned with the stroke of the pen. Wrongly colored residents were given eviction notices.

"Did the government draw new lines for the native location?" Jason Singleton said that the people gathered under the yellowwood tree had come from the farm and from a native location.

"Maybe, ma' baas. The white man across the river said it is so. He made a new fence and put up signs telling us to stay off his land. Abraham took the matter of the fence and the river to the sister of the madam."

Abraham Zolta had traveled to Johannesburg to settle a land dispute and ended up in the middle of a violent attack. Zweigman estimated a period of two to three days before the schoolteacher would be able to answer questions. It might be a week or more before he made it home.

"You've heard what happened to the madam's sister?" Emmanuel asked, realizing that the chances of that were slim.

"I know nothing, ma' baas." The woman's shoulders stiffened in anticipation of bad news. Abraham had gone to the city even after she'd begged him to stay close to familiar things.

"Some men . . . thieves . . . broke into the house where your husband was staying in Johannesburg. They hurt the madam's sister, her husband and also Abraham. Now Abraham is in Baragwaneth Hospital. He will come back to Clear Water when he is well, but it will be many more days before that happens."

"He lives?"

"He does," Emmanuel said.

The woman looked to Shabalala for confirmation. The

word of a white man and a black man together *had* to be the truth.

"Abraham lives," the Zulu detective said. "He will return to you and the little one soon."

The woman scooped the baby from Shabalala's arms and held it close, seeking the comfort of plump limbs. "God is good, but my heart is heavy. What did these robbers take in exchange for the harm they caused?"

"A motorcar." The wrongness of the theft again stuck Emmanuel. If the red Mercedes were the prize, the actual break-in made no sense.

"We will leave the madam's name and telephone number with the hospital in Johannesburg," Shabalala said. "When it is time for Abraham to come home, they will call the madam and let her know."

"When must I come to hear news?" the young mother asked.

"Go to the back door of the farmhouse in three days' time and knock. Be at ease, the sergeant will tell the madam that you are coming. She will expect you." Shabalala paused so the woman understood that approaching the big house without explicit permission would not cause offense. "What the hospital tells the madam, she will also tell you."

"My thanks, ma' baas. I will do as you say. *Salani kahle.* Stay well, the both of you." The woman swung the baby onto her back, tied it snugly into place with the cotton wrap and then walked the path leading to the river.

"What is on your mind, Sergeant?" Shabalala asked.

"The two European suspects could have opened the garage, hot-wired the car and driven off with no fuss," Emmanuel said. "Instead, they forced their way through the back door, beat the Brewers to a pulp and then stole the Mercedes. It doesn't make sense."

"The men were looking for money and valuables in the house." The Zulu detective came to the logical conclusion. "They used the boot of the car to carry away what they had stolen."

"They wrecked the furniture but left a row of silver picture frames on the mantelpiece and a stack of presents under the Christmas tree. Not one thing in the lounge room had been touched." Emmanuel visualized the crime scene in vivid detail: the smashed hall stand, the ripped telephone wires and the shards of broken glass lying in the doorway. "Why stop outside the lounge?"

Shabalala thought for a long while and then said, "Maybe they found what they were looking for and had no need to search further."

"Huh . . ." Emmanuel considered the implications of that statement. "The thieves were searching for something other than money or jewelry. They found it and took the car on their way out."

"Maybe so," Shabalala said.

"*Who gives a shit why those men broke into the Brewers' place?*" the Scottish sergeant major said. "*It's not your problem, soldier. The Shabalala boy is safe. Let sleeping dogs and corrupt police lieutenants lie. Forget about Mason. Forget about the robbery. Walk away with what you have.*"

25

THE SUN HUNG lower on the horizon and the shadows lengthened across the grass. They'd make Jo'burg just after nightfall if they moved now. Glimpses of the farmhouse walls flashed between rows of corn. A high-pitched squeal cut through the air. Emmanuel expected to find Jodie, the youngest of the children, hanging from the porch rafters like a bat.

"Don't you run away from me." Delia's voice carried from the kitchen. "You stay where you are, miss."

The back door opened and a bright-haired girl of about twelve scooted outside with a hessian bag slung over her shoulder. She sprinted across the porch with her red pig-tails flying and the hem of her dress tucked into her under-pants for extra mobility. Delia had no chance of catching up. The girl glanced back and smiled, sure she'd made a clean getaway. Her toe caught the edge of an uneven tile and she pitched forward and hit the ground hard. Delia grabbed a leg and the older maid, brown wig now askew atop her head, gripped an ankle.

"It's not for me." The girl tried to kick free. "I'm telling the truth."

"You're stealing food for your darkie friends," Delia said. "Just like you did last week. Don't lie to me."

"For shame . . ." the elderly maid panted. "How can the madam believe the stories coming from your mouth, child?"

"I'm taking the food and the water to a sick person," the girl screamed. "That's the truth."

Zweigman and the rest of the Singleton children came around the far corner of the house at the same time that Emmanuel and Shabalala reached the altercation. The native men sitting under the yellowwood shuffled in for a better view.

"So, this is Julie." Emmanuel glanced briefly at his watch and allocated five minutes to defusing the situation before he took the long road home to Davida. He crouched down. "How did she get into trouble so fast?"

"Look in the sack." Delia kept Julie pinned. "See for yourself, Detective Cooper."

He picked up the hessian bag and pulled the ties loose to reveal the contents: four buns, a leather canteen, a mango and a collection of cotton scraps of the sort normally used to sew patchwork quilts.

"What are the rags for?" he asked. He remembered that

his sister, Olivia, had kept rags to dress up her collection of "grass dolls," long tufts of wild grass, which she'd plaited into cornrows before tying the ends with vines and bits of cloth.

"I have to bandage the sick girl's leg." Julie tugged the hem of her skirt over her knees and sat up. She looked Emmanuel over from head to toe with an interest that he found disconcertingly adult. "The cut on her leg has sand and blood in it."

The specific nature of the answer caught Emmanuel off guard. Either Julie lived in a detailed fantasy world or the bizarre story had an element of truth.

"Who is this girl?"

"I don't know her name, but she's from the Lion's Kill farmhouse. The big man kept her locked in a little room, but she got out. Must be that's how she got hurt . . . by kicking in the window."

"Lion's Kill?" Delia's grip tightened, which caused Julie to wince. "You know not to go onto that property after what happened. You've read the warning signs."

The nursing mother had mentioned the new fence and the signs put up by the white man across the river. Abraham, the mystery man found in the Brewers' garden, had traveled to Johannesburg to check the legal boundaries of the adjoining farm.

"Where is the girl now?" Emmanuel focused on how he, Shabalala and Zweigman could do the most good. Rescuing an injured girl they could manage. Land disputes were out of their jurisdiction.

"She's in the hills." Julie lifted her chin in the direction of the three peaks. "I gave her bird eggs to eat, but she's got no water and her lips are cracked."

"Sunstroke and dehydration." Zweigman made a long-distance diagnosis. "A fatal combination if untreated."

Delia's fingers loosened and she leaned in close to Julie. "These men are police. You'd better be telling the truth or it's jail for you, miss."

Jason and his siblings squatted, barefoot and ragged, by their mother's side. The younger ones observed Julie with pink, milk-washed eyes. A hundred times "sorry" wouldn't fix things with the police. Their sister was in for it now.

"Cross my heart and hope to die . . ." Julie looked Emmanuel in the eye. "Boy-Boy and Precious from the location also saw her. She asked me to stay but I couldn't. I told her that I'd come back later with more food. I said I'd try."

"This is dangerous business, Cooper," the sergeant major said. *"Call the nearest police station. They'll lead a rescue while you drive back to Johannesburg. Remember the mission objective. Get Cassie's statement to the Dutch lawyer before Mason lights a fire under your arse."*

"I can't just walk away."

"You can and you will, soldier. Do the right thing by Aaron and by Davida. Keep a low profile and slink off down the road. I'll not hold it against you."

Emmanuel turned to Delia, who knelt on the cracked paving stones with slumped shoulders. Evidence of her failures lay in every direction: dried corn, filthy children, natives milling unattended at the back of her house and a daughter who'd rather roam the bush than read a book or bake a cake.

"Call the local police," he said. Hard times made for hard choices and he chose Aaron's freedom and Davida's safety above all else. "They'll conduct a thorough search of the hills and the farmhouse on Lion's Kill. We don't have the resources for a proper rescue."

"The police constable won't come," Delia said straight off. "He steers clear of Lion's Kill. No charges have ever been laid against the owner, Leonard Hammond."

"There've been complaints?"

"Dozens, but nothing's ever come of them. People say it's because a retired detective owns part of the farm and knows the higher-ups in Pretoria."

"Sergeant," Shabalala spoke in a low voice. "If the little one knows the way, we can reach the hills before dark. I will bring us back by the full moon."

Emmanuel motioned the Zulu detective away from Delia and her family. Zweigman joined them to form a tight circle.

"Do we believe Julie's story?" He asked the question to establish a common starting point from which to plan the rescue.

"I think the child is telling the truth," Shabalala said.

The doctor mulled over the complexities of the situation, then said, "If the injured girl does not exist, we will look foolish for having believed a lie. If she is real, we will have saved a life and our conscience will be clean. If we drive away, we will never know either way."

"Aaron . . ." Emmanuel prompted. Shabalala had the most to lose from delaying the journey back to Jo'burg. He had till dawn to call Elliott King and suggest an early departure to Mozambique for all the residents of the Houghton house—a temporary solution to the threat posed by Mason.

"My son will not be released tonight even with the new statement." The Zulu detective had calculated the hours and weighed the risks. "The lawyer can do nothing till the morning."

Emmanuel picked up the hessian sack and gave it to Zweigman. "See what else we need."

The doctor checked Julie's cache and added blankets, more food, water and flashlights to the supply list. Jason and the younger children raided the house for the items after Delia gave a weary "go ahead." She believed in luck and knew hers had run out. A sick girl rescued from imminent death could be the charm that opened the doors so good luck could walk in. Shabalala emptied the hessian sack and reloaded it with supplies for the journey. Zweigman packed extra disinfectant into his medical bag while Julie hunted the yard for stones to arm her slingshot. The five remaining children ran laps around the swimming pool and sent the resident frogs into a frenzy.

"We are ready, Sergeant," Zweigman said, and joined Shabalala at the start of the path that ran down to the river. The sun showed more orange than yellow and the sky had turned a softer blue, with tendrils of green at the horizon line. Twilight closed in fast.

"We'll be back after dark. I can't say when," Emmanuel told Delia. "If you leave a light on and the curtains open in the kitchen, we'll find our way back faster."

"Of course," Delia said. "You keep an eye on my Julie, Detective Cooper, and stay away from the Lion's Kill farmhouse."

Emmanuel thought over that last piece of advice as he walked down the path. Jason Singleton had said his father died while on a hunting weekend at Lion's Kill. Delia's tension suggested there might be more to the accident than a misfired gun.

"*N'kosi* . . ." One of the elderly men who'd squatted under the tree for the better part of the afternoon approached Shabalala and spoke in a low, urgent voice. He gestured to the hills and then moved back to join the others in the shade. Julie ran ahead with a pocket full of stones and her slingshot in her right hand. Emmanuel drew level with the Zulu detective, who balanced the weight of the hessian sack on a broad shoulder.

"Let me guess. The old man warned us against going . . ."

"*Yebo*. That is so," Shabalala confirmed. "He said the men across the river like guns and they like beer. When they drink they load their guns and shoot them at whatever moves."

"*One warning from Delia and another warning from the old man,*" the sergeant major said. "*Could this bare-arsed rescue be anything but a bad fucking idea?*" Emmanuel ignored the Scotsman. The journey would finish when the girl in the hills was safely brought back to Clear

Water and not before. Zweigman and Shabalala felt the same.

They followed the course of the river upstream for roughly fifteen minutes before coming to a chest-high wire fence that blocked access to the bank.

"This way." Julie took Emmanuel's hand and tugged him in the right direction. "We have to go into the fields now. It's more fun walking on the sand, but we can't do that anymore."

They switched from following the riverbank to tracing the fence line for another quarter hour. Up ahead, a collection of mud huts and cinder-block dwellings stood in a wide field. A dozen footpaths led from the huts to the river, access to which had been cut off by construction of the new fence. Emmanuel stopped. Julie kept hold of his hand.

"This is why Abraham Zolta went to check the boundary lines," he said. "The people living in the native location have to walk a mile in the direction of Clear Water to gain access to the river."

"The new border gives the white man's farm the river," Shabalala said, and stepped off the path so three women carrying empty buckets on their heads could pass. "In this dry season, he is king."

"Is the fence legal?" Zweigman asked with a raised brow.

"If the government approved the expansion under the Group Areas Act, then yes, it's legal. Our man in Baragwanath Hospital went to Johannesburg to double-check

the maps—a bold move for a black man living on an isolated farm."

Julie tugged Emmanuel's hand and pointed to a board
attached to the chain-link fence by a wire. A skull and
crossbones was spray-painted above a red-lettered warning: PRIVATE PROPERTY. KEEP OUT. TRESPASSERS WILL BE SHOT
AND FED TO THE LIONS."

*"It's time to sit up and pay attention, soldier. You're
walking into a cluster-fuck. I can feel it."*

Emmanuel accepted that the mad Scotsman had a point.
They were entering armed territory with one Webley six-
shooter revolver, a child's slingshot and a hessian sack
filled with relief supplies. They had to get in and out fast.

26

*S*LEEP CAME IN *snatches, but the pain lingered. The cut in her leg throbbed and burned. Alice wedged herself deeper into a rock crevice high off the ground. Clawing her way up to the narrow sanctuary had taken hours and turned her muscles to jelly. She peered into the blue-and-crimson sunset. Light reflected off the windows of the farmhouse where the big man lived. He and his visitors were home: eating, drinking and enjoying their shelter from the heat and the sun. It wasn't fair, but when had her life been fair? The red sky faded to the color of ashes and night dropped like a curtain overhead. So many stars . . . She rested her forehead against the side of the rock and closed her eyes, determined to sleep and dream.*

The crunch of footsteps and the timbre of male voices came from the thorn trees. Alice held her breath, made herself small. A wild animal grunted in the darkness, but she paid it no mind. The most dangerous predators were the men and they were moving closer, their torch beams shining across the ground.

"This is the place," a man's voice said. "I see her prints."

Alice cupped her mouth and muffled a scream. The big man had brought in a tracker to hunt her down and drag her back to the cell. That's who must have been in the car that sped through the dirt road this afternoon.

"Where has she gone?" another strange voice asked.

"Not far. She is hurt and dragging her leg across the dirt."

Twin light beams converged on the place where she'd rested against the rock. Broken eggshells littered the ground. The shafts of light tilted suddenly upward and caught Alice in their glare. She cried out and scrambled to her feet. Her legs gave way and she fell from the crevice like a fledgling out of a nest. Wind ruffled the hem of her dress as she dropped through the air and she tensed, waiting for impact. Strong arms caught her midfall and laid her gently to the ground.

"See?" a girl's voice said. "I told you she was here. Look, there's the cut on her leg."

"Julie?" The name came thick and slurred from Alice's mouth. "You came back."

"Ja. I brought men with me. Police."

Alice dug her elbows into the dirt and wriggled backward. She'd encountered the police before—most of them unsympathetic or looking for a sexual favor. Rescuing prostitutes was not their highest priority. An olive-skinned man with messy white hair and gold-rimmed glasses leaned into the spotlight. This one, she sensed instantly, was kind.

"I'm Dr. Zweigman," the man said in a foreign accent. "Drink first and then I will look at your leg."

She gulped water from a canteen held to her mouth by a tall black man wearing a suit. Broad-shouldered and with arms strong enough to catch her body in midair, he'd be more than a match for the monster who'd snatched her from the alley. The thought of the big man beaten and cowed by a black man made her smile. Water gurgled from her mouth and spilled to the ground.

"That is enough for now, Shabalala," the foreign one called Zweigman said. "Sergeant Cooper, please cut a piece of fruit with no skin for the patient while I attend to the wound."

"Not choking . . ." Alice grabbed a muscular forearm and held tight. "Laughing . . ."

The black man, Shabalala, said, "This water is for you alone. There will be more soon. I promise."

She believed him. The white doctor and the well-dressed detective were unlike the men she knew back in Johannesburg. They were gentle. If she'd been naked, Alice believed that they would have treated her with the same degree of care.

"Light please, Detective Constable," Zweigman said.

Shabalala set the canteen down and picked up a silver flashlight. He aimed the beam at her legs, which were scratched and filthy. Strange that she cared what a native thought of her physical condition, but she did. A darkened shape crouched at her feet and peeled a mango with a penknife. Zweigman had called that one Sergeant Cooper.

Julie stood by the sergeant's side with her hip pressed to his shoulder. He took her weight, neither encouraging nor disapproving of the intimate contact. Cooper's relaxed posture made Alice think, He's used to female company. Women like him and he's good with them.

Cooper got to his feet and moved to her side. Julie followed with a torch, and the detective sergeant and the girl squatted opposite Shabalala. Alice squinted into the confusing darkness and made out a clean-shaven jaw and a bruised cheek.

"What's your name?" the sergeant asked.

"Alice."

"Open wide, Alice," he said, and slid a piece of mango into her mouth. It tasted delicious, like the fruit on her grandmother's farm. "Another one?"

"Please." The juice stung her lips, but the pleasure of eating the fruit outweighed the pain. Cooper leaned in with the second piece held between thumb and forefinger. Built leaner than the black detective, he moved with a confidence that Alice associated with men who took their looks for granted. Dark hair, light-colored eyes, a face composed of clean-cut lines . . . he'd never paid for it in his life. The sergeant wasn't precious about his appearance, though; the bruised face and the raw knuckles made him appear strong. He was the kind of man you could depend on when there was trouble.

"More light, please, Sergeant," the doctor said. Cooper exchanged the mango for Julie's torch and angled the beam onto the cut on her leg. The doctor's gentle fingers probed

the wound. Alice thought of home and tried to find some comfort there. She'd mend and grow strong. It would take a while to scrape up the courage to return to the alley. She'd have to work the streets in the meantime, making less money as a result. Memories of the three men and the red-haired girl would fade and she'd be left to take care of herself again.

"Almost finished." The doctor picked out dirt and glass with a pair of tweezers. "I cannot stitch the cut until it is absolutely clean and I cannot be sure of that till there is proper light to see by. A bandage will suffice for now."

Disinfectant stung the wound, but it was a good pain, a healing pain, unlike the hurt inflicted by the big man. Alice pushed herself into a sitting position and watched the doctor apply the bandage. Physicians who took on prostitutes as clients rarely had such steady hands.

"More water for the young lady," Zweigman said to the black detective, who uncapped the canteen and handed it to her. She drank deep, enjoying the sensation of wetness in her mouth.

"When last did you eat?" the doctor asked.

"I got fed twice." Alice tried to unpick dates and times and failed. "I don't remember which days."

"Have the rest of the fruit but try to go slowly. Your body needs time to get used to having food in the stomach," Zweigman said. "Please rinse the young lady's hands, Shabalala."

The black policeman motioned for her hands, which she held out to her side. He poured water into her cupped palms and waited till she'd scrubbed away the dirt before repeating the action. Julie handed over the mango and wiped her sticky fingers on the front of her dress while Cooper peered across the crop of thorn trees to a pinprick of light shining in the window of the big man's house.

"Is that where you were?" he asked after the mango flesh had disappeared.

"Ja. *In a little cell with a cot and a bucket.*" Alice chewed at the pip like a starving dog. "We came from Jo'burg, but I don't know where I am now."

"You're in Northern Transvaal, off the main road to Rust de Winter," Cooper said. "Did you miss the road signs?"

"They put a hood over my head," Alice said. "I couldn't see anything . . . not till we got to the farmhouse."

"How many are there?"

"Two, the big man and his little friend. Other men came to visit, but they didn't stay."

Cooper and the black detective exchanged a quick glance. The description of the big man and his smaller friend meant something to them.

"The big man is the boss." Julie spoke with authority. "He's the one you have to look out for. The little one is scared of him, that's for sure."

"The small one is a coward," Alice agreed. "Another car drove to the farmhouse this afternoon. I don't know how many men were in it."

"How long before we can make a move back to Clear Water?" the sergeant asked the white-haired doctor.

"That depends on our patient," Zweigman said. "If she can stand and put weight on her injured leg, we can leave right away. I would prefer that we wait till she is better rested."

Alice gritted her teeth and got to her feet. The cut hurt worse than before. She placed half her weight onto the injured leg and felt the muscles quiver. Walking was out of the question, but with help she could limp. The black policeman offered his arm. She clung on tight and hobbled in the direction from which she'd seen the rescue party come. If the big man found them, he'd kill the policemen and the doctor; of that she had little doubt. Her fate and that of the little girl she dared not think about. They moved slowly into the cover of the thorn trees.

"I'm glad we found Alice," Julie said to the sergeant. "The other girls just disappeared."

—

"Other girls?" Emmanuel stopped in the darkness and stared at Julie. He felt the hairs on his neck stand up.

"Last holidays it was a lady with long black hair and black eyes." Julie continued in a matter-of-fact way. "I didn't see the one before that, but I heard her crying in the small room."

"Did you tell anyone about the women?" he asked.

"I'm not allowed onto Lion's Kill. Same goes for Precious and Boy-Boy from the location. We'd get a thrashing if our parents found out that we played here."

"Fair enough," Emmanuel said. Speaking up meant a

beating, while silence gave Julie the freedom to roam with her friends. He switched the rope handle of the hessian sack to his left shoulder and walked over to Shabalala and Alice. Zweigman flanked the pair, shining a light onto the ground with a torch.

"Were you the only woman at the farmhouse?" he asked Alice.

"Yes." She stopped to catch her breath. They'd walked but a few yards from the start position and Clear Water was still miles away. At the rate they were traveling, they'd make Delia's farm by dawn and Johannesburg by early afternoon. "I found a hair clip under the cot. That's when I figured out that other girls had been locked in the room before me."

"Tell me how you got from Jo'burg to here." From her low-cut sateen dress and rough accent, Emmanuel guessed she was a working girl.

"I was in my usual spot, waiting for offers." Shabalala took the full weight of Alice's body while she talked. "The big man came from one end of the alley and started moving toward me, slow like. I didn't like the look of him, so I took off. I almost made it to the road before the little man blocked the way. I slammed into him and hit the ground. They caught me. They put a hood over my head and pushed me into a car with leather seats and it smelled of cigarettes. After that, I didn't see anything."

"When was that?" Emmanuel asked. The big man who led the raid on Fatty's club had picked through the women like a gold prospector, searching for a "new one" to take home.

"Friday night," Alice said. "I thought they were rich, but the car is the nicest thing about them. The house and the yard are falling apart."

Shabalala turned in the direction of the farmhouse and listened intently to a sound that barely registered in Emmanuel's ears. Julie ran back to where they stood and pointed across the plains.

"A car," she said. "I saw the headlights."

"It is coming in this direction. They have seen us, Sergeant. Switch off the torches," Shabalala said.

Three beams shut down simultaneously. The group stood in the moonlit darkness, breathing slowly, waiting for the threat to pass. The sound of the car engine grew louder. Alice moaned low in the back of her throat.

"Move," Emmanuel said. "We have to be gone by the time they get here."

"The river is this way." Julie darted ahead, familiar with the landscape and the location of the fence line. Shabalala scooped Alice into his arms and ran. Zweigman and Emmanuel followed, ducking and weaving through thornbushes. A brown buck sprang from a stand of mopani trees, giving away their location. The car engine revved; the driver shifted into fourth gear.

"In here." Julie dodged hard right into a thicket of red-spiked aloes. She slipped between the trunks and moved deeper into the heart of the forest. The plants grew thicker, their fleshy leaves touched together like outstretched fingers. Emmanuel crouched low and caught a glimpse of Zweigman and Shabalala hidden in the moon shadows.

The Zulu detective held Alice tucked close to his chest. Julie was gone.

High beams cut the darkness, flooding the aloes with light. Emmanuel breathed deep and stayed down. The engine whined as the driver shifted down a gear and kept the vehicle close to the outer edge of the forest. Tires spun in the sand and the car stalled. Emmanuel snapped open his holster with his thumb and gripped the Webley revolver's smooth handle.

"None of this aiming-for-the-leg bullshit, Cooper. These men have kidnapped and hurt God knows how many women. And they're connected to the Brewer mess and the club robbery. You know it, too. They will kill to keep their secrets," the sergeant major said. *"For God's sake, shoot straight like I taught you. Get the bastards before they get you."*

The engine started up and the driver tapped the accelerator. Emmanuel slipped the Webley free from its holster and rested it on the curve of his knee. The car tires spun, kicking up stones. A male voice cursed. The tires found purchase and the vehicle continued along the sandy edges of the aloe grove. Emmanuel held the gun steady and waited until the mechanical sounds faded into silence. He crab-crawled across the dusty ground to Shabalala and Alice.

"The car is heading for the river," the Zulu detective said when Zweigman and Julie came out of hiding. "The driver knows we must follow the fence line and then cross over to the native location. He will wait for us there."

"There must be another way off the farm." Alice looked from one face to the next, desperate to hear the right answer.

"We could take the farm road and follow that back to Clear Water, but it will take a long time," Julie said. "The other river crossing is at the far end of the fence and it will take us a long time to get there, too."

"We have to be off this farm by dawn," Emmanuel said. If they failed, they would be on the wrong side of a turkey shoot in the morning and he'd miss the deadline to call Davida's father and warn him about Mason. He thought through options and came up with a possible way out. "Shabalala and I will draw them away from the river, give the three of you time to cross over to the native location. We'll circle around and come after you."

Julie moved closer, nudged a shoulder against his leg. "I want to stay with you, Detective."

"You have to guide Alice and the doctor across the river and back to Clear Water," he said. "I'll be back in time for breakfast. That's a promise."

He'd broken that promise to his ex-wife, Angela, at least once a week during their brief marriage. He made Davida no promises. She returned the favor.

They crossed a dry field, keeping to the tree line. Julie pointed to the river, running silver under the moonlight. A multitude of stars dusted the night sky over the plains that stretched to the horizon. A parked car aimed its high beams at the space where the fence stopped short of the riverbank. Cigarette smoke curled from the windows.

"Two men, maybe more," Shabalala said. "They are settled. Only a fire or a storm will move them."

"*Good idea,*" the sergeant major said. "*Put a match to the homestead, stand back and watch the bitch burn. That will get their arses in gear.*"

The tinder-dry bushland made the perfect kindling for an inferno that could easily spread to the native location and to neighboring farms. A bush fire drew oxygen from the air like a living being; it jumped and ran and roared with life. It took instructions from no one.

"A pity there's no safe way to start a fire in a drought," Emmanuel said. "Or call down a flood."

"There's a braai pit at the back of the homestead. Boy-Boy jumped into it and the sides come up to here." Julie touched a finger to the top of her forehead. "Me and Precious rolled a big stone into the pit so he could climb out."

The light shining in the window of the Lion's Kill homestead pierced the darkness. A fire built in a deep pit would barely register over the same distance.

"We run," Shabalala said. "The men in the car will follow. It is human instinct."

A breathtakingly simple plan, Emmanuel thought. No fire, no flood: just the two of them running like rabbits in a hunter's headlights. The plan would work. Sitting surveillance stretched the time, made minutes feel like hours. Nicotine took the edge off the boredom, but only for a while. The men would give chase.

"We must move fast to the gap in the fence line and into their light, Sergeant." Shabalala stood up and scouted the fall of the land, which dipped down to the riverbank. "If we run to the river, the men in the car will lose sight of us and begin the chase."

Emmanuel's lungs burned in advance of the sprint through the headlights and across soft sand.

"A fine plan, gentlemen," Zweigman said. "Except for one detail. They are in an automobile and you are on foot."

"There are no roads," Shabalala pointed out. "We are free to move into the rocks and through the thorn trees where a car cannot go."

The doctor gave a weary shrug, accepting that the detectives had made up their minds and were prepared to, literally, run for their lives. Once more he'd be left with the care of the sick and the needy. He healed wounds and mended broken bodies and he did it well. Some called it a gift, even a blessing. On occasions like this one, though, he longed for some of the pure physical strength and quick reflexes that Shabalala and Cooper took for granted.

"To the right, across the headlights and then down the ridge to the river." Emmanuel fixed the sequence of events in mind, imagined the fall of each step onto hard ground and then the change in texture to fine sand.

"*Yebo*, Sergeant. Ready?"

Alice stepped closer and licked her dry lips. "If you get to the homestead . . ." She addressed the space between the detectives' shoulders, unused to asking for favors from the police. "Could you check the little room? They might have brought in a new girl. I saw a car drive to the house this afternoon. She might have been in the car. She might be trapped in the cell. She might never get out."

"We will." Emmanuel had his own reasons for checking the Lion's Kill farmhouse. He turned to Julie and said, "See Dr. Zweigman and Alice home to Clear Water. When the car leaves, take them across the river and over to the native location as quick as you can."

Julie nodded. Emmanuel split to the right of the group with Shabalala, both preferring to skip the good-byes and the good-luck farewells. Their survival depended on the most basic physical elements: speed and stamina.

"Run fast," Julie said. "And keep running."

27

LIGHT FROM THE high beams hit the back of Emmanuel's retina, momentarily blinding him. Shabalala ran a half stride ahead, loose-limbed, graceful. Emmanuel stayed glued to the Zulu detective's shoulder, heard the muffled cry of male voices and the sound of a car engine turning over. Bait taken: now to avoid being landed and gutted like a fish.

They hit the downward slope to the river and dropped from sight. Shabalala poured on the speed, aiming for a slender path winding up through the grass. The sandbank had no shelter on either side, no safety from enemies on higher ground. The bump of car wheels on the ridge confirmed that the chase had begun, just as they had anticipated.

They scrambled up the path and hit the flatlands at a sprint. The car came from their left, headlights burning bright, its engine running in top gear. In thirty seconds the car's silver fender would collect their legs and knock them clear into the thornbushes. Fear pushed Emmanuel hard. He drew even with Shabalala. The car closed in. They simultaneously bolted slightly to their left and the car's silver fender whipped past them, collecting the tails of their jackets and fanning a breeze.

"Close. Too close, boyo."

A flat stretch of land dotted with acacia trees lay before them. It might as well be a four-lane highway. Car wheels spun in the dirt, kicking up stones. Emmanuel and Shabalala had no option but to keep running, just like Julie said. A stand of trees, five deep and two hundred yards off, beckoned. They set off with the car's headlights licking the darkness, seeking them out. The sound of the engine cranked up as the car closed the distance to impact.

"Split," Emmanuel said. "Now."

Shabalala peeled to the right and Emmanuel went left. A space opened between them, wide enough for the car to drive between. Brakes slammed. The driver threw the gears into reverse and swung the wheel hard in Emmanuel's direction. Emmanuel ran flat out. Knives stabbed at his side, the pain hot and sharp. The trees came into range. Emmanuel tripped and he pitched forward onto his knees. So close were the trees that he was able to make out individual leaves and the sharp ends of thorns.

"Fuck . . . this is like dying on the last day of the war."

A hand snaked out and dragged him bodily into the woods. Car brakes slammed, giving off the acrid smell of burning rubber. Emmanuel pushed onto all fours and scrambled into the trees. He found a kneeling position. Shabalala crouched low in the gloom and sucked in lungfuls of air through his open mouth.

"We must draw them further away from the river," Shabalala said. "The girl's leg is bad. It will take time for the doctor to walk her across to the location. He is not strong enough to carry her."

"More running?" The pain had dulled to needles pricking his lungs, which made breathing difficult.

"To the big rocks." The Zulu detective pointed through the trees to a mass of dark shapes looming from the dry veldt. "The car cannot follow us into such high ground."

The rock outcrop looked to be miles away with no safe place to stop and draw breath. Meanwhile, the car circled the trees like a shark, waiting for them to break cover.

"First, I need to grow fresh lungs." Emmanuel's breath came in short, noisy gasps. "Give me a year."

"You can run the distance easily," Shabalala said. "When you find the rhythm of your body, the strength will flow."

"Are you seriously talking to a white man about finding rhythm?" The idea was funny, even in the circumstances.

"Tonight," Shabalala said. "You and I are the same. We go together as one."

Nice theory but a bad idea. Lagging behind would put them both in danger. What if they didn't make it? The thought of Shabalala's wife, Lizzie, becoming a widow chilled Emmanuel. His lungs seemed to repair themselves instantly.

"All right, but we split when I say." That way, at least one of them would get to the rocks in safety. "With luck, the car will chase *you* this time."

Shabalala grinned, not bothered by the thought. They moved to the edge of the trees closest to the rocks. The car, a black Dodge, cruised by with the windows rolled down and bony elbows jutting over the metal.

"Come out, come out, wherever you are . . ." the driver called. "I know, I know you're not very far."

The lyrics of a Frank Sinatra song used as a threat; Emmanuel gave the driver points for musical knowledge. The vehicle circled past the hiding spot and continued around to the other side of the trees. Taillights glowed red in the dark.

"Empty your mind," Shabalala said. "Listen only to the breath coming into your lungs and then going out again."

They broke cover and sprinted. They made the half-way mark before a car horn blasted three times, signaling the second phase of the chase. Emmanuel's head reverberated with the sound of rattling bullets from long ago and the cries of men as they were cut down. He'd run for his life under an iron sky on Sword Beach in Normandy, hid from snipers and huddled in mud trenches. Most of what he remembered now was the fear.

As he had many times before, Emmanuel pushed the fear away, although he knew he would never fully rid himself of its power.

"Breathe, Sergeant. Breathe with me."

Shabalala's voice broke through the memory and pulled him back into the present. The throttle of the car engine surged and faded. He released a long breath and drew in another in time with Shabalala. Five more synchronized breaths and the world simplified. His body fell into rhythm. He was whole and intact—a survivor. He felt as if he could run forever. The rocks rose up from the earth like the walls of a citadel. Emmanuel jumped, found a foothold and scrambled over the craggy surface to a ledge high off the ground. The Dodge braked and spun a circle. The boot smashed into the rocks and metal groaned. Car doors opened and feet hit the ground.

"Fuck." Two bullets ricocheted off the granite wall to the right of Emmanuel. He pressed into the shadows, certain the shots were fired blind and in anger.

"How did they do that? They disappeared into the rocks," a male voice said.

"Who cares how they did it? All I know for sure is that we're in big fucking trouble. Help me push the car free. She might be good to drive."

Emmanuel pressed his palms flat to the granite and worked around to a patch of starlight at the far end of the ledge. He jumped to a lower level, landing in a crouch. Shabalala was somewhere in this field of wild grass and boulders. The driver and his passenger swore a red streak as they struggled to push the wrecked Dodge free.

"We made it," he said when the Zulu detective stepped out from the shadows and walked across the dry ground on cat's feet.

"I had no doubts," Shabalala answered.

The rock ledge where Emmanuel had sheltered cut a black slash into the rock face. How he'd gotten up that high, he had no idea.

28

MUMMIFIED ORANGES LAY scattered on the ground of an orchard planted in uneven rows. Their plan was to circle away from the crashed Dodge and then switch back in the direction of the river, giving the armed driver and his passenger a wide berth. From there, they'd join Zweigman, Alice and Julie at Clear Water Farm.

Emmanuel crossed the orchard, the dead fruit crunching underfoot. Branches threw shadows on the ground and a windmill creaked in the dark, a sound both lonely and bleak. He and Shabalala stayed silent, aware of a light shining up ahead. Lion's Kill homestead, no doubt. They stopped at the tree line and looked out to a whitewashed structure so unloved that the moonlight hitting the silver roof turned it gray.

Gravel stretched from the edge of the orchard to the

front door. Tire marks crisscrossed the gravel, but the yard was empty of cars and the traditional plantings of hardy aloes and lavender bushes.

"She said that a second car drove onto the farm this afternoon." A light glowed in a front room. It might have been left on to guide the men in the Dodge back home. Or it might be illuminating an occupied chair.

"Maybe the visitor left," Shabalala said from under the branches of a native tree. "Maybe the house is empty."

There was only one way to tell. He'd promised Alice that he'd check what she'd called "the cell" for a new prisoner. He peered across the yard and made out a broken window boarded up with cardboard. The metal grate covering the opening was bent out of shape.

If his suspicions proved right, then Davida had escaped being thrown into this very space by the big man.

"Sergeant." Shabalala held out a cut stem with withered leaves. "Look. *UmPhanda*. The raintree."

"Same as the branches hiding the red Mercedes."

"The very same," Shabalala said.

Emmanuel ran a hand over the trunk of a near tree and felt dried sap and raw timber where branches had been hacked off.

"This is the house of the men who beat the principal and his wife and then stole the car." Shabalala nodded to the forlorn dwelling. "The big man and the little one."

"I know it. The same men also broke into Fatty Mapela's dance hall. If the big one had had his way, then Davida would be the one locked in that house right now. Let's check the cell and be gone. When we're back in Jo'burg we'll find out who owns this place and drop the names to the Pretoria police."

He stepped from the shadows onto gravel. White stones marked the perimeter of a hole dug out close to the side of the house, the braai pit that Julie had mentioned. Ash and bleached animal bones lay on the bottom. Shabalala went wide and scanned the area ahead. Emmanuel pressed to the wall and moved to the window in which the light shone.

He'd seen piss-poor farms before and had lived on one during adolescence, so the bleak interior of Lion's Kill was no surprise. The uncurtained windows, paint peeling off the walls and dust on every surface were familiar. Likewise, the paraffin lantern on the foldout table, the threadbare couch and the stuffed animal heads mounted on the wall. The beds would have lumpy sisal mattresses and the kitchen a woodburning stove that belched smoke.

"Empty," he said of the room. "Swing around the back, check the other exits and entries. I'm going in."

Shabalala lifted a brow, asked the nonverbal question, "Are you sure that's a good idea?"

"If that car engine starts up, those men will be back here soon. We have to move fast." He crossed to the front door and turned the handle. The door opened. Folks in the country rarely locked their doors, but they often kept loaded guns on hand in case of unwelcome guests. Shabalala disappeared into the night. Emmanuel slipped into the corridor of Lion's Kill homestead. It was darker inside than he'd thought. The lantern glow drew him into the front room like a Neanderthal seeking fire.

He moved to the table. A paper-thin map, yellowed with age, spread over the tabletop. The words *Northern Transvaal* ran along the bottom in black ink: of all the things to find in a backwater farmhouse. He picked up the lantern and held it high to cast more light. A small detail snagged his attention and slowed his exit to the corridor. A black leather-bound Bible lay on the arm of the couch, its thumbed pages slotted with strips of paper to mark the locations of favorite verses. The men in the Dodge weren't the praying kind and they'd be back as soon as the motor ticked over. He stepped into the corridor. The lantern flame threw circles of white light onto the walls and the wooden floors. Crickets chirped and the windmill turned outside. The two bedrooms each contained twin iron cots with rough sisal mattresses and cotton sheets. There wasn't much to see in the kitchen beyond a small dining table, a wood stove and a chipped cabinet stocked with mis-matched crackery.

A door led off to the side of the kitchen. He opened it and entered a tacked-on annex made of thin wood panel-ing. Dust blew in under the gap between the concrete floor and the bottom of the walls. A flight of stairs led down to a subterranean space. The little room: Alice's holding cell. His heart kicked harder with each downward step; the old battlefield terror pressed a weight to his chest and coiled into his windpipe like a snake. He pushed his fingertips against the metal door and it swung open. Nothing good waited behind an iron door built below a wooden annex. He entered the concrete cell with the lantern held high. Shadows flickered. He moved deeper into the room and allowed his eyes to adjust to the gloom. The rusting cot and mattress gave off the smell of sweat and dried blood. A primal dance, older than the advent of speech, had taken place here.

"Get in and then get the fuck out," the sergeant major said. *"That was the plan. Now follow it. This place gives me the shakes."*

No hostage, no reason to stay. One call to the Pretoria police and a carload of detectives would flood this cell with a bunch of foot police pinned behind them. Alice was white, thank God, and a worthy victim.

The soft shuffle of feet across the concrete floor snapped him around to face the door, too late to draw his weapon, too late to do anything but experience the rush of fear flooding his veins. A large man stood in the doorway.

"Keep the lantern high. Unclip your weapon and kick it into the corner," a familiar voice said. "I have my revolver aimed straight at your gut, just above the navel, and at this range I won't miss."

"Lieutenant," Emmanuel said. "This is a surprise."

"It's a surprise and it isn't, if you catch my drift," Mason said. "You and I have business to settle. Now do like I said and drop your weapon."

Emmanuel unclipped the Webley left-handed and placed the revolver on the floor. He kicked it, heard the barrel scrape against the rough concrete surface then come to a stop someplace he could not see. The initial rush of fear drained. Meeting Lieutenant Mason again felt more like fate than coincidence.

"Have you figured it out yet?" Mason moved closer, let the lantern light find the black metal barrel of a Browning Hi-Power. "Have you made the connections?"

"Trying to. The gun pointed at me isn't helping," Emmanuel said. Thoughts rolled into black corners, leaving only a faint kind of sense. Mason here at Lion's Kill. The Bible belonged to him, but so what? He found one clear thought and held on to it: Mason was far from the big house in Houghton. That's what really mattered.

"Come on. A clever man like you must have some ideas." Some men, less experienced than the lieutenant, held their weapons too high and miscalculated the strain of the gun's weight on their shoulders and wrists. Mason held the Browning like it was an extension of his hand. "Take a guess, Cooper."

"You're the detective who owns part of this farm and all of the local police."

"Spot on," Mason said. "And there are no local police, just a single constable. He and I have an understanding. He understands that I will beat the teeth from his head if he interferes with me and mine."

Me and mine was an odd phrase to describe the men driving the Dodge. Emmanuel associated the term with blood relatives, family. Mason's words still translated the same, though: Expect no help from the law. You are alone.

"What are you doing here, Cooper?"

"We ended on a bad note the last time we talked. I came to apologize, make sure there were no hard feelings."

"Funny . . ." Mason said deadpan, and slammed the butt of the Browning Hi-Power to Emmanuel's head. Emmanuel felt the breeze generated by the gun slicing through the air and then the crunch of his bones hitting the floor. He blinked hard, thinking, Jesus, that was fast.

"The first thing that you should know about me, Detective Kaffir-fucker, is that I do not have a sense of humor. Never have. Even as a child." Mason knelt down and the light from the fallen lantern threw shadows across his chalk-white skin. "Second thing is, I have a very short fuse. If you don't answer my questions quickly, I will beat you down every single time there's a delay. I will continue doing that till the mountains fall into the sea if necessary. Understand?"

"You sound like my father," Emmanuel said. "He had a short fuse."

In five minutes, maybe ten, Shabalala would come looking for him. All he had to do in the meantime was take a beating. He'd done it before and wasn't looking forward to it. Mason rubbed the barrel tip of the Browning Hi-Power against his cheek, itching a scratch with the safety off and a finger on the trigger.

"Do you have children, Cooper?" The lieutenant sounded genuinely interested.

"I'm single. How could I have children?"

Mason grinned. "Being single doesn't mean anything in the world that we live in. And a man of your proclivities wouldn't flash photographs of his half-caste offspring around the office. You could have a dozen little bastards stashed away."

"I like nonwhite women." Admitting to the lesser sin of fornication might camouflage the greater sin of unsanctioned procreation. "That doesn't mean I'm ready to settle down and have a family with one of them . . . even if it was legal."

"A man without a son leaves only bones when he dies. You waited too long, Cooper. Who's going to bring flowers to your grave?"

"I'll be buried on your land, so I'm hoping you'll do the honors once a year on my birthday. No carnations. Wildflowers are fine."

"*Here it comes . . .*"

The punch lit up a constellation of stars behind his eyelids. He fell back, breathing hard. Where was Shabalala?

"I did warn you." Mason took a reasonable tone. "Now tell me what you're doing on my farm."

"Passing through, thought I'd say hello." Emmanuel willed his muscles slack, like a drunk driver about to make impact with a wall. The lieutenant's fist connected with the weight of a brick thrown by a giant. Shabalala had better come soon.

"Tell me the truth," Mason said, almost kindly. "Believe me when I say that beating you to a puddle gives me no pleasure."

From the low vantage point of the floor, Emmanuel found that he believed Mason's statement. The word *joy-*

less best described the lieutenant's attitude and perhaps the very fiber of his being. Happiness and humor were nowhere to be found, even outside the confines of this cell. Behind the dead pools that were Mason's eyes, Zweigman had glimpsed fear and sadness. Emmanuel saw only a void that couldn't be filled. The years of boozing, violence and whoring had dug the pit deeper and made it impenetrable to light.

"Now that you've tracked me down, you've got nothing to say." Mason rocked back on his heels, thinking. "Curious."

"If you want my opinion, you could do more with this space, Lieutenant. Replace the broken window, get some curtains, put a rocking chair in the corner and you'll have a nice reading room." Every cut and bruise throbbed, but he'd heard the soft crunch of a footstep in the gravel yard. Shabalala would enter the house soon, moving in the darkness, part of the darkness. Between them, he and the Zulu detective would take care of Mason. Somehow.

The lieutenant remained still in the cell's murky atmosphere. No fist, no slap, no reaction at all to the rocking-chair comment. He spoke after a long pause. "When a person deliberately tries to provoke me to violence, I stop and ask why. Does that man enjoy being beaten or is he hoping, for example, to cover the sound of footsteps approaching the house? You brought friends with you."

"I'm alone."

"Are you sure about that, Sergeant Cooper? I hear a person moving around out there."

"I came alone." He emptied all thoughts of Shabalala from his mind. He imagined himself deep in a mountain stronghold and far from Mason's probing gaze. Gravel hit the cardboard square pushed into the cell's empty windowpane, killing the element of surprise.

"You've got no idea who's creeping around the house perimeter?" Footsteps moved away from the front door and in the direction of the braai pit ringed by white stones. It didn't sit right—Shabalala stumbling and raising noise. The first you knew of the Zulu detective was *after* he'd materialized from the air and stepped to your side. He didn't stumble or go bump in the night.

"It's probably your men," Emmanuel said. "The ones in the Dodge."

More footsteps crunched across the front yard and a male voice called out, "Quick, there's one over there. Come round."

Mason stood up and kept the Browning in a relaxed grip, as if he were shaking hands with a good friend. He said, "Pick up the lantern and walk to the door slow. I'll be right behind you. Run and I'll put a bullet in your back. Understand?"

"Perfectly." Run? He could barely stand. His bruises throbbed and his bones ached. Mason's solid right hook had reopened a cut sustained during the fight in Fatty Mapela's club last night. The wound pulsed in time to the beating of his heart and a trickle of blood ran down his cheek and onto the lapels of his shirt. A dry-clean job for sure.

"Move," Mason said.

Emmanuel raised the lantern and darted a quick look into the corner, hoping to find a glint of silver in the gloom. Darkness stared back. The Webley might as well be invisible or locked in a gun safe for all the time it would take him to find it.

"You'd never make it to your weapon in any case." Mason stated the fact. "Glad to see it crossed your mind, though. I had you down as one of those pretty army officers with no guts."

"I was in the field, not behind a desk," Emmanuel said. Held at gunpoint, bloodstained and beaten, yet he still felt it necessary to clarify his position as a combatant: a fighter, a soldier who'd been in the mud at the business end of the war. His military vanity appeared to be resistant to fear.

"Eyes front. Make it fast, Cooper."

Mason tapped the Browning's barrel to a middle vertebra, pushing Emmanuel out of the cell. Noise increased in the yard, rushing steps overlaid with hard breathing and raised voices. Emmanuel gained the stairs, certain that the men from the Dodge were chasing shadows.

"Into the lounge, Cooper. You know the way."

He cut through the kitchen, turned into the corridor and stopped by the side of the decrepit sofa with the Bible sunk into the arm. Dead animals stared from the wall with glassy eyes that absorbed the lantern glow. Not a family portrait to be seen.

"Sit," Mason said.

Emmanuel sat. The front door slammed against the interior wall and the floorboards creaked under the weight of people entering the house. Two men at least, most likely the driver and the passenger from the wrecked Dodge.

"You can run but you can't hide," a man's voice said. "I got you good this time, boy."

"True. You got him good," said another.

"In here," Mason called, and then moved directly behind the couch, ready to empty the Browning's loaded barrel into the crown of Emmanuel's head or into whoever walked through the door should they displease him, craftwork he'd learned working undercover operations. "Slowly."

A small man entered first, grin strung from ear to ear like he'd just been given a puppy for Christmas in addition to the four-speed bike that he'd had on the top of his list for two years running. Shabalala came next, arms raised to shoulder height, his face a blank canvas of skin stretched over bone. If the gun pressed to his neck gave him any bother, it didn't show. The last man in was tall, broad-shouldered and had blue eyes.

"Lenny and Crow," Emmanuel said, surprised but not entirely. Meeting the big and the little man who'd ransacked the Brewers' house and broken into Fatty's club also felt like fate. "We weren't properly introduced last night. I was too busy beating the shit out of you and your men."

The tall one, Lenny, surged into the lounge, his face a patchwork of purple-and-blue bruises, his fist cocked. He landed a few punches but nothing compared to Mason's right hook. The Bible fell to the floor, spilling tabs and fanning pages marked with red ink.

"That's enough, Leonard," Mason said. "Frisk the kaffir for weapons. Make sure to check the socks. They like to keep knives tucked in there."

Lenny and Crow took opposite sides, each patting the Zulu detective down from shoulder to ankle. The paper with Cassie Brewer's statement written out in a cramped hand rustled under Crow's palms. Shabalala's throat tightened, his Adam's apple pushing against the skin to make a hard lump, but otherwise he seemed calm.

"Nice threads for a kaffir," Crow said, and ran baby fingers over the fine cotton. He reached into Shabalala's jacket pocket and withdrew Cassie Brewer's statement. Shabalala blinked hard and for a moment Emmanuel thought he might cry.

"Give that to me," Mason said, and motioned to the couch. "Sit him down next to Cooper."

29

E MMANUEL MET SHABALALA'S gaze and tele-
graphed the question, *How the hell did you end up
sitting next to me in this crap hole?* The Zulu detective sat
down and looked to the window, giving an answer that
Emmanuel didn't understand. Out there lay churned
gravel and acres of thornbush and none of it worth dying
for. Mason came around to the front of the couch, side-
stepping the fallen Bible.

"What are you doing on my farm, gentlemen?" He
held Cassie's statement between pinched fingertips, having
read the contents. "You got the truth from the girl. Excel-
lent job. Why risk it all by coming to Lion's Kill?"

"We were in the area and thought we'd drop by. We
should have called first," Emmanuel said. "For that, I
apologize."

Mason would intimidate Cassie Brewer into withdraw-
ing her statement. He'd walk Alice to a lonely spot and

then bury her deep in a field. Harm the daughter of an educated middle-class couple and the police station phones would ring hot; one more missing whore, who'd notice?

Mason raised the Browning and swung down hard. Emmanuel again felt the fanning breeze of metal displacing air then heard the wet smack of metal finding flesh. Not his flesh this time but Shabalala's. The impact threw Shabalala back and bounced his head off the sofa's wood frame. Emmanuel stood up, hands balled into fists, driven by pure instinct. Mason swung around, pressed the Browning to his forehead and applied pressure. Emmanuel sat down, breathing hard.

"You told that constable at the crime scene that 'Blood is blood. It looks, smells and stains the same no matter who's doing the bleeding.' Let's put that theory to the test, Cooper. I will work on the kaffir and Leonard will work on you. We'll see who bleeds the most before answering my questions. That sounds fair, doesn't it?"

"Did you learn that in your Bible?" Emmanuel said.

The lieutenant snapped his fingers and called Leonard over like he was a drinks waiter at a fancy restaurant and he, Mason, was in need of a refill. The smaller man, Crow, raised the lantern to shed a light on the experiment. Mason tucked Cassie's statement into his breast pocket.

"You reap what you sow." Leonard pushed close to Emmanuel's face so their noses almost touched. Until the cuts and bruises faded, Leonard belonged to a new race group of "purple-and-blue" people. "I'm going to repay you for last night with interest, my friend. See how you like pissing blood."

The fight at Fatty's could have been five minutes ago or a year for all that Emmanuel remembered of the specific details. The evidence suggested that he'd beaten Leonard with a scientific thoroughness. What fleeting memories remained were the rage that burned through him like a fever and the bright blue eye that showed through a hole in the stocking mask. There was something in the color, a familiarity he couldn't place at the time.

Mason stepped back and drove a fist into Shabalala's shoulder. Leonard did the same to Emmanuel, putting weight into the punch, stepping into it like a professional boxer.

"Why are you on my farm?" Mason asked, only slightly winded from connecting with Shabalala's body.

Emmanuel looked directly into a pair of eyes a lighter shade of blue than Leonard's and saw the near-identical shape of brow and jawline shared by the two men. He said to Mason, "We came to talk to your son about the break-in at the Brewers' house, the manslaughter of Mr. Brewer and the theft of a Mercedes-Benz cabriolet from the crime scene."

"Bullshit," Leonard said. "Nobody saw us. You've got no proof we were there."

"I do now."

Mason blanched the color of sea foam and gritted his teeth. "You and your kaffir friend won't live to see the dawn, let alone the inside of a police station."

"Killing two detectives is a sure way for you and Lenny to end up sharing a cell and pissing in the same bucket. That's until the hanging. A father-and-son execution will make the *News of the World*."

Emmanuel took a hit to the stomach but felt it was worth the pain. He'd opened the door to Mason's worst nightmare—two graves side by side, both naked of flowers.

"What's the alternative, Cooper? That I give up my son to save a black boy from the slums?" Mason turned, fixed Leonard a hard stare. "My boy's a killer, I know. But you've got to understand that everything he did was for my benefit. My prayers for his salvation have gone unanswered, but my boy will be all that remains of me when I'm gone. No deals. Accept that you and your kaffir friend are dead."

"This place is called Lion's Kill, yet there are no lions," Shabalala said out of the blue. "Very little buck also."

"What?" Mason was flummoxed.

"The house is filled with dead animals, but the farm is empty of live ones," Shabalala said. "What is there to hunt in this dead place?"

"Besides detectives, you mean?" Emmanuel said.

Shabalala laughed, drawing on the diamond-hard reserves of a black man who'd seen through the pale skin of the "superior race" to their weak and cowardly hearts. Sound worked its way from Emmanuel's stomach, up to his windpipe and out through his mouth in a chuckle.

"A hunting reserve with no animals to hunt. That is funny."

"They killed all the animals," Shabalala said.

"I'm going to let my boy work on you one at a time." Mason's mouth held a smile but his eyes filled with spite. "There'll be no laughing then. I guarantee it."

"I believe you," Emmanuel said. Leonard tortured women for sport.

A fleck of gravel hit the window, soft enough that it might have been blown by the wind. Crow jumped. Lenny put a hand into his jacket pocket and gripped something there. A knife, Emmanuel thought, the same one that had dispatched Vickers, the Afrikaner railway man, to the great train yard in the sky.

"It's the whore," Crow blurted. "I told you she'd come back."

"Shut it." Leonard broke a sweat and wiped a hand across his forehead. "It's the wind, you idiot."

Mason stood at ease, shoulders loose, arms hanging by his side. A face peering through the window would see a calm man, a man in total control of his emotions. You'd have to move closer, pay attention to the deepening lines at the side of his mouth and the narrowing of his eyes to recognize the rage building under the impassive expression. Emmanuel had experience. He could read the signs. Mason's fuse was burning fast.

"Crow, cover our visitors while I talk to my son," Mason said in a gentle voice that was worse than shouting.

"Yes, sir." Crow put the lantern on the map unfurled on the table and fumbled a snub-nosed revolver from his jacket pocket. He held it in unsteady hands.

Mason placed his palm on the crown of Leonard's head, a loving touch, but all wrong in the details. His fingers tightened. He jerked Leonard back by the roots of the hair and slammed him to the floor. Emmanuel winced at the sound. He remembered Davida being dragged across Fatty's club with Leonard's fingers twisted through her hair. Lenny had learned the technique from the master.

Mason worked two punches into Leonard's side, finding the kidneys. Emmanuel checked the exit to the corridor, calculated the distance. Shabalala's body coiled tight, ready to make a run. Crow's hand shook. Mason kept a firm hold on the Browning.

At this range, either man could hit a vital organ or nick an intestine. Emmanuel and Shabalala exchanged a look. Too dangerous, they decided, but the odds of living were better than ten minutes ago. Something was changing.

"You disobeyed my instructions," Mason said to Leonard, who lay dazed on the floor. "How long did you keep her after I gave the order?"

"A day."

"How long was it really, Crow?"

Crow rolled over without resistance. "Two days, sir. I told Lenny what you said, but he wanted to keep the girl for a bit longer."

Mason patted Leonard's cheek and found a bruise. "You disobeyed me, boy. Under normal circumstances, I'd turn you black and blue, but Sergeant Cooper got to you first." He leaned closer. "Have you got any idea where she is now?"

"I . . . I don't know." Leonard spoke through clenched teeth. "She ran off. It's summer. There's no water for miles. I figured she'd make her own grave."

Mason looked up and caught Emmanuel in a predatory gaze. "You found the whore," he said. "You and the black."

"Don't know what you're talking about, Lieutenant."

"Sorry, Pa." Lenny flipped and found a fetal position. "I'm sorry I disobeyed you."

"Shhh . . . quiet now. I need to think." Mason got a chair from the table and placed it directly in front of Emmanuel. He sat with his arms resting across the top rail, the Browning hanging loose in his right hand. "Where is she?"

"Who?"

"Lenny's friend."

"Don't know."

"Bullshit. She's at Clear Water. I'll stake my life on it."

"You mean you'll stake Leonard's life on it," Emmanuel said. "After the Pretoria police dig up that orchard, he's the one who's going to swing. And you'll swing with him, Crow."

Crow's hand shook, sent the gun barrel jigging right to left. "I'm clean. Getting those girls was Lenny's idea. He kept them to himself."

So Alice was right. More than one girl had occupied the cell before her.

"Shut it," Mason said. "Cooper is lying but not well enough to fool me. Ten years working undercover, I can sniff out a liar blindfolded."

"Is that why you read over my files . . . to catch me out in a lie? And how many times did that happen, Lieutenant? Not once, I'm guessing. I'm from Sophiatown, I was born lying to men like you."

A flicker of emotion crossed Mason's face. Fear, followed by the determination to export that fear to others.

"Clever will get you just so far, Cooper. You are in my house now. It's not like any place you've been before." He nudged the tip of his shoe into Leonard's ribs. "Get a chair and sit next to me, Lenny."

He waited for his son to take a seat directly opposite Shabalala. "Where did you first encounter these two men?"

"By the river fence. They ran down to the bank and we chased them."

Mason nodded. "They moved from the mountains, where the torchlights were shining, down to the river and then back in the direction of the farmhouse."

"I never thought of it that way but, *ja*, that's what they did."

Emmanuel caught the moment the geography clicked in Mason's head and could think of no way to undo it. Shabalala brushed dirt from his trousers, pretending a calm that neither of them felt.

"You came on foot from Clear Water," Mason said with undisguised pleasure. "Somebody that side saw the whore and you came to the rescue. You risked your skin and the Brewer girl's statement for a tramp that nobody will miss, not even her clients. What kind of a fool does that? I'm curious."

Emmanuel shrugged off the question.

Mason rubbed the stubble on his chin. "In all the rush I forgot to make the proper introductions. This is Leonard Hammond. My son. His mother and I never married, so he kept her name. He gets his looks from her and his height from me. From both of us he inherited some very bad habits. Tell Sergeant Cooper and this kaffir the ways that you have erred."

Lenny hesitated and received a fatherly nod from Mason.

"I drink, I steal, I take the Lord's name in vain, I lie, I fight, I bare false witness, I . . . I . . ."

"Come. Don't be shy. Tell Cooper the worst of your habits . . . the one that gives you the most pleasure."

A second hesitation on Lenny's end prompted a second nod of approval from Mason. Emmanuel wondered where this conversation was leading.

"I take women off the street and teach them the error of their ways."

"All kinds of women?"

"No. Just the bad ones."

Mason turned to Emmanuel while he talked. "Tell me about the woman Cooper danced with at the rail yards. Was she one of the good ones?"

Emmanuel tried to keep a neutral expression and knew he'd failed when Mason smiled.

"A mix of both," Leonard said. "She danced like one of the cheap ones, but up close she smelled of roses and talked like a girl who does music lessons. I wanted to bring her home."

"Of course you did," Mason said. "You found a diamond in the rubble and wanted to keep it. Unfortunately, that gem already belonged to Cooper. He thrashed the white off your skin when you laid hands on her."

"If he hadn't surprised me, I would have had him."

"No, that would not have happened. Do you want to know why?" Mason continued before Leonard replied. "A man will fight, give everything he has, to protect what he loves. Is that not so, Cooper?"

Emmanuel shrugged stiff shoulders and heard the breath sucking in and out of his lungs. He dared not talk for fear that he'd beg Mason to leave Davida out of their business, to forget that she ever existed. Or worse still, that he'd threaten acts of violence he was in no position to dish out. Either way he'd sound weak.

Mason's smile widened to a grin. "Yes, I thought it was something like that. You'd kill for that girl . . . almost did, in fact. And I know where she is. Figured it out just now."

Emmanuel said nothing.

"*Ja*, really. See, I did my homework. I asked around about your private life and got back zero. What I do know is that you're not the type to fuck and run, not least with a woman like that one. You'd take the night and then steal the morning in bed with your coloured bit."

"Interesting theory," Emmanuel said.

Mason laughed, discovering a sense of humor. "Oh,

I'm on the money. I see the truth in your eyes. There's no hiding it, Cooper. Your woman is in that Houghton house . . . probably waiting for you right now with the sheets turned down."

Emmanuel turned to Shabalala, seeking a guideline. He could not control his expression. He'd lost the ability to hide the fear and rage churning inside. His brain had taken the long hike back to Sophiatown days when his father, vengeful and self-pitying drunk that he was, smashed the chairs and plates that he'd neglected to break the week before.

Shabalala turned, gave him a calm face and deliberately looked to the window. Emmanuel did the same. Moon shadows streaked across the dusty glass. Beyond the glass, black sky and stars.

"There's something out there," Crow said. "We can't hear it, but the kaffir can."

"Rubbish," Mason said. "Cooper and his friend came here alone. Heroes don't need backup. Isn't that so, Sergeant?"

A second piece of gravel hit the window, too loud to be windblown, too deliberate to be ignored. Crow swiveled and took aim at the glass. Leonard pulled a knife from his pocket and flicked the blade, both of them skittish as alley cats.

"Go out there, Crow," Mason said. "Check the house perimeter and report back."

"Yes, sir." Crow slid the revolver into the waistband of his pants and headed out. The front door opened the same time as a stone hit the window, fracturing the glass. Cracks fanned across the surface to make a webbed pattern.

"How many out there?" Mason asked Emmanuel.

"Don't know. It must be the wind." For once, he spoke the God's honest truth, which sounded like a lie.

"Answer or I'll gut the kaffir like a fish." Leonard stood and pushed his knife to Shabalala's jugular vein.

30

A ROCK SMASHED a hole in the fractured window, showering shards of glass into the room. Fragments pinged against the table and the hardwood floors. Leonard pitched forward, stuck in the neck by a splinter. Shabalala pushed the couch backward to avoid the knife blade. The sofa flipped. Emmanuel hit the floor, raising dust. He sucked in a breath, aware of bodies slamming and rolling to his right. A thin whistling sound came from outside the broken window. Animal heads stared from the wall like high-court judges sitting on the bench. He had no idea what had just happened.

A hand slapped the side of his head. He sat up, caught a glimpse of Mason standing ashen-faced in the doorway. The fear and sorrow that Zweigman had seen hiding behind the lieutenant's face now seemed to leak from every pore. Emmanuel swiveled right to follow Mason's gaze. Leonard sprawled across the ground with his body pinned under Shabalala's weight. A knife handle protruded from his chest, the blade stuck deep into his sternum. Blood poured across his shirt. His blank blue eyes stared at the ceiling.

"Go after the father, Sergeant," Shabalala said. "The son has passed over."

Emmanuel followed Mason into the house's dark interior. The journey led through the kitchen to the top of the stairs that led to the cellar. All light died on the third rung down. He crouched and crossed the threshold of the concrete cell. He jagged to the left and in the direction of the discarded Webley revolver.

Mason's voice floated from the pitch black. "My boy is the reason I read through your files, Cooper. I wanted to know how a white kaffir from the slums made it to the Detective Branch instead of checking in and out of prison. How did you slither out of that hole? Why didn't Leonard find the right path? He won't have that chance now. Your kaffir stabbed him. Took my son . . ."

Emmanuel could not think of anyone more deserving of being stabbed to death than Leonard. He inched across the concrete floor with both hands sweeping the surface for a touch of metal.

"Leonard tried to do good," Mason said. "He got me the original surveyor's map showing the boundaries between the native reserve and Lion's Kill. The new boundaries will stand now that there's no proof to contradict our land claim. My son got me the river."

"He could have bribed an official at the Lands Department to lose the map like a normal person." Emmanuel could not let that sugarcoated version of Leonard's actions pass.

"The Brewer bitch took the map from the office, told everyone it had been misplaced. Leonard knew that she and her kaffir-lover husband were going to let the blacks from the reserve have it. If she'd done that, Lion's Kill would have turned to dust in the drought."

"Your son beat Martha Brewer into the emergency ward and Ian Brewer into the grave for that map on the table upstairs?" Wars had been fought over access to water and cities had fallen for the lack of it. Water in a dry land had a price above rubies.

"All things considered, one death in exchange for river frontage is a good deal," Mason said. "Lenny understood that."

"Leonard got what he deserved. It's just a pity he died so fast," Emmanuel said, and heard Mason suck in a breath as if he'd been hit in the gut.

"I'm going to kill you and your friends, Cooper. Afterward I will drive to that house in Houghton and introduce myself to your woman. Not a polite introduction, you understand. I will share the present darkness of my soul with her and leave her in pieces."

Mason's feet scuffed the floor as he moved closer.

Emmanuel blocked images of Davida and Rebekah from his mind, blocked out the fear. His left hand extended and touched a handle, then the metal barrel of his Webley.

He righted the gun in a two-handed grip, arms locked in firing position.

"You've got nothing to say?" Mason's voice came from directly ahead. "Are you afraid she'll enjoy my—"

Emmanuel squeezed off two shots and heard a grunt, then the sound of Mason's body dropping. Footsteps pounded the cellar stairs and the light from a lantern cut through the gloom. Mason lay on the floor. Blood poured from two wounds on the left side of his chest. "Let me live." The lieutenant grinned, enjoying a private joke with God or the devil. "I promise not to tell anyone about her."

Emmanuel pressed the muzzle to Mason's heart and pulled the trigger. Shabalala moved into the room and the light from his lantern grew brighter. Emmanuel reached into Mason's pocket and removed Cassie's statement before blood soaked the paper. He gave it to the Zulu detective. They walked out in silence.

31

EMMANUEL, SHABALALA, JULIE and Zweigman trekked the moonlit veldt and came to the edge of the river. Behind them, lost in the great stretch of aloe and thorn trees, stood the Lion's Kill homestead, home to two corpses inside and Crow, lying broken at the bottom of the braai pit. Zweigman and Julie had seen Alice safe to the native location and doubled back to Lion's Kill armed with a slingshot and cunning. They'd risked their lives so that Emmanuel and Shabalala might defeat the enemy. And they had.

Shabalala hesitated, then said, "We cannot carry the blood of the dead and wounded with us. We must wash before going back to the world of ordinary things."

They had all brushed up against death to varying degrees. He and Shabalala had killed with a knife and a gun. Zweigman had bloodied his hands examining Mason and

Leonard to confirm their departed status and Julie had driven Crow into the braai pit under a hail of stones.

"We can do that," Emmanuel said.

He felt certain that Shabalala recognized the dangerous pleasure he'd taken in killing Mason and thought it possible that the Zulu detective had taken equal satisfaction in killing Lenny. The killer in both of them had to be washed off and left behind in this arid place. They undressed together, stripped down to cotton undershorts and, in Julie's case, a threadbare vest and knickers. The water ran silver around Emmanuel's ankles and swirled to his thighs and chest the deeper he walked. He dived. The current rinsed the stain of Mason's blood from his hands. Mason wanted the river. Now he was part of it. Emmanuel broke the surface and gulped warm air. Shabalala and Zweigman bathed on either side of him, the water beading on their skin.

"Look," Julie whispered.

Two lionesses walked along the bank with the grace of wild-born things. They crouched and lapped at the water, the river's silver surface reflecting in their eyes. Thirst extinguished, they turned and disappeared into the bushlands.

"No lions on Lion's Kill, you said." Emmanuel gave Shabalala a look. Legend had it that Shangaan hunters could track a drop of rain in a thunderstorm.

"There aren't any lions," Julie said. "There haven't been any since before I was born."

—

Emmanuel undressed in the candlelight and climbed into bed. Davida turned like a flower seeking the sun and kissed him on the mouth, drawing him closer. He tasted mint on her tongue and spread his palms flat against her back. They fit together, skin to skin and heart to heart.

"You smell of dirt and rain," she said.

"I washed in a river," he said, though washing and actually getting clean were two separate things.

"Why?" She tangled her fingers through his hair and shook loose grains of sand. "Did you get dirty?"

"Yes," he said. He couldn't explain. To truly understand, Davida would have had to have been there, standing on the moonlit riverbank with Shabalala, Zweigman and Julie.

Bedsprings creaked and Emmanuel smiled against the warmth of Davida's neck. He was washed clean in the river and reborn in her arms. This perfect state would not last—could not. He knew it. The present darkness that Mason talked of had the country in a grip that would not let it go. Now had to be enough.

He smoothed Davida's hair against the pillow. He loved the contrast of dark and light created by her cinnamon skin against the cream sheets. Moonbeams glanced off the white candles on the bedside table, the yellow flowers in the vase on the windowsill and the bronze of Davida's mouth. So many colors together, he thought, and every one of them beautiful.

EPILOGUE

EMMANUEL SMOOTHED THE newspaper flat, careful not to disturb Rebekah, who slept pressed to his chest. He skimmed the headline, "Four Bodies Found on Northern Transvaal Farm," and read the article.

> *The Pretoria police yesterday unearthed the remains of four unidentified women buried on an isolated farm outside of Rust de Winter. Acting on a tip-off from a neighbor, the police raided the property and made the grim discovery. Two men with long criminal histories, Leonard Hammond and Danny Crow, were killed during the raid. A senior policeman, Lieutenant Walter Mason, was shot at close range and died at the scene. The police commissioner praised the brave actions of the Pretoria Detective Branch and the constables who helped search the grounds.*

"Once again the South African police force has proved its worth. A brave man, Lieutenant Walter Mason, was lost during the operation, but good ultimately defeated evil. Let us take time over the Christmas break to remember those who work so tirelessly to keep our country safe."

A black-and-white photograph of two Pretoria detectives accompanied the write-up. In the photo, the detectives leaned on shovels with their shirtsleeves rolled up to the elbows. Sweat patches under their armpits proved that South Africa's policemen were determined to restore order after the chaos.

Emmanuel remembered it differently. In reality, it was Shabalala who'd located the shallow graves. Shabalala had insisted that the shovels be put aside and the bodies uncovered by hand so as to show respect for the victims. In the end, the truth mattered little. The local police got the glory while he and Shabalala walked away from three dead white men with no public explanation necessary. No charges would be laid. No internal police investigation would ever reveal the poison inside the police force's own ranks.

Thanks to Colonel van Niekerk.

"I'll fix it," the Dutch colonel said when Emmanuel took the precaution of calling his boss to report Mason's death. "The last thing the commissioner needs is a dirty detective thrown onto his doorstep before Christmas. I'll call him. Explain that the lieutenant he praised in the newspapers a few days ago was part of a criminal gang that kidnapped and murdered women."

The pleasure in van Niekerk's voice was sharp: the thrill of gaining the upper hand an unexpected Christmas present. The police commissioner now owed him a debt. A substantial one. And the Pretoria Detective Branch would not forget who threw them the biggest case of their careers.

Emmanuel placed a palm to the crown of Rebekah's head, felt the silky hair and fragile bones. He remembered Lion's Kill. He closed his eyes and he was back in the grim yard where the noon sun beat down and the windmill creaked. Black sedans and beige police vans choked the driveway. A mortuary van idled at the front door. Four mortuary attendants carried out the bloated bodies of Mason and Lenny on stretchers. Flies fed on the dried blood of their wounds.

Shabalala stood in the shade of a grapefruit tree with a human skull cupped in his palms.

"Four," he said when Emmanuel joined him in the orchard. "Their bones are scattered all around. The graves were shallow and the animals dug them up."

That could have been Davida . . . The thought hit Emmanuel hard, took the breath from his lungs. *Those bones could belong to my woman, my wife. Or my little girl, fifteen years on.*

"Are you all right?" A voice came from far and near at the same time.

The soft exhalation of Rebekah's breath tickled Emmanuel's neck. He opened his eyes. Davida stood an arm's length away, alive and radiant in the morning sunlight. His girls were safe and Lion's Kill was just another place to forget. If he could.

Davida's gaze flicked to the newspaper. "You were there," she said.

"Yes. I was."

He'd decided to tell Davida the truth as much as possible and to keep lies for the outside world. This situation, however, called for some omissions. The identity of the man who'd grabbed her at Fatty's club and how close she'd come to the horrors of Lion's Kill, he'd keep a secret.

"Those poor women." Davida read the story over Emmanuel's shoulder. "You did a good thing. You stopped those men from hurting more people."

"That's what I have to remember," Emmanuel said. "The good."

He focused on all the things that went right.

There was Alice, rescued and then restored by Zweigman's skilled hands. Tough, unbreakable Alice. The girl had more guts than any soldier Emmanuel had ever known. Dropping her back into her old life felt wrong: a waste of potential and a missed opportunity.

"She would make a wonderful nurse," Zweigman said when Alice woke early to help mix a solution of milk and honey for the Singleton children's infected eyes.

Emmanuel and Shabalala agreed.

So, Zweigman made plans. He arranged for Alice to stay at Clear Water until her wounds healed and she was ready to reenter the world. He left her with a promise. "If you wish to finish your schooling, my wife and I will help you. We will give you whatever shelter you need."

It seemed to Emmanuel that the German doctor was re-creating the family he'd lost in the war. A year ago, Emmanuel would have found that need for family strange, even a weakness. Now, sitting outdoors with his daughter's warmth nestled against his body and Davida close by, he understood.

He understood completely the joy on Shabalala's face when Aaron walked free of the juvenile prison on the police commissioner's personal order. Father and son had approached each other slowly, warily. Shabalala broke first. He took his son into his arms and held tight. Aaron tensed then relaxed into his father's embrace, their years apart forgotten, their differences forgiven.

"What are you thinking about?" Davida smiled to see Emmanuel smile. She sat down next to him.

He leaned over and kissed her mouth.

"You," he said.

PRESENT DARKNESS

MALLA NUNN

READERS CLUB GUIDE

EMILY
BESTLER
BOOKS

WSP
READERS
CLUB

INTRODUCTION

From behind his desk in the Johannesburg major crimes
squad, Detective Sergeant Emmanuel Cooper is counting
the hours until his holiday in Mozambique. Then a call
comes in: a respectable white couple has been assaulted and
left for dead in their home. The couple's teenage daughter
identifies the attacker as Aaron Shabalala—the youngest
son of Cooper's best friend. Though others in the office
aren't interested in hearing evidence to the contrary, Cooper knows the boy is innocent and is determined to ensure
justice for Aaron. With the help of Shabalala and their
friend Dr. Daniel Zweigman, Cooper sets out to find the
truth. Their investigation uncovers a violent world of
Sophiatown gangs, thieves, and corrupt government offi-
cials who will do anything to keep their dark world intact.

TOPICS AND QUESTIONS FOR DISCUSSION

1. Race is incredibly important in the highly structured world of apartheid Johannesburg, but Emmanuel, a white kaffir, seems to almost float between the races. How does his past allow him access to the world of Sophiatown? How is his thinking shaped by his parentage and his personal history?

2. Emmanuel, a detective sergeant sworn to uphold the law, has an illegal mixed-race family and reflects on his status, thinking that "he was, in reality, already across the line that divided the dirty cops from the clean ones" (p. 31). How does this belief affect Emmanuel's actions? How do his inner conflicts inform how he behaves throughout the book?

3. Think about the ways in which the treatment of "non-whites" is different from the treatment of Europeans in this story. Do you see similarities to our society today? Why or why not?

4. "A white man and a black man cannot be friends in this country. . . . It is written in their law books" (p. 144). In what ways do you see the laws, meant to control citizens' actions, being constantly subverted? In what ways are they inescapable?

5. "Fix had loosened Bakwena's tongue in minutes. Violence worked" (p. 228). Do you agree with this sentiment? In what ways does it prove to be true in this story, for both the protagonists and antagonists? Discuss an instance in which it backfires.

6. What did you make of the sections told from Alice's point of view? Did you find them intriguing? Confusing? Discuss the function that they serve in broadening our view of life in apartheid South Africa.

7. Think about the differing landscapes that make up this book—Johannesburg versus Emmanuel's home in Durban; the neat, ordered world of Parkview; the chaotic streets of Sophiatown; the dusty fields of Clear Water Farm. How do the different settings shape what happens there? Are we inevitably shaped by our environments?

8. Discuss the complicated role of Mason's religion in the story. Is he sincere in his belief? How does it affect his actions? Do you believe, as Negus does, that "the rain wets the leopard's spots but doesn't wash them off" (p. 46)?

9. The specter of his World War II service continues to haunt Emmanuel. How is he affected by his experiences in the war through this story? How are the other characters, such as Zweigman, influenced by their war experiences?

10. What is the role of family in the story? How important is family to each character? What is each willing to sacrifice for the people they love?

11. Discuss the elements of magical realism that inhabit this otherwise realistic story—the lions, though there are no lions left at Lion's Kill; Emmanuel's unlikely, almost miraculous climb up the rock face. Is there meant to be a logical explanation for them? Do these mystical touches make the story more or less "real" to you?

ENHANCE YOUR BOOK CLUB

1. Apartheid in South Africa ended only in 1993, when Nelson Mandela was elected president. Mandela was a beloved figure on the world stage and was mourned by world leaders when he passed away in 2013, and yet his public and private lives were not without controversy. Research the life of Nelson Mandela and discuss the impact he had on South Africa and on the world at large.

2. One of the dishes that Cooper, Shabalala, and Zweigman enjoy at Mama Sylvia's in Sophiatown is a dish called funeral rice. Prepare this dish, or another South African dish, and enjoy together at your next meeting. You can find a funeral rice recipe here: http://www.food.com/recipe/funeral-rice-11409.

3. Get a taste of the diverse musical styles that make up South African music. The website of *Cape Town Magazine* has a virtual jukebox that allows you to sample music from a variety of South African artists: http://www.capetownmagazine.com/south-african-music/. Listen to the samples as a group. Can you hear resonances with the book in the music?